A Love to Remember

Peter Samuel

Published by Clink Street Publishing 2024

Copyright © 2024

First edition.

The author asserts the moral right under the Copyright, Designs and Patents Act 1988 to be identified as the author of this work.

All rights reserved. No part of this publication may be reproduced, stored in a retrieval system or transmitted, in any form or by any means without the prior consent of the author, nor be otherwise circulated in any form of binding or cover other than that with which it is published and without a similar condition being imposed on the subsequent purchaser.

*ISBN:
978-1-915785-27-5 - paperback
978-1-915785-28-2 - ebook*

CHAPTER ONE

Amadeus Rupert, what a name. Often teased about it throughout his school days.

Born on the 3rd of September 1914, the year the great war began.

He had learned from his mother how his father, Thomas Rupert, volunteered and marched off to war with the Coventry pals. An architect by profession, he was drafted into the Royal Engineers, saw action in the early years of the war, then was killed in 1916, when the British forces continued their push on the Somme battlefield.

Amadeus never knew his father, but he knew his mother. As he got older, they would sit by candlelight while his mum would open the photograph album, then reminisce over the times, before he was born, when she and his dad walked the boards of the Empire theatre: acting in amateur dramatics, taking part in operas. Hence the name Amadeus, taken from the Amadeus Wolfgang Mozart opera *The Magic Flute*, which was their favourite.

It was often thought that young Amadeus would follow in his parents' footsteps but that was not to be. Although educated in the arts, Amadeus was to choose a different role in life, much to the disappointment of his mum. He always seemed to have his head stuck in a book. Puzzle books mostly, and it wasn't long before his school teachers recognised that that they had a genius in their class. Amadeus excelled in Maths and Literature, always top of the class in most subjects except sport, he had no time for playing football or cricket, although he did enjoy athletics. He was doing the *Times* crossword at the age of ten.

He was devoted to his mother, who had struggled after the war to put food on the table. But the theatre rallied round to give her secretarial and typing work, and the firm that his dad had worked for also pitched in to give Amadeus an easy beginning.

Then came the decision as to whether he would go to Cambridge University, or join the Metropolitan Police Force in London, the latter was his choice; that made his mum weep.

He sent off the application, and received a quick response that he was to report to the Hendon police college in London, to commence training.

Billeted in the college dormitory, he was fed, watered and most of all, had easy access to the library where he spent many an hour of his spare time with his head stuck in a book, although he made it a point to travel back home at weekends when there was no tutorial.

The year was 1931, a lot was going on in the world, especially in Germany.

He was sitting in the lounge enjoying the break from his lessons, browsing through the *Times* newspaper, deciding to leave the crossword until later.

Amadeus did not know it then, but his life was to change dramatically, when a tall blond-haired recruit sat down beside him. Holding out his hand, "Colin Freeman," he said with a strange accent. Amadeus put down the newspaper, then introduced himself.

"Yes, I've been studying you over the past few weeks, you don't say very much and don't go out a lot," the stranger said with a large smile.

"I go home occasionally, but right now I'm here to study and, hopefully, get through my finals." He attempted to pick up the newspaper.

"I have no doubt you'll succeed, Rupert. You, my friend, are the academic type. So fear not because there are great things in store for you."

"I take it you have a crystal ball in your dormitory." Amadeus smiled.

"Don't be so presumptuous, Rupert. I wouldn't live here if you paid me." They both laughed. "I have an apartment in Mayfair. You're welcome to attend the parties, if you get bored with life in the box room." This brought another laugh. It was from that moment on that the two became close friends.

Colin explained why he spoke with a foreign twang. "I was brought up in Munich, Germany. My parents saw the writing on the wall when the brown shirts, they were the Nazi party enforcers, a truly ruthless mob, took to the streets and began to persecute the Jews. That's when we moved to England and changed our name by deed poll, from Friedman to Freeman. My dad kept his first name of Jacob, but it was advised by relations living in England for me to change from Gustav to Colin, and Frau Anna Friedman, my mother, to Anabela Freeman." Colin hesitated as if he had said too much, but continued, "It was a wise move by my parents. You only need to look at the way Germany is run today, by thieves and murderers. Herr Hitler especially."

Colin Freeman said no more, but Amadeus knew the young teenager was hurting.

"Come on, let's go and take in a matinee at the Odeon cinema, that will release us for an afternoon." This was to become one of their escapes from reality.

Colin kept his passion for flying a secret, until one Saturday he and Amadeus drove up to North London in the Austin 7 which Colin had taught Amadeus to drive.

As instructed he helped Colin push the Tiger Moth aeroplane out of the hangar, turned the propeller, then chocks away. He watched as the flimsy aircraft trundled down the grass airfield then lifted off into the blue cloudless sky.

Colin had invited his friend on many an occasion to sit in the gunner's seat of a borrowed aircraft. "No chance, Freeman. I'll keep my feet on the terracotta clay if you don't mind."

However, Amadeus was intrigued by Colin's skill and decided to put his life on the line, joining his friend in the air. It wasn't long before Amadeus found a passion for flying, and with Colin's instruction, soon began to take off and land of his own free will. There were times when they would just sit in the draughty hangar and learn about aircraft maintenance from an aircraft mechanic.

But Amadeus still kept hold of his passion to become a member of the Metropolitan Police Force, much to his friend's annoyance when he refused to join him at the airfield.

"You must study, Colin. Flying is one thing but your commitment to passing your exams is another." Amadeus would try to encourage his friend to get his head into the police manuals. "There's a preliminary exam coming up, so you better get studying or you're out." It was a warning that Colin paid attention to, and he would burn the midnight oil, to play catch-up on what he had been taught in the lectures.

Much to the surprise of their tutor, both friends passed the final exam that determined whether they were capable of becoming policemen or not. The tutor made it clear that Amadeus was not a problem, but shook his head when Colin was mentioned.

"Don't worry, sir, I'll make sure he doesn't waste your time." Amadeus studied the tutor's face before he turned and walked to the library.

The two cadets had become firm friends, relying on each other's wisdom, passing on any advice that they held and sharing their present situations. It came as a surprise that Colin was in fact very rich. Amadeus never realised that Colin Freeman was part of the Freeman empire, who had stores all over the south coast of England, including counters at the large department stores in the city, although he often wondered how Colin could afford the luxury of owning a car, an aeroplane and a luxury apartment in a residential area of the city. However, he never questioned his friend on his apparent wealth. It was none of his business.

Colin had frequently asked his friend to move out of the police dormitory, and move into the luxury apartment, but Amadeus knew that would be fatal. Because of the parties and Colin's lifestyle, no work would get done, so it was always a polite refusal explaining why.

With careful persuasion, Amadeus was able to guide his friend through the rigorous moments of study, and it was now approaching their finals, where the boys would be separated from the men. The day that would reveal the outcome of the past two years.

The results were posted on the notice board. It came as no surprise when Amadeus Rupert topped the class with a pass mark of 92%. Those that had a high mark were also mentioned, but the police examiners were more discreet, by mentioning those who had scraped through without revealing their percentage mark, and not listing those who had failed at all. The two chums studied the board with enthusiasm. Needless to say, Colin had scraped through, and didn't really care what mark he got, as long as he succeeded in the game. That was his considered opinion of all this study and the boredom of the tutorials.

His life would be up in the air, and nothing would change that. However, it took all of his friend's resolve to encourage him to stick it out.

The pass-out parade was held in the Hendon College square where Amadeus received the honour of being the best recruit and accepted the challenge trophy, for the best team out of four. A coveted trophy that had taken in lots of sports, especially athletics.

Amadeus was proud to see his mother and uncle David in the crowd of onlookers, as the cadets were put through their marching drill.

It was on that day he was first introduced to Mr. and Mrs. Freeman. He was quite impressed by their manner, there was no sign of "look who we are" they were just ordinary parents, proud that their son had achieved something in his life.

There were a lot of handshakes and introductions, the cadets posing with their parents and family for photographs. Amadeus and his family were invited to join the Freemans for lunch at the Ritz, but Amadeus turned the invitation down. He wanted to spend as much time with his mother, Emily, and uncle David, as possible before they caught the train back to Coventry.

"Some other time then," Jacob Freeman said, slapping Amadeus on the back, then indicating to his wife and son it was time to go.

Amadeus and his family went to the food hall, where a buffet had been laid out. There was lots of chatter, and more introductions.

The time had finally arrived when Amadeus saw the family off on the train. "Stay safe" was his mother's parting advice, with tears flowing down her cheeks as the whistle blew and the steam train moved with a jerk. He stood waving until it was no longer possible to see the carriage that carried his mother away.

There was still work to be done at the college. Desks had to be cleared, beds changed and made, a tidy up of his dormitory, and two weeks of sheer bliss as the college tutorials and students began to disband, after allocations of police stations were received by the grateful cadets.

Knowing he would eventually be asked to vacate his box room at the police college, Amadeus was lucky to find alternative accommodation quickly. London was not the easiest of places to find affordable places to live; however, he managed to find a basement flat that was affordable to his income. It was handy, since he had been allocated to Holborn Police Station. His basement flat was situated in Eagle Street, not too far from there, so in a way he considered himself lucky.

Colin helped with the decoration, and the moving of accumulated bits and pieces. He had been posted to Chepstow, so there would be little time for fun and games, and Amadeus's friend seldom visited the basement flat, since he had to settle into his own station.

Colin appeared on the doorstep of the flat one morning, with that huge grin on his face.

"We have another week before we take up our attachments. So come this weekend I have booked us into a hotel in Bournemouth. It is a holiday weekend so there should be plenty of spare crumpet walking about." He saw the look of consternation on Amadeus's face. "No arguments please. This is my treat; my way of saying thanks, for all the help you gave me during the police college days, but most importantly, helping me at the airfield. So be packed and ready for Friday. We need a break after all we've been through."

Amadeus knew it was futile to argue, so nodded. "Okay, Friday it is."

Amadeus had no idea just how much his life was about to change, as he packed his suitcase with shorts and tee shirts for the weekend in Bournemouth. They took the train from Paddington and travelled down to the English Riviera, arriving in the resort in the early afternoon. They booked into the Highcliff Hotel, before taking a walk into the town to explore, with a refreshing walk along the pier, to stretch their legs before dinner. Much of the afternoon was spent going in and out of shops, until they agreed that a nap before dinner would set them up for the evening's search for a girl in need of company. Which Colin was all too eager to indulge in. Amadeus reserved his thoughts on the matter, not wanting to be seen as a predator, or a prude in his friend's enthusiasm.

After dinner, they set off into the town, and while walking on the promenade, Amadeus pointed up to a clifftop pub. So they made their way up the steps. Out of breath, they took a seat and ordered beer. They sat in the corner, eyeing up who came in and who left. They got into conversation with an old one-armed soldier, who insisted on telling them about the days of the trenches in World War One. This reminded Amadeus of the stories his mother would tell him, and he was glad to be distracted by two teenagers who took a seat by the guard rail overlooking the bay. He said nothing to Colin since he was intrigued by the old man's stories. They had bought him plenty of beer, as his exploits got grander. He finally changed the subject.

"Those two girls, that came in a while ago, keep looking over here as if they might be interested, certainly not in me." He gave a loud laugh. "That two at the bar are preparing to pounce so you better be quick."

It was Colin who took the initiative. Springing from his seat, he walked over to their table. "You girls look as if you're in need of company and a good time."

"Bugger off," the dark-haired girl said, blowing smoke up into his face.

"Amadeus, get over here," he ordered, paying no attention to the rejection, while pulling a chair over to their table. He quickly introduced them. "This is my friend Amadeus Rupert, and I am Colin Freeman, both in need of company."

The dark-haired girl guffawed. "I suppose you're going to tell us you're part of the Freeman jewellers empire, just sod off will you?"

Amadeus had already drawn in a chair and sat beside the quiet blonde, who paid little attention to the intrusion, and her friend's outburst. The waitress brought over their pints from the other table

"What I want to know is where your friend got his name from, some famous composer no doubt, and why is he not wearing his traditional yellow checked trousers, red polo-neck jumper and scarf?" She laughed at her own inference to Amadeus.

The quiet one spoke up. "Be quiet, Veronica. You, my dear, are becoming a pain in the arse." Her face went beetroot when she realised what she had said. "Sorry for my outburst." She encouraged Amadeus to move his chair closer.

She introduced herself as Deborah Fox, and her friend Veronica Courtney, both from the village of Welwyn, in Hertfordshire. The conversation became more civilised after Colin had bought them a drink. They had spent two weeks living with Deborah's aunt Ada, and needed some excitement.

"Boring," Veronica said as she lifted her vodka and tonic, swallowing it without a break.

Deborah sipped her white wine. "Pay no attention to her, she just wants to get back to the art school."

It was Amadeus who picked up on the conversation. "Art school. So you're an art student, Veronica?"

There was no response as she tapped her empty glass on the table.

"Yes, she's a student, and a very good one at that," Deborah said coming to the rescue. "If she works hard she'll become a name in English art and sculpting."

"What's your occupation, Deborah?" Amadeus leaned towards her and got a whiff of her perfume.

"I'm at the teacher's training college. I still have eighteen months to do, then hopefully I'll graduate as a teacher."

"God help the little brats," Veronica said as she tapped her empty glass again. The conversation was more relaxed as the four sat discussing what they did, their plans for the future, and the holiday weekend. That conversation took pride of place with Colin and Veronica, who were determined to have a ball in the short space of time that was left. So after a few more drinks, they paired off, with Colin and Veronica, who were well matched, and Deborah and Amadeus, who were, as they say, caught in a whirlwind romance. It was love at first sight for Amadeus, although Deborah played her cards close to her chest.

Closing time and the foursome made their way out of the lounge entrance. It opened out into a broad street, high above the beach and promenade. Victoria and Colin decided to go to a party that Veronica and Deborah had been invited to, but the latter said she was tired and preferred to walk back to her aunt Ada's flat. So they split up, each couple going their separate ways.

The walk along the Clifton road was refreshing, and the full moon cast a yellow pale shadow on the two who walked hand in hand in silence towards Deborah's accommodation.

They stood for a moment. Deborah leaned forward and kissed him on the cheek. "What about tomorrow?" Amadeus asked before she was about to go indoors.

"What about tomorrow?" Deborah teased.

"Well, I thought we could go to the beach, have a picnic, or even take one of the pleasure boats and do a trip along the coast." He could hardly get the words out before she answered.

"That might be awkward, Amadeus. You have your friend and I have mine; we might want to do something different. So I suggest we leave it at that. Just go and enjoy your weekend."

Amadeus made a move towards her but Deborah turned quickly and ran up the steps to the main door where she was greeted by the security guard on duty.

He was sure he saw a curtain twitch on the second floor as he looked up to admire the building. Slightly disappointed, he walked back to the hotel alone.

The next morning he was down in the dining room early, and settled for a full English breakfast with coffee and toast.

Colin appeared looking the worse for wear. He moved his clenched fist up and down.

"What in heaven's name is wrong with you, Freeman, have you got wind or something?" Amadeus said loudly. He knew exactly what Colin was asking before Colin got it out.

"Well, did you or didn't you? I gave you every opportunity to give her one," he said with the hint of a smile.

"Certainly not, Freeman, and if I did I wouldn't disclose it to you." Amadeus was slightly put out at the intimate question. "Right, I'm off into the town. I'll meet you at the boating pond cafe."

"Failure," Colin said as the waitress took his order. "I'll tell you one thing, my friend, Veronica held nothing back; we ended up in bed together, what a girl. However, things began to get out of hand at the orgy so I left while she was smoking her joint, and when she began to kiss a stranger, that was it for me. But it turned out a very good first night." He paused for a moment. "I have to go down to Cornwall to look at a car. I arranged it last night. If you want to come, that's fine, otherwise you can spend the time here with Deborah." He buttered his toast.

"That's not going to happen, Colin. We parted company on amicable terms. She's more considerate towards you and Veronica, so we'll say no more about it."

"Come off it, Rupert, I saw the way you looked at her, and she at you; it nearly made me throw up." He hurried with his breakfast. "Needs must, Amadeus, I have a train to catch." He snatched a piece of toast. "See you tonight, my friend." His breakfast remained on the plate, and he was gone.

Amadeus picked up the *Times* and studied the crossword as he sipped his coffee.

It was a sunny August morning so after a shower he dressed in shorts, a light shirt and sand shoes before setting off for the town. There was little to see that he and Colin hadn't seen last night. Although he did check out the theatre, nothing interested him so he walked along the pier, eventually settling down to get stuck into the *Times* crossword, He ordered a cold lemonade with cake before turning to the back page. He tapped his teeth with his pen. Five down always was a bugger.

Nicely settled in the shade, he was deep in thought when a soft voice spoke to him. He shielded his eyes and looked up at the handsome girl. "Deborah," he said with glee in his voice. He looked around for Veronica. No sign, so he asked the obvious question.

Deborah looked hurt. "She came in at half three in the morning much the worse for wear, her face bruised, and her clothes covered in vomit. I cleaned her up and put her to bed, and that's where she is, unable to face the day. Aunt Ada is absolutely furious with her, so we're cutting our holiday short and leaving Bournemouth on the morning train for London."

"Take a seat, Deborah. Let's get you a refreshing drink with cake." She sat down quickly.

Amadeus thought he detected a tear in her eye, but she turned and looked up at the waitress to order, then blew her nose gently.

"I'm at a loose end as well. Colin has gone off to Cornwall, so perhaps we could join forces and spend the day together."

"I'd like that very much, Amadeus," she said looking into his eyes.

They finished their cake and juices, then strolled along the pier, taking time on some of the joy rides, and getting photographs taken in Victorian period attire. There was fun to be had on the dodgems, with much laughter on the swing boat.

They were totally at ease in each other's company, talking about their upbringing and their dreams of the future. After a fantastic lunch, they decided on the cinema, an afternoon matinee, then sadly it was time to say goodbye at Aunt Ada's apartment block.

Amadeus was sure he saw the curtain move on the second floor, just like the night before. He was about to mention the fact when Deborah spoke softly, "I'll see what Veronica has planned for tonight, but I'm not going to be dragged to one of her parties. However, you mentioned a picnic, so let's do it tomorrow. I know an ideal spot that the family used to use in the past, very secluded with plenty of beach to sunbathe." She paused. "I'll make up some sandwiches if you buy some orangeade, then we can take the number eleven bus out to the beach." She gave a radiant smile at his reaction.

"Alright, I'll meet you here at the tearoom, say ten a.m., and we can take it from there." After the cinema, he walked her back to Aunt Ada's apartment. He didn't care who was watching. He took her in his arms and kissed her passionately. She responded by holding him close.

Amadeus watched her hips sway as she climbed the steps, then disappeared indoors.

He whooped and jumped into the air several times, as he made his way back to the Highcliff Hotel. There was no sign of Colin before he turned in for an early night. Much as he adored his friend, he didn't really care, because his mind was only on one thing. After a good breakfast, he made his way down to the store, he bought a number of items, including two beach towels and sun cream. Two bottles of juice and a packet of digestive biscuits. He put the items into his haversack, then walked to the promenade tearoom to meet Deborah. He was early, so ordered a coffee to pass the time. There was no way he could concentrate on the *Sunday Times* crossword so he left it in the haversack, then sat back, awaiting the love of his life.

Deborah arrived on time, turning down the offer of tea or coffee. "Come on, we have five minutes before the bus leaves, and being a Sunday service there's not another for two hours."

Amadeus grabbed the haversack and took her hand as they made their way to the bus stop. Eventually it arrived, Deborah paid the return fare, and told the conductor where they wanted to get off. The distance was three miles, so the journey did not take long. They alighted quickly and heard the two bells rung by the conductor for the driver to proceed. They climbed over the fence and made their way through coarse grass to the secluded beach. Amadeus was amazed at the long spit of sand. "You haven't seen anything yet," she said, releasing his hand. "We have our own private swimming pool, if my memory serves me correctly."

They spread the beach towels out, then stripped down to their bathing costumes. Running towards the sea, Deborah suddenly stopped in her tracks. "We have to wait on the tide to turn. The ebbing tide has strong currents. However, follow me."

They made their way over a sand dune. Suddenly it appeared. Amadeus gasped at the natural large pool of clear water, trapped by the ebbing tide in a pool. They waded into it and began to swim. Amadeus commented that it was like being in a large hot bathtub.

They hugged, then swam, then hugged again. Amadeus had never known such pleasure, and he told her so.

They both settled onto the beach towels to sunbathe, letting the heat of the morning dry them off. Deborah turned him over, then began to apply the sun cream to his back, then he did likewise to her. He watched her cover the rest of her body with the cream. They gave each other a hug before lying back to sunbathe.

Now the tide had turned, and they frolicked in the sea, splashing each other with hilarity, Amadeus lifting her out of the water, then throwing her into the surf again. They had much fun, embracing and kissing each other with affection, before running up the beach to the towels. They lay for a moment, before turning to face each other. They knew what each other wanted, and it wasn't long before they lay naked together, touching each other's private parts, Amadeus rolled onto her gently. "Be gentle with me," she husked. "I'm still a virgin."

This did not deter them, as they made love in the heat of the day. They both got so much pleasure from their encounter that the sun was sinking in the west before they cleansed themselves in the sea. "So much for lunch." Deborah giggled.

"We can eat the sandwiches on the bus back to Bournemouth," Amadeus said laughing. They gathered their belongings and made their way across the rough grass to the bus stop, sitting eating their sandwiches before the bus appeared.

The journey back to town was travelled in silence. They both knew that this was their last time together for some time to come. Addresses and phone numbers were exchanged in the silence. "Our train leaves tomorrow morning at eleven a.m. Will you come and see me off?" she asked as they strolled up the steep road to her aunt's apartment.

"I'll need to check my diary, but it should be okay," he said in fun.

Deborah nudged him in the ribs. "If I got down on my knees and pleaded with you, would that change your mind?" She was about to drop down on one knee, when he held her close.

"Wild horses and an army wouldn't hold me back from seeing you off." He kissed her with added hardness. "You must come up to London and visit me," he added before they finally broke free of their embrace. The curtain moved on the second floor, so he cheekily waved to the person responsible.

"That'll be Aunt Ada," Deborah said with a smile.

Amadeus gave another cheeky wave before kissing Deborah for the last time that evening.

His heart was filled with joy as he made his way back to the hotel.

An alarm call was arranged for the Monday morning early. He set his own alarm clock, just in case, then ventured down to the dining room for dinner. There was still no sign of Colin, and he became anxious. However, when he finished dinner, reception gave him a message that read, *Car deal done, returning tomorrow morning. C.*

Amadeus had a pint of beer before retiring for the night. He wrote a short note: *Gone to see Deborah off on eleven a.m. train, meet back at hotel, eventually.* He slipped it under Colin's bedroom door before he finally went to bed.

Next morning he was up at the crack of dawn. With time to spare, he packed his suitcase before having breakfast. He assumed that he and his friend would be driving back to London later in the day, but first things first. After breakfast he walked to the railway station and sat in the waiting room, patiently awaiting his lover.

The voices on the platform made him stand up and go out to check who it was.

Deborah and Veronica held their suitcases while an older woman looked at her watch. He assumed this must be Aunt Ada; what a battle axe she appeared to be: tweed skirt, a tweed poncho, thick grey stockings, with brown brogues on her feet that stood with legs apart.

Amadeus ignored her, then embraced Deborah, giving her a kiss on the cheeks.

"So you're the flavour of the month, Rupert. Just like a peacock, strutting about outside my apartment. I was tempted to throw a bucket of cold water over you to cool you down."

"Oh do be quiet, Aunty, and allow me to introduce him." The introductions were made.

Amadeus couldn't believe Deborah's description of her aunt on the beach, but now he understood. A woman not to be messed with or lied to. He shook her tight grip with vigour, not letting go until she decided to let go of his hand. They heard the train approaching from the bend in the tracks. A solitary figure ran across the overhead bridge waving his arms. Colin bounded down the steps as the large steam locomotive shuddered to a stop. "Glad I made it, Deborah," he said trying to catch his breath.

Amadeus lifted her suitcase and walked to the first-class compartment, placing the case in the overhead luggage rack. They stood in the corridor kissing and making promises. The guard arrived to close the door and Amadeus stepped out onto the platform, making sure that the carriage door window was open. He stretched up and kissed her before the whistle sounded and the train began its journey to London. Everyone on the platform was waving frantically, as the carriages disappeared out of sight.

Aunt Ada spoke in a harsh voice, "You take care of my niece, Rupert, or you'll have me to answer to." She briefly shook his hand before hailing a taxi.

Colin laughed. "You have your hands full there, my trusty friend. However, come and see my little beauty that I have purchased." They walked to the red M.G. Convertible two seater. "What do you think?"

Amadeus just nodded, his mind was elsewhere.

CHAPTER TWO

The journey back to London by car was comfortable enough. They talked about the weekend, but it was the only secret he ever kept from his friend.

Amadeus said nothing about his experience on the beach the day before. In fact, the conversation became muted when Deborah's name was mentioned. Arriving in London, Amadeus was dropped off at his basement flat, after promising to keep in touch.

It was now time for work, each friend made their way to their appointed police station location.

It was quickly recognised that P.C. Rupert had an uncanny knack of solving cases quickly with method and ability. Therefore, it wasn't long before his name was mentioned in the confines of Scotland Yard. Soon enough, he was transferred to serious crime duties and his skill became the talk of the top brass. He was rapidly promoted to detective sergeant.

He had settled into his position, solving bank raids, serious assaults, and other crimes that embraced the city. Always keeping in touch with Deborah, three, four times a week, more when he could find the time. She would visit him whenever possible, and their time was spent mostly in a horizontal position, in bed.

Then came the news he had least expected. She had become pregnant, due to their unprotected sex on the beach that special afternoon in Bournemouth. She had held it back from him. However, she was now starting to show, and her teaching profession would eventually have to cease until she could resume her studies.

A marriage ceremony was hastily arranged, at the Bow Street Marriage Centre in London.

It was a simple ceremony, with Colin as best man and Veronica as maid of honour.

They stepped out into a cold November wind; Amadeus felt strange. It was all over so quickly that he did not feel married. However, love conquers all and, after a dinner, they made their way by taxi back to the basement flat where they would stay until their son Colin was born.

Amadeus was always on the lookout for something better. A place they could call their own, now that he was earning a reasonable wage. That was to improve as he was promoted to Inspector. It had a nice ring to it: Inspector Rupert of the Yard.

This was a name that struck fear in the minds of the crime syndicate bosses in London.

When Inspector Rupert was on a case, it was only a matter of time before an arrest was made; that was how he had gained his reputation. However, everything in the garden was not rosy. Deborah was not completely happy with city life, and they had many heated discussions on the subject. She felt her profession had been snatched away from her, and, with the help of her parents, wanted to resume her studies at the teaching academy in Welwyn, Hertfordshire. This was becoming an everyday discussion at the dinner table. She had informed him there was a place vacant to take up her studies. So it was agreed that she would go back to Welwyn where her step-mum could look after baby Colin. Amadeus could make an application for a transfer to the Hertfordshire constabulary.

That was the way it was to be, much to the disappointment of his senior officers, who insisted it was a bad move, and London was where he belonged and would in time climb the promotional ladder, emphasising that Welwyn was a backwater with little action.

Everything had fallen into place. Deborah had resumed her studies, eventually graduating to teacher status. Amadeus had been accepted into the Hertfordshire constabulary, who were only too glad of an officer with such high esteem from the Scotland Yard team.

There was some hope on the horizon. However, as two new towns were proposed to eradicate the growing housing problem. The first to be built at Letchworth, and another to follow called Welwyn Garden City. The Welwyn Garden City project had been started in 1919, when plans were laid out by the private sector, and mostly bungalows and villas had been built. Then in the interim period it was slowly taken over by the public sector, which started to build a new primary and secondary school, an art college and a teacher's training college. The police headquarters were to be moved from Stevenage to a large five-story police building, which pleased Inspector Rupert, who had to commute around the county (a position commonly known as a floater). The new building might prove that he would be kept in the area. He found a way of combating that by keeping himself busy, he moved around the county whenever the local force needed help. He just had to be patient, and allow things to change at their own speed.

It was on one of those boring days as he stood in the Welwyn police office that he thumbed through a missing persons case in the rotary card system. A case caught his attention dating back to 1933, but there was a much more recent case that he intended to follow up.

A woman had been reported missing over a year ago, in 1937, and the case was not followed up. He understood that after a time most missing persons were traced or simply turned up, it was not listed as a grade one incident until a week had passed, but this was over a year ago; something had gone badly wrong in the missing persons procedure. He would keep a close eye on the situation. Each day he came into work, he focused on the missing woman from Hatfield.

Her name was Molly Stacey, a factory worker from Hatfield, so he took the decision to put together a small team, comprised of a woman police constable and a male police constable, who in fairness were the best of a lethargic bunch.

He called a meeting of every officer in the station.

"Okay, at ease," he said calmly. "It has come to my attention that there seems to be a lack of enthusiasm in this station and beyond." He paused. "I didn't spend my time with Scotland Yard making things easy for lazy officers. Therefore, my uniformed friends, that is about to change. W.P.C. Buckingham, and P.C. Bowman will assist me in the investigation I'm about to undertake."

He looked at the smiling officers. "Working with me will not be a walk in the park. I will expect you both to be at my beck and call twenty-four hours a day, is that understood?"

They both nodded sheepishly.

"As for the rest of you, I expect you to go about your police duties with some enthusiasm, and be ready to assist in our investigation." There was a whispered response. "Right, come tomorrow, Molly Stacey will have been reported missing for over a year. Therefore, I intend to reopen her file. That gives me the opportunity to commence our search for her. Meanwhile, I'll report my intentions to H.Q. in Stevenage, and while I'm doing that Buckingham and Bowman can revise the case by starting with who made the report and when, along with a name and address we can start with in the morning."

The trio made their way to Hatfield. As they stepped out of the police car, P.C. Bowman commented on the state of the garden and house, a semi-detached that only needed a lick of paint. Inspector Rupert ignored the comment. "You go round to the back, Bowman, there's a good chap. Right, Buckingham, you're with me."

Inspector Rupert spotted the rusting Austin 7 parked in an overgrown driveway. It took him back to the days when he and Colin would drive up to the airfield, with him at the wheel. They walked carefully up the broken slabs of the uneven path.

He knocked on the door, getting no answer. He knocked louder. Still no response. He opened the letter box and shouted, "Police, open up." That did the trick.

A badly dressed man appeared, clutching a bottle of beer, a heavy stubble on his face. "What now? Can a man get no peace in his house? I know nothing about any break-ins," he said taking a drink from the bottle.

"It's not about any break-ins, Mr. Stacey; it's regarding your wife's disappearance. You were supposed to inform us if she turned up. So the question is, has she turned up, or have you heard from her over the period since you reported her missing?" He brushed past the surprised character into an untidy living room.

"The cow's never been in touch with me or our two children. Off she went with some lover who was shagging her at the time. Does that answer your question?" He took another drink, spilling some of it onto an already stained jumper.

"Not quite, Mr. Stacey." Inspector Rupert paused. "You must understand that if your wife hasn't turned up, then it's our job to find her." He noticed there were only photos of children on the mantlepiece. "I see from our notes that you were questioned by the Hatfield police, who had you down as their chief suspect, so much so that they turned over your gardens, back and front but found nothing. Therefore I was wondering if you can remember anything else that might give us a clue as to where she is?"

"Bloody police left the garden the way you see it today, and no, I have nothing to add to the statement I gave them at the time. So you and your hounds can bugger off. I want to listen to the first race."

Inspector Rupert rubbed his chin. "I wouldn't take any more of that beer, sir, not if you want to keep your children. A social service is available, but they can take the children into care if they think they are not being looked after properly."

"Listen, Inspector, I adore my children, and they are looked after, so you can drop that accusation." He put the bottle of beer on the mantlepiece, attempting to bring the intrusion to a swift end. Inspector Rupert sat down on the stain-covered couch. "I see that you were a sergeant in the army. I thought they would have instilled some discipline into your life, and yet you continue to live in this—" He waved his hands around in the air, about to say "Hovel" when P.C. Bowman appeared.

The Inspector got up quickly. "I'll arrange for the council to tidy up the garden since it was us that left it like this. However, I want you to think about anything you can add to your statement. I will be making my own inquiries in the meantime, so take heed of what I've just said, and get a grip of yourself." He made his way to the door then turned. "Your wife worked as a machine operator in a factory. Give W.P.C. Buckingham the address, or her last place of employment." He urged Buckingham to take down the information, then walked quickly out of the stale house into the fresh air.

As they drove back to Welwyn, Inspector Rupert spoke earnestly, "I can see that you pair are as keen as mustard. Therefore, I have a proposition to put to you." He paused. "I will recommend to the top brass that you take up the position of detective constables, and in time, who knows? You might manage promotion if you can prove your worth."

They both agreed wholeheartedly.

"Okay, let's look at this case; I notice that Justin Stacey is listed as the only suspect. However, I want you both to keep an open mind, because by all accounts his wife Molly was a bit of a girl. She must have known plenty of people who worked in the factory." He paused again. "You heard what Mr. Stacey said about his wife having extramarital affairs before going off with her lover. So we have to find that lover, and why he wasn't listed as a suspect I'll never know."

The Inspector got out of the car and leaned on the roof. "That's a job for you, Bowman. The best place to start would be her place of work; question any friends that she mixed with, both at work and in her leisure time. Buckingham and I will question Justin Stacey again, after he's had time to think, and sweat." He relaxed his stance. "When you're at Hatfield, give the council a kick up the backside. I know we're not social workers, but I think if we play ball with Mr. Stacey, he just might remember something of his wife's lover and disappearance."

They walked into the police station and set up an incident room. The scant information was pinned to a board, with a black marker explaining what was what.

After lunch, Bowman made his way back over to Hatfield. He visited the council first, then made his way to the factory where Molly Stacey had worked.

He picked up some valuable information about Molly, from her acquaintances and friends.

It had taken most of the afternoon to question each one at length, much to the annoyance of the factory foreman, who bleated that production was being lost. It was with perseverance that he extracted who Molly Stacey's lover was. A name and address was given, so he decided to make a name for himself and pay the lover a visit. He was quite surprised at the affluent area that he drove into. Detached bungalows, no broken windows and street lights that worked. The night was creeping in when he tapped the door lightly, then remembered how the Inspector got a response, so rapped the knocker loudly and was about to lift the letterbox when he heard a woman's voice. "Hold your bloody horses," she said opening the door.

P.C. Bowman introduced himself, showing his warrant card. "Is Mr. Tarell at home, as I need to speak to him?" he said sternly, so the woman would not take his visit lightly.

"Sorry, he's away on business. Can I help?"

"No, it's Mr. Tarell I need to speak to. When will he be back?"

"Friday." She attempted to close the door, but Bowman had learned early. He jammed his foot in the opening before she could close it. "It's most urgent that Inspector Rupert of Welwyn Police Station talks to him." Bowman scribbled down a phone number from his notebook. "Make sure he contacts us on his return. We don't have time to waste coming to get him." He withdrew his foot from the door before the woman closed it.

He sat in the police car feeling pleased with himself before driving back to Welwyn. There was nobody but the desk sergeant to be seen, so he went to the incident room, and pinned up the information he had acquired.

This drew the attention of Inspector Rupert as he studied the information board the following morning. He realised that Bowman must have worked late the previous night to acquire such information. He never mentioned it as the team began to assemble in the incident room, where it was agreed that every officer would report to the duty sergeant, sitting at the table.

The debate began with the usual reports of drunken behaviour and fighting in the street. However, these petty crimes were left to the woolly suits, as the detectives gathered around the information board.

He addressed the throng, who chattered loudly when allocated their beat in the small town.

"Listen up, children, I want a couple of officers to do a door-to-door in the Hatfield area where Justin Stacey lives: when was Molly Stacey last seen? What were her movements, apart from going and coming home from work? Were there any vehicles that picked her up or dropped her off? Sergeant Whelan will allocate who does what, but I want information about her." He thought for a moment. "Okay, D.C. Bowman, and D.C. Buckingham will go and put pressure on Mrs. Tarell again. Find out what her husband does, find out what company he is with, something that Detective Constable Bowman should have asked last night." He smiled. "You'll notice I use the term detective constable, because the top brass agreed it was time for Welwyn to move forward, so congratulations to Bowman and Buckingham. Now it's time for work." Inspector Rupert turned and walked quickly out of the incident room.

He made his way over to Hatfield, calling into the police station to see if they had any other information on Molly and Justin Stacey. There was nothing of any extra interest so he drove down to Justin Stacey's house. It was in the same state as he had left it yesterday.

"Good morning, Justin, just a few more questions regarding your wife. When she left for work on the day she disappeared, was she picked up by anyone, a neighbour perhaps?"

Justin Stacey coughed and spat into the fire. "Not that I know of, Inspector. What is all this? My wife took off leaving me to bring up two children. I had to give up work. That's why we're in such a state today."

Inspector Rupert listened intently. "You mentioned work, what was your occupation, and who did you work for?"

"I'm an electrician by trade, time served and taught by the armed forces, when I done my national service. I was what you'd call freelance, working for different contractors in the area, but the days of plenty were over when Molly walked out."

Inspector Rupert nodded. "I want you to write down every contractor you worked for. Not now, take your time and give me a complete list the next time I call."

He watched Justin Stacey twitch. "Some were years ago, Inspector. How do you expect me to remember them all?"

"Just do your best, Mr. Stacey; we can trace any firm you worked for if need be. However, this way it will be quicker, so do as I ask. I'll also need recent bank statements, which points me in the direction of an accountant, so that in itself would be useful, because they tend to keep records for years gone by, a name and address would be most helpful."

"Brightman Accountants on the high street, they handled my business and tax returns. As for recent bank statements, well that's a joke. Where am I going to get any money to put in an account?"

Inspector Rupert nodded. "Just one more question, Justin, did your wife Molly have a separate bank account or was it in joint names?"

"Neither, Inspector, it was in my name, or I should say the firm's name, from which she was given an allowance, for rent, food, etc. That was all listed and handed to our accountant at the end of the financial year." He hesitated. "No, I' m wrong. She did have a separate bank account that she paid part of her wages into, and spent part on clothes. However, she never showed me her wage slips in the brown pay packet, and to be frank, I was making money back then, so didn't really care." He stoked the fire noisily. "Right, I have to pick the children up from school at lunchtime, so if you don't mind, Inspector."

"Thanks, Justin, keep yourself available and don't leave the area without informing us."

Inspector Rupert made his way out to the police car. He noticed the two constables making door-to-door inquiries. He felt that things were starting to move. On what, he hadn't decided yet, but kept an open mind about Molly Stacey.

He sat in the police car, watching the curtains in the neighbouring houses move. Justin Stacey stood on the doorstep with arms folded, then gave them the V sign, before he walked down the uneven path.

Inspector Rupert decided to go back to the Hatfield police station, he had in his possession another name he had taken from the index card about another missing woman, which he kept close to his chest. However, it was time to ruffle a few feathers, as he walked into the police station.

The desk sergeant paid him little attention. "Yes?" he asked in a drawl.

"Stand up when you address a senior officer, and put that cigarette out now."

The sergeant sprang to his feet when Inspector Rupert flashed his warrant card.

"Sorry, sir, I was concentrating on something important," he said softly, buttoning up his tunic

"Well, Sergeant, concentrate on this," the Inspector said harshly. "I want to talk to a senior officer who was in charge of two missing persons cases. The first was a nurse called Marion Fletcher, aged twenty-five of Scottish origin, then there is another name which I inquired about here before and was fobbed off. But not this time, Sergeant, so do what you must, but get me a senior officer who was attached to those cases." His voice had risen a decibel. The sergeant hastily lifted the telephone and pressed a button. He spoke quietly with his back turned to shield the conversation. "Superintendent Bovey will be down shortly, sir. Please take a seat."

Inspector Rupert ignored the gesture, and paced up and down in front of the desk.

Eventually an older man came from behind a door. Introductions were made with the usual handshakes before Inspector Rupert followed his boss upstairs.

"Two missing women, Superintendent," he said before they made themselves comfortable.

"Marion Fletcher in 1935, then Molly Stacey in 1936, yet no official statement was ever made that the women had been found. There is another that goes back to 1933, but I haven't had the chance to look at that case just yet."

"Indeed, Inspector, let's start with Marion Fletcher." He took out a file from the cabinet. "Born in Arbroath in Scotland, came to work at the Hatfield general hospital in 1934, family relations in Ireland. It was assumed that she took off because of the string of debt she had left behind. The Scottish force said they would check her family out, to see if she had returned to Scotland. However, we never got word back, and assumed she had been found or had gone to Southern Ireland."

Inspector Rupert screwed up his face. "That was two years ago, sir; why was this not pursued to conclusion?"

The Superintendent ignored him. "Now let's move on to Molly Stacey. Her husband was the chief suspect; we even turned over his garden, back and front, and found nothing. After a wasted search, it was assumed that Molly Stacey had gone off with her lover to London."

Inspector Rupert couldn't believe his ears. "Did you follow up on that, sir? I know, having worked with Scotland Yard, that people don't just disappear. A paper trail would be left to follow. It takes a very special criminal to make a body disappear, sir, and frankly I don't believe a word of it until I can prove otherwise." He stood up quickly before the Superintendent had time to draw breath. "Thanks for your time, sir, I'll do a little digging myself, to see what I can come up with." He started to make his way out of the office.

"You listen to me, Rupert, I don't want you opening up old wounds that are dead and buried. You may have served with the Met and Scotland Yard, but you're in the Hertfordshire constabulary now, and you obey our rules."

Inspector Rupert ignored the slight, opened the door, and leaving it open marched down the corridor and out to the police car.

He didn't take it to heart, but thought carefully about what the Superintendent had said, and would use it in the future. But now there was more work to be done.

He looked at the reports on his desk, before making his way to the incident room. The door knockers had found out nothing, neighbours had used the time factor as an excuse. However, one man had noticed that there were a lot of visitors to the house, and one vehicle in particular stood out, a Ford Zephyr, but he had paid no heed to the registration.

There was nothing from the Arbroath police regarding the missing nurse Marion Fletcher, so he kept an open mind on what had been suggested. It was possible that Marion Fletcher had left a string of debt, then skipped off to Scotland or Ireland.

And Molly Stacey could have disappeared with a lover. Yet her so-called lover had been traced, living happily with his wife and three children in Hatfield, yet to be interviewed, but his place of work could be approached and questioned over the suspect's character. When he returned from work duties the time would come to put the pressure on him and his wife.

Every clue, every avenue that Inspector Rupert had, was checked and double checked: the various people that were connected with Molly Stacey, including Mr. and Mrs. Tarell, which left Mrs. Tarell in tears, and her husband having to explain his extra marital trysts.

This was now getting out of hand, one or two leads, but nothing concrete. They needed a break, something to set the ball rolling, something to follow up.

Molly Stacey's bank records corresponded with her weekly wage payments from the factory. Something didn't add up. However,: the fact that so many men were visiting her house during the day, when her husband was out on a job, made him suspicious.

Inspector Rupert asked himself, "How can she be entertaining men at the house, when she was clocked in and out of the factory, her time card stamped and up to date?" There was an answer to that conundrum, somebody could have been clocking her in and out, and that someone would have to be a shift supervisor, or floor personnel.

He called D.C. Bowman aside and explained what he wanted done at the factory. "Okay, Bowman, you go over to Hatfield and question Justin Stacey again, ask him if he has any photographs of his wife, something we can pin up on the board. I'll follow you down later when I've sorted out my in tray."

Everyone went off to carry out their specific duties. Inspector Rupert cleared his in tray of what was to be done, as well as the missing persons cases.

After putting them into order of response, he drove over to Hatfield. D.C. Bowman was leaning on the fence reading his newspaper.

"Anything interesting, Bowman?" the Inspector asked tersely.

The D.C. folded the paper quickly. "As you can see, sir, the council have started cleaning up the garden." He was trying to divert attention from his being caught when he should have been working.

"Never mind that, Bowman, has Stacey revealed anything else?"

"No, sir, nothing that he hasn't already told us," Detective Constable Bowman said lightly.

The Inspector rubbed his chin. "Okay let's go over to the factory, and find out what Buckingham has come up with."

When they arrived, she had a works manager sitting in his office, looking nervous.

"I could lose my job if this gets out." The works manager had apparently been signing Molly Stacey in and out of work, using the excuse that she was sick or had some doctor's appointment.

"You should have thought of that at the time, Mr. Sugden. Please, tell the Inspector what you've just told me," D.C. Buckingham said tersely.

The nervous manager began to speak softly. "Molly Stacey was a very generous woman where sex was concerned, Inspector. On certain days of the week, she entertained men while her husband was at work. She operated her sexual favours like a hairdressing salon, with each client booked in for a certain time, and having a fifteen-minute break to shower and prepare for the next one. Three times a week she did this, giving me a freebie now and again, but more important, payment for my services rendered." The manager drew breath. "Molly Stacey was making a fortune, Inspector. She'd been at it for years, not only in her house, but she'd visit the streets of the surrounding towns and villages occasionally, keeping a note of every client. She was meticulous with her book keeping."

Inspector Rupert leaned forward in the chair. "Are you telling us that Molly Stacey was a prostitute and on the game?"

"I suppose that's the bottom line, Inspector." He hesitated before speaking again. "There was one particular client that she saw on a regular basis. I never met him, simply because he always parked a safe distance from the factory gate, but he was there every Tuesday and Friday without fail. It was probably him she took off with. Leaving me to lie and scheme to cover her tracks."

"Registration, make and model of the car?" Buckingham asked hopefully.

The manager just shrugged his shoulders. "Will this need to come out, Inspector? I've got a wife and family to care for." There were tears in his eyes.

The Inspector said nothing and signalled with his head for the two detectives to follow him out to the car.

They stood for a moment before Inspector Rupert spoke. "So now we have Molly Stacey on the game, and whatever else she was up to."

He rubbed his chin as D.C. Bowman asked, "What else could she have been up to, sir? We surely have the big picture from the manager."

"Blackmail, Bowman. I think Molly Stacey was a blackmailer, as well as a prostitute. She'd found herself a sugar daddy with a dodgy past, then set about her illicit trade." He paused. "And if I remember words of an old colleague in the Met, 'where there's one on the hook, there are bound to be more'. Let's keep in mind that Justin Stacey was in the army, so what better opportunity for having free movement and a place to carry out her sex trysts in the early days. So dig a little deeper into her past, something's sure to surface. Meanwhile I'll go back to visit Justin Stacey; I'm sure he's hiding the truth from us. There must be a ledger of income somewhere. I suspect all her payments were made in cash, and if her illegal income's not in a bank account, then where is it? You come with me, Buckingham, meanwhile Donald can retrace our steps to the Tarell household, find out if Mr. Tarell was being blackmailed, and if he knows of any other fly that was caught in the spider's web. The more names we get the quicker a can of worms will open up and point us towards Molly Stacey's killer."

"Killer, sir? You're surely getting ahead of yourself," D.C. Buckingham said with hesitation.

"No, Buckingham, I believe we're now dealing with a murder. I think Molly Stacey's been murdered, due to the fact she was blackmailing the wrong man, and knew too much of the murderer's past. So let's get to it with new vigour, because this is the opening I've been praying for."

They went their separate ways. Inspector Rupert took the wheel and drove back to Justin Stacey's house.

"Have you crowd got nothing else to do?" Justin asked blandly.

"Time for the truth to come out, Justin. If you don't come clean, then I'll have no alternative but to arrest you and take you to the Welwyn police station, for more questioning."

"For God's sake, Inspector, I've told you all I know, how many times must I repeat myself?" He slumped back onto the couch spilling his bottle of beer.

Inspector Rupert stared at the suspect, letting the accusation sink in.

"I have no idea what you're talking about, Inspector, certainly there was talk, but that happens when you're popular, like Molly was, with many friends; people are just jealous."

He leaned back and took a swig of beer, not bothering to wipe the dribbles from his cardigan.

"You're either very gullible or very stupid, Justin, not to realise what your wife was up to, especially when you were in the army, and at work with your business." He paused. "We now have evidence that your wife was, in fact, a prostitute, and that she was also a blackmailer. I'm waiting on a report, and if you want my opinion, I think your wife is dead, which makes you my number one suspect, Justin." He was starting to put pressure on the nervous man, who squirmed where he sat, staring into space.

"I've killed no one. I keep telling you but you're not listening. I know my rights, that you and your bunch need a search warrant. In fact, you and your bosom pal shouldn't be questioning me without legal representation being present, my legal representative, therefore I must ask you to leave, now." He emphasised the last word.

"If I have to leave here, I'll be taking you with me, and we can carry on this conversation at the Welwyn police station, that's your choice."

"What about my children, Inspector? I'd be lost without them."

Inspector Rupert sat silently.

D.C. Buckingham said softly, "We can arrange to have them taken into care, while you're held in custody, Justin."

That made Stacey sit up. "Alright perhaps I did know my wife was having extramarital relations, but I swear, I never knew she was on the game. I know absolutely nothing about a ledger book or her income, apart from her wages." He held his head in his hands. "There is one thing I do know, Inspector, I was never allowed into her bedroom. Another thing was her late nights, and when I questioned her about how she could keep so many late nights and work in the factory during the day, she told me to mind my own fucking business, in those exact words."

Inspector Rupert couldn't help himself. "Look at you, Justin, you're a disgrace to depression. Now show me her bedroom."

He waited until Stacey had finished his beer, then followed him upstairs. The strange thing was that the bedroom was tidy and spotless. He mentioned this to Justin Stacey, who told him this was now his daughter's room, it was her sanctuary which she lived in most of the time.

Inspector Rupert walked around the room. "The wardrobe has been moved, Justin; look at the marks on the linoleum."

"Not by me, Inspector, and certainly not by my daughter, Christine. She could never move this on her own." He walked over towards the large Victorian wardrobe.

"Let's move it away from the wall, just to see what's behind it," the Inspector said quickly.

They moved it quite easily, and that was when the wall cupboard came into view. The Inspector slid back the bolt, to reveal the contents of the walk-in cupboard. Black notebooks and ledgers piled on top of one another, there was a large trunk in the corner that was padlocked. He ordered D.C. Buckingham to fetch the wrecking bar from the car. She returned quickly taking the stairs two at a time.

The Inspector edged the bar between the padlock and the chest. The lid sprang open. He gasped in amazement at the money the chest concealed. "Wow," was all he said, turning to Buckingham. He stood in silence totally dumbfounded.

"This is what we've been missing, Buckingham. Get some officers down here to remove this cache. We'll also need fingerprints and a photographer. You see to it, while I continue to question Justin." He stared at the black books and trunk with a huge grin on his face. "Right, Mr. Stacey, let's go downstairs and get this find cleared up."

CHAPTER THREE

They sat in the incident room sifting through the black books. Most were like an accountant's ledger, even listing taxi fares to and from towns and local areas.

"This is dynamite, Buckingham, feast your eyes on this one." He slid the black ledger across the desk. "Molly Stacey earned more in a day than I earn in a month." He changed the subject. "What does still leave a sour taste in my mouth, though, is wondering if Justin Stacey knew about his wife's game all along, helping himself occasionally, to help prop up his business."

"And live the lifestyle he's living sir? I doubt it, because if it was me, I'd be living the high life with expensive clothes and cars." She shook her head. "I think Justin Stacey is innocent, even if he had killed his wife, why live in poverty?"

The D.I. nodded. "Yes, I'm inclined to agree with you, Buckingham; so tell me what you think of the evidence in front of you."

"It wipes the theory that Molly Stacey ran off with a lover, because, firstly, she wouldn't have left thousands of pounds, and the risk of it being found." She screwed up her face. "Secondly, she would have destroyed all the black books that linked her to the crimes. Let's for argument's sake call it a paper trail." She thumbed open another page. "I think we can say conclusively that due to what we have found, and the names listed in this book, Molly Stacey is a dead woman, murdered by a person or persons unknown. She was also a blackmailer; you only need to look at all the names and addresses she kept, with regular payments at the end of each month, with the crimes associated to the person involved: shop lifting, incest, homosexual activities, etc. etc. etc." She drew breath. "What a list, sir, dynamite, just as you said."

"Well done, Buckingham, I couldn't have said it any better myself. So now it definitely is a murder inquiry, and when you go through the rest of the black books, look out for Marion Fletcher's name. I'm sure it will appear somewhere."

A Love to Remember

Buckingham nodded. "I'm convinced those aren't the only women involved. It might be worthwhile checking each area for missing persons, because this could be the action of a serial killer."

"Please, Buckingham, I know you're enthusiastic, but let's keep this within the bounds of sanity." He smiled and left her to carry the black book ledgers to his office where he and she could study each one without interruption or distraction. They worked late, listing every name and address, typing them out, and then carbon-copying each sheet ready for the officers to start the investigation in the morning

His wife Deborah wondered what had happened to him, he normally phoned home to report he would be late. However, on this occasion he was more interested in getting the work done. He was met with a frosty reception. "Your dinner is in the oven, ruined as usual," she said before going to bed.

Amadeus sat with a glass of wine, pleased as punch that they had finally got a breakthrough. He explained this to Deborah, while lying in the dark. She turned over and went to sleep without a word of sympathy and understanding. D.I. Rupert was first in the incident room. He looked at the information board that could now be upgraded. He pinned up a copy of the names and addresses When the morning shift were recalled to the police station, and the team began to assemble, he held up one of the large ledgers. This contains figures of Molly Stacey's income and expenditure." He waved it in the air. "One of the team can concentrate on the figures, who was paying for what, how much and, most importantly, the amount. Look for a steady pattern that we can cross-reference with the names and addresses. Each of you will receive a copy of those names and addresses. Take Note that they are not all in Hatfield, but cover different locations in Hertfordshire." He pointed to the information board. "We have twenty-six names to follow up, so get your heads together with D.C. Bowman, and decide who is going to knock on the doors and where. If the person who was being blackmailed is not at home then make it a point that you will return." He pointed at the list. "Take note that some of those who were targeted might have moved away, or might even be deceased. Only then will you delete the name from the list, and we will update your finds every morning." He tapped the board lightly. "Somewhere in this list is the killer of Molly Stacey, who I am now convinced is dead. You will note that Marion Fletcher's name is on the list, so let's keep an open mind on that as well." He made his way to the office, followed by Buckingham. "Why do your colleagues call you Queenie, Buckingham?"

She gave him a scowl. "Christened Victoria, sir, Buckingham palace. Does that answer your question?"

The D.I. Changed the subject immediately. "Take a look at this name, Buckingham, this man was paying for sex. However, look at the dates and markings. S is obviously for sex, but much later in the year he has a U.A.S. marked against him, with an amount of £250 that then doubles to £500. Any suggestions?" He folded his arms awaiting an answer.

"I think the S again represents sex, sir. I would hazard a guess that the U.A. is underage, and if Molly Stacey had this information on such a prominent business man, Strewth, it would open up Pandora's box." She leaned on the desk. "There is also the fact that his name is the last entry in this notebook, which moves him to the top of our suspects list because that was around the time Molly Stacey was reported missing."

The Inspector nodded. "So our first course of action this morning is to pay Captain Ernest Foster a visit, to ask him exactly why he was being blackmailed."

They walked across town to Wheatfield Villa, that lay in its own grounds, a mile from the road. They walked at a steady pace, eventually reaching the villa. Inspector Rupert rang the doorbell, then rapped heavily and loudly on the letterbox. The door was answered by a maid. "I wish to speak to Captain Foster, is he available?"

A voice came from the background. "Who is it, Cynthia?" The lady of the house made an appearance.

"Inspector Rupert, and D.C. Buckingham." They showed their warrant cards. "I wish to speak to Captain Ernest Foster, if he's available."

The pretty petite blonde handed them their cards after studying them. "Sorry, Inspector, the Captain is away on business, can I be of any help?"

Inspector Rupert shook his head. "No, I need to speak to the Captain urgently, so when he returns, please phone this number, and ask him to wait until we arrive." He watched the woman's reaction.

"Can I ask what it is about, Inspector? My husband is a very busy man."

Inspector Rupert pointed at the slip of paper. "Just tell him to phone that number." They turned to walk away, as the door was slammed shut in their face.

They walked back to the police station. Detective Constable Buckingham had trouble keeping up, as the Inspector had a spring in his step.

She was glad when they reached the comfort of the incident room, where she slumped onto a chair. Realising what she had just done, she stood back up quickly despite her aching legs.

Inspector Rupert went directly to the information board and wrote down two names, Cynthia Foster and Ernest Foster. He turned to Buckingham. "I want this pair checked out, the usual scenario, any police record, that can give us ammunition when we question the so-called captain." He paused. "That's something else to check, Buckingham, get onto the armed forces records, find out what regiment and battalion he was in, whether it was infantry or whatever." There was a silence as Inspector Rupert rubbed his chin. "Have his medical records checked while you're at it; something just might pop up, you never know, but I want to be prepared when Captain Foster turns up. We'll give him to the end of the week before venturing any further with an arrest warrant."

Buckingham took notes. "About this unexplained U.A.S. listed in the ledger, sir, shall I follow that up as well, when I get my breath back?" She watched him smile.

"I think we can leave that until we meet and question Mr. Foster. However, you could do a little digging into his family life. That might help when we meet the man, but it is important you attend to the first few items." He stopped suddenly, looking at his watch. "I think I'll go over to Hatfield and drop a few hints to Justin Stacey about our interest in Captain Eric Foster, you never know what his response might be, so you get on, and I'll expect some information when I get back this afternoon."

He heard the D.C. mumble, but paid little attention, as he made his way out of the incident room.

The drive did not take long. He noticed that the front garden had been tidied, and painters were giving the house a lick of paint. He was pleasantly surprised when Justin Stacey opened the door and stood smartly dressed, with polished shoes.

"This won't take a minute, Justin." He was invited into a clean and tidy living room. No beer bottles were on display. Inspector Rupert did not waste time. "Tell me, Justin, have you ever come across a man called Foster, Ernest Foster, with a prefix of captain?"

"Don't mention that name in this house, Inspector, a character of ill repute, who never pays his bills on time, and owes me money from years ago. I chased him for it, but couldn't afford the lawyer's fees to take him to court."

Inspector Rupert nodded. "Does he owe money to anyone else, Justin?"

"Practically anyone who did work for his company, plasterers, plumbers, my electrical work, you name a trade and I can guarantee that Foster owes them money, and what's this captain business? He's no more a captain than I am. He was a kitchen orderly in the army. Scrubbing pots and pans, that's what Foster was, before he met his wife, who had money and set him up in business."

Inspector Rupert smiled. "I'm glad to see you've smartened yourself up a bit. Keep it up, there are openings out in the real world for smart men with a trade." He paused. "Tell me Justin, have the Fosters any children?"

"There was talk that he had a daughter to his sister-in-law, a Mrs. Jennifer Steadman. The reason I know that is because I done work for her, but that was a while back, and I got paid direct from Mrs. Steadman, whose daughter told me that Ernest

Foster was her father who had interfered with her, but I dismissed it as a childish story, poor little mare."

"You would have mentioned this to your wife at the time?" Inspector Rupert was interested in the answer.

"I suppose so, those were the days we discussed our work. However, I wouldn't mind betting it was Foster that was shagging my wife, and gave her a dose of the clap, although I could never prove it. I had doubts, and we argued constantly about it."

Inspector Rupert thanked him and walked out into the sunshine.

He decided to go home for a bite to eat. Deborah was in a buoyant mood. She had attained a position in the secondary school, which meant higher income. Now they could afford a small bungalow, similar to the type Amadeus had been brought up in. She placed the estate agent's photographs on the table pointing to one in particular.

"I'm sorry, darling, but I'm far too busy at the moment to be house hunting or moving. I have an investigation under way and about to open up."

She yelled, "You always have something on the go, Amadeus. I sometimes wonder what comes first, me, or the job?" She apologised for the outburst. "Just do me a favour and consider it when you get a minute." She kissed the top of his head then poured the tea.

He thought congratulations were in order, and told her how happy he was for her, expressing his concern that it would be a bigger workload, with bigger classes and more examination papers to correct. However, the decision had been made to accept the appointment, and this made Deborah very happy indeed, in fact it had been a while since he had seen his wife so happy. He kissed her, then made his way to the police station.

Detective Constable Buckingham had done her homework. "Guess what I've discovered, sir?"

"I don't have time for guess work, Buckingham, get on with it."

"Captain Ernest Foster contracted a venereal disease." She paused to let the information sink in. "I didn't get this information from his doctor, but the army medical corps were more open about his syphilis, so I went onto the register, kept by the National Disease Records, and found four people connected to Ernest Foster: his wife Cynthia; Molly Stacey; a young girl who was in a children's home in Stevenage at that time, her name is Amanda Smith; then we have Jennifer Steadman who you already know about."

The Inspector nodded. "You've done well, Buckingham. I want you to go to the orphanage and question the older staff, who might know where Amanda Smith has moved to. I'll take the chance to pay Jennifer Steadman a visit. I have a few questions that need answers."

He decided to walk to the outskirts of the expanding village. The Victorian villa stood on a grassy knoll, above the treelined street. He checked the number, 27 Mayflower Gardens, obviously an affluent owner. He pressed the doorbell, and when nobody answered he kept his finger on the button until a smartly dressed woman opened the door.

"Jennifer Steadman, Mrs. Jennifer Steadman?" He asked in a monotonous tone. "Inspector Rupert of Hertfordshire Constabulary." He flashed his warrant card. "Just a few questions, madam, can we talk inside?" He didn't wait on an invitation. He quickly brushed past the woman, and waited in a large hall to be shown where to go. He followed her into a large bright room with a bay window.

"I'll make this as brief as possible, Mrs. Steadman, there are a few sordid questions I need to ask, just to help me clear up a few anomalies." He watched her light a cigarette and blow smoke into the air before offering him tea or coffee. "No thanks, Mrs. Steadman, a busy afternoon ahead for some." He smiled. "Okay, let's start with your sister Cynthia. She is married to Ernest Foster, is that correct?"

He watched her inhale deeply. "Yes, that is correct, Inspector," she said softly. "Captain Foster is my brother-in-law."

"I think we can cut out the crap, Jennifer; we know that Ernest Foster is no more a captain than you are, so let's stick to the facts." He took out his notebook.

"We have certain information that you and the so-called captain had an affair, is that correct?"

She inhaled the smoke again, then blew it into his face. "A lot of water has flowed under the bridge since then, Inspector. Is this what it's all about? Because it's not illegal. It might be shameful, but I have no regrets."

"Partly, Jennifer, because we know that you contracted V.D. from him. It is said that you had a daughter to him a few years back. Is this true?"

Jennifer Steadman sat silent and shocked at the revelation.

"Let's leave that for now, Jennifer. However, I will come back to it at some time in the future." He rustled the notes around for effect. "Tell me, Jennifer, have you ever heard of a woman called Molly Stacey?"

She shook her head. "Never heard of her, Inspector, who is she?" She inhaled again.

Inspector Rupert shook his head, then raised his voice. "Don't waste my time, Mrs. Steadman. Molly Stacey was blackmailing you and Ernest Foster when she found out that you and Foster were having an affair, then along comes your daughter, so Molly Stacey upped the stakes and demanded more money, and that's when the pair of you killed her."

"Don't be ridiculous, Inspector. How could I kill this Molly Stacey if I don't know who she is." She sat back on the Chesterfield couch. "I don't deny that Ernest and I were an item at one time but, as I've said, that was a long time ago."

Inspector Rupert eyed her nervousness closely before continuing. "Perhaps you can explain then, since you don't or didn't know Molly Stacey, how come your name is in her black book, with listed payments? And I'm sure that if we dig into your bank account we'll find withdrawals for the blackmail amount with dates to match. There's also the marking of U.A.S. beside your name. Now I'm willing to take a stab in the dark and assume that Ernest Foster was also interfering with your daughter, who would have been underage at that time." Inspector Rupert sat with his arms folded awaiting her to respond.

"Yes, Inspector, that's why I ended the affair. As for Molly Stacey, she was a conniving bitch, who threatened to expose us to my sister. However, much as I hated her, I would not stoop to murder. I don't have that in me."

"That gives you a very strong motive, Mrs. Steadman. People have been killed for less." He pursed his lips. "I'm prepared to give you the benefit of the doubt, Jennifer, and a piece of advice, stay away from the Foster house, no phone calls, until I get this mess sorted. You can advise your bank to cancel your monthly transfers to Molly Stacey's account. She has no need of money any more." He stood up quickly. "One more thing, Mrs. Steadman, a colleague will call tomorrow for a statement, so make yourself available, and leave nothing out, because wasting police time is a serious offence."

He was about to leave and then turned around to face her. "Have the names Margaret Fletcher or Amanda Smith ever been mentioned when you and Ernest Foster were sleeping together?" He waited until she lit another cigarette. "What about Felicity Roach? Although her name goes back a bit to the early thirties."

"No, Inspector, and that's the truth. Don't say they were on Molly Stacey's list as well, what a cow."

Inspector Rupert walked out of the Victorian villa and made his way back to the station, going over in his mind what Jennifer Steadman had confirmed. Now all he had to do was wait until Ernest Foster returned from his business trip.

D.C. Buckingham had returned from the orphanage. "I managed to question a few of the staff, sir. However, a lot has changed in the time scale, retirement, deaths." She gave a wry smile. "There was one older member of staff who knew Amanda Smith quite well. She was a bit younger then, when Amanda absconded, but the strange thing is, she never took any clothes with her. It was thought that Amanda had gone off with her sugar daddy at the time, often expressing her urge to go to London with her rich boyfriend, so her clothes were given to charity and her room let to another child. That was that. So I decided to check for missing girls from the Stevenage area but drew a blank. According to Miss Heysham, the staff cook, Amanda took a bracelet and a gold sovereign on a chain from another girl's room, something that was totally out of character, and the cook blamed the company that she was keeping, especially at such a young age. But Miss Heysham said that Amanda was a young girl with an old head on her shoulders, well versed in the birds and the bees, that used to shock the staff of the orphanage, and other young orphans." Buckingham closed her notebook. "Any joy with Jennifer Steadman?" she asked, changing the subject.

"Just confirmation, although we now know that Foster was having sex with his daughter. That was the U.A.S. abbreviation listed in the ledger and black book." He paused, rubbing his chin. "I want you and Bowman to get a statement from Jennifer Steadman tomorrow morning. While you're there take her fingerprints, simply routine, you know the script by now, Buckingham. Incidentally, where is Bowman? He was sent to the Hatfield hospital to check on Margaret Fletcher, not to have heart bloody surgery."

Buckingham ignored the outburst. "Is that it for the day, sir, or is there anything else you want me to do?"

Inspector Rupert looked at his watch. "Hell's bells is that the time? She'll crucify me; we're supposed to be celebrating our anniversary with a dinner at the White Horse, so that's it for today, Buckingham. Oh, please give me a lift home. I need to get flowers and a gift." He hurried out of the incident room without another thought of the case.

He was just in time to catch the jewellers before they closed. When he arrived home he opened the door furtively only to hear laughter coming from the living room.

"Colin, what on earth brings you so far north?" He embraced his friend then hugged and kissed his wife, handing her the flowers.

"I was checking something out for the Air Force. I haven't always been on the beat or stuck in a police office you know."

"Can I ask what it is, or is it confidential, my friend?" Amadeus laughed loudly.

"Very hush hush, old boy, things are starting to liven up across the channel, with Herr Hitler marching into the Rhineland. Where next is the big question?" Colin smiled. "I think the Sudetenland, then Austria. But Herr Hitler is so unpredictable he could go anywhere, although we do have concerns about Poland, since we are one of her allies. Then, with Ribbentrop signing a peace pact with Soviet Russia, things could get a little sticky for us, but we'll cope; we always have and we always will." Colin gave a wry smile.

"We're going out to celebrate our anniversary. Late." Deborah laughed. "Why don't you join us? You know you're always welcome," she said taking hold of his hand.

"No. I'll leave you two love birds to celebrate in peace, besides I'd just bore you with flying tactics. I have a long drive back to London." He hugged them both, promising to make his visits more often, before making his goodbyes then, off at speed in his Morgan sports convertible.

Amadeus knew it would be a long time before he saw his dear friend Colin again, and was thankful that his friend had saved the situation and prevented another argument with his wife, which was becoming more frequent as the days, months and years passed.

At the anniversary dinner he slipped a beautiful emerald and diamond ring onto her finger.

"This is for eternity, my darling," he said admiring her glittering eyes in the candlelight.

"Yes, Amadeus, I shall wear it for eternity. Now get the bill, and I'll give you my present when we get home."

They made love, the way they used to do, welcoming the dawn chorus, exhausted but totally satisfied in each other's arms.

What could he say, after a night of passion like that? It was clear they still loved each other intensely, and he blamed the pressure of work on these tedious arguments. Now he had to get on and bring charges against the rich contractor, Ernest Foster. He had all the proof he needed, and settled down in his office to type up the charge sheet. He sat, considering that, if Jennifer Steadman was involved, had he given her enough rope to take off into the blue horizon? That thought was interrupted as D.C. Bowman entered the office.

"Just reporting on the nurse Marion Fletcher, sir. Apparently she was seen entering a dark Zephyr car the day she went missing, and failed to turn up for her shift." He looked at his notes. "Somebody didn't like her, because the information we have is that Marion Fletcher took off leaving a string of debt in her wake. Well, nothing can be further from the truth. Apparently she was of good character and reliable, because I checked her work pattern over the four years she was at Hatfield General, and Marion Fletcher never missed a day." He continued," I contacted the Arbroath police again, and asked them to get a move on, and quiz the family as to whether she had arrived back in Scotland. Word came back eventually that she had not returned home, or gone to Ireland to stay with relatives. So I think we can safely place Marion Fletcher on the missing persons register."

Inspector Rupert nodded. "We've made quite a bit of headway, while you were strutting around the nurses quarters, Bowman. I'm waiting on Buckingham returning with a statement from Mrs. Jennifer Steadman, but I have all the information to arrest Ernest Foster for the murder of Molly Stacey. So when she gets back, have her statement typed up and carbon copied, because we'll need it for Mr. Foster's lawyer."

He had just finished talking when Buckingham appeared. She handed him the written copy of Steadman's statement. "Why do we not bring her in for further questioning, sir? She is after all a suspect in all this and apparently she knew that Foster and her daughter Anne were having illegal sex, so that in itself deserves an arrest."

"Later, Buckingham, just let her sweat, and see what she does next." He took the sheets from her and handed them to D.C. Bowman. "Right, Bowman. You know what to do, and meantime we'll go over to Wheatfield Villa to see if Mr. Ernest Foster has returned."

They took the police car because it was the Inspector's intention to bring Ernest Foster back to the station once under arrest. When they arrived at Wheatfield Villa, it was obvious that the police were expected, the door opened and a large blond man stood in the entrance.

Inspector Rupert jumped out of the moving vehicle. There was no introductions; he walked up the marble steps. "Ernest Foster, you are under arrest and will be charged with the murder of Molly Stacey. You don't have to say anything, as it may harm your defence in court. Do you understand, Mr. Foster?" Buckingham put his hands behind his back and then handcuffed the accused suspect.

"Cynthia, call my lawyer, darling, explain what's happened." He was led to the car and gently ushered into the back seat, joined by the Inspector. "You'll suffer for this, Rupert, yes I know your name, and so do a lot of my work colleagues, and among them I have powerful friends."

Inspector Rupert had heard it all before, and ignored Foster, who continued to curse and swear as Buckingham drove to the police station and parked the car.

"Take him to the cell, Buckingham. We'll await the arrival of his lawyer before we hold the formal interview, but after you put him in the cell, you can set up in Interview Room One, just make preparation."

He went to his office hoping that Bowman had completed his task.

Eventually the high-flying solicitor arrived. Desmond Simkin had things all tied up in the Welwyn area and beyond. He had built himself a reputation, sailing close to the wind as far as the law was concerned, but managed to get results, and charged plenty in his fees for services rendered, adding a few pounds to the bill for expenses.

It did not take long for him to put in an appearance, realising Mr. Foster's position as a respected member of the Round Table in the area.

"Rupert, Rupert, have you gone completely loopy, do you know who Captain Foster is?"

"My name and rank is Detective Inspector Rupert to you, Simkin. Kindly remember that when you address me in future.

As for the suspect, Foster, he is not a captain, that's a title he bestowed on himself to impress his wife. He is being held in the cell block, so you have thirty minutes to confer before Foster is charged with murder."

"You have the charge sheet and any other relevant documents, Inspector?"

Inspector Rupert removed the paperwork from the desk drawer. "There will be other charges to follow, Simkin. So don't think your client's going to get away easily."

"Such as, Inspector? I take it those charges are not on this charge sheet?"

"No, Simkin, it's the murder of Molly Stacey we are concerned with for the present, while we make further investigations into other crimes that include incest."

Mr. Desmond Simkin was livid as he walked to the cell to interview his client.

CHAPTER FOUR

Once again it was D.C. Buckingham that interrupted Amadeus in his office as he studied the paperwork, preparing to charge the accused. He looked at his watch. "What is it, Buckingham? Can't you see I'm busy?" he said, irritated at being disturbed.

She quickly approached his desk and sat down without an invitation. "I'm a bit concerned, sir, that we're putting the cart before the horse." She laid her notebook on the table. "I've been having a think about this case and come to the conclusion that we don't have enough evidence to charge Ernest Foster with murder." She looked at the pages in her notebook before speaking. "I'm not saying that Foster's not guilty. What I am saying is we have three suspects, namely Justin Stacey, Ernest Foster" – she lifted her finger – "and what about Jennifer Steadman? She had the motive and opportunity when she contracted V.D. but do we have enough proof it was Foster that gave it to her? I personally don't think so. However, I do believe it was the other way round, because I think Molly Stacey was the original carrier of the disease. She and Foster were having an affair while Justin was doing his national service. Therefore that puts the boot on the other foot." She paused. "We only have Justin Stacey's word, a man that contracted the disease, blaming Foster. However, who's to say that Justin Stacey is the innocent party in all this? Again motive and opportunity."

The Inspector held up his hand to silence her. "So you're saying I got it wrong, Buckingham?" he asked tersely.

"Not wrong, sir." She paused. "No, I think you've got it right, but we need more proof, sir. The first thing Foster's lawyer is going to ask is if we have a body. Which we don't. Then he'll question your case, sir, and dismantle it piece by piece, and if it ever reaches the courts, which I doubt, then any legal team would destroy you and the case in cross examination. That's why I urge us to be cautious sir. That's why I urge you to be a little careful before charging him. It could only backfire on us, sir."

The Inspector stood up. "What you're asking me to do is stop the interview, Buckingham, and that means I'll have to release our main suspect without charge. Don't be bloody ridiculous. I know Foster is guilty."

"Then prove it, sir. Before you make a grave error of judgement, let's just inform the solicitor we have fresh evidence that doesn't point the finger at his client. Give Foster some rope to hang himself, put his mind at ease, entice him into a false sense of security while our investigation continues."

"Then what do we do about the incest charge, Buckingham? Do we drop that?"

"Ah yes, the incest charge." She paused. "There's a wide gap between incest and murder, sir. Again, is this revenge on Steadman's part, have we questioned the daughter? The answer to that is no, we don't have a clue where she is. That's something we can follow up before charging Foster. Let's keep him in the dark before we eventually charge him with incest, and murder, but now's not the time, sir."

Inspector Rupert rubbed his chin then sat down. "Alright, D.C. Buckingham. I'll go along with that for now. Arrange for the suspect to be brought from the cells."

After Buckingham had left, he sat considering her logic. He knew she was right, there were so many flaws that any reasonable solicitor would pick at. Common sense prevailed as he looked at the papers on his desk, then deposited them back into the safe.

The interview room was stuffy as he entered and sat down quickly.

"I must apologise to you and your client for bringing you here at such short notice, Desmond. However, I must tell you that something has come up, and entered into our investigation, that throws the question of doubt at your client's involvement." He sat and watched the suspect grin broadly, before Ernest Foster stood up. "In future you will address me as Captain Foster, Rupert, and stop trying to patronise my solicitor by addressing him by his first name."

The solicitor spoke loudly. "You have waisted Captain Foster's time, and mine, Rupert, so I will be making a complaint to the Chief Constable, and I'll go further if need be. You have to face it, Rupert, you and your team have got it wrong." He paused. "We will be lodging a complaint with the Crown Prosecution Office for wrongful arrest, so that will give you something to chew on while you stumble in another direction with this case. I was ready to rip you and your case apart, Rupert. You have escaped lightly, and one more thing: you will address me as Mr. Simkin, just as my client has said, should our paths ever cross again. You might speak to your subordinates that way, but not me." He signalled to his client. "Come, Ernest, we're finished here." The two men exited the interview room without another word spoken.

"I'll nail that bastard, see if I don't, Buckingham." He covered his face to hide the disappointment.

"I'm sure you will sir, can I suggest we go to the tearoom and have tea and cake?"

"A good idea, Buckingham. Let's go over what we have again, a cuppa, and a pot of tea should do the trick."

They left the interview room in a sombre mood.

Making their way to the tearoom, it started to rain. Buckingham smiled. "It never rains, but it pours, sir. Never mind, we'll get another crack at Simkin and his client, of that I am sure, sir." The tearoom was closed for refurbishment.

"I never wanted tea anyway." Inspector Rupert turned and walked back to the police station with Buckingham struggling to keep up. She decided to buy a newspaper and a chocolate bar, that would help stem the disappointment of the tearoom being shut.

They sat in the office going over old paperwork, that had been studied so many times before. "I want you to go back to Steadman, and find out about this elusive daughter. I'll go over to Hatfield and question Justin Stacey again. There's something we're missing and I have to find out what it is, and quickly."

Buckingham unfolded her newspaper. "There was an advert for landscape gardening. "Take a look at this, sir. Remember earlier this morning I mentioned that we don't have a body? Well, this advert has drawn my attention to the fact Molly Stacey just might be buried in Foster's garden, or Steadman's for that matter. Justin

Stacey's has already been turned over so I think we can rule him out, but the other two." She was interrupted.

"You've done it again, Buckingham. Why did I not think of it in the first place?" He stood up, quickly tossing the statements onto the desk. "I'll hazard a guess that Foster's is the garden we need to search. He looked at the wall map. "He could have buried her anywhere in this area, but thankfully there are lots of trees so it's doubtful he'd dig through roots to bury a body. Therefore the most likely place is the large garden at the back of his house." Inspector Rupert rubbed his chin. "Okay, let's start by getting an order to dig up his patch, because he will not give permission to dig if there is a body there." He paused. "You get over to Hatfield and find a firm with an excavator."

"Why don't we use the advertisement firm, sir? They're bound to have that machinery and labour; we can tell them what the digging is about without jeopardising the investigation."

"Yes, Buckingham, I'll need to clear that with headquarters, but I'm sure they'll agree. Go ahead and set that up please."

Buckingham had never heard the Inspector use that coin of phrase before. However, she never mentioned the word "please" and got on with her duties.

Inspector Rupert drove down to headquarters at Stevenage to obtain a search warrant and permission to hire the landscape company.

With everything in order, he drove back to Welwyn and awaited word from D.C. Buckingham. She was excited as she and Bowman walked into the office.

"All arranged, sir, all they need is a start date."

The Inspector clapped his hands. "Get this right, and I'll recommend you pair for promotion to detective sergeants. Meanwhile, let's go and wipe the smirk from Ernest Foster's face and tell him we'll be digging up his garden tomorrow morning."

"Do you think that's a good idea, sir?" Bowman said softly. "Why not just surprise him?"

"Because I want Foster to have his lawyer present when we start to dig. Which reminds me, organise a photographer to take various snapshots of the garden as it appears today. We don't want to leave a mess, now do we?" He smiled. "Okay. I want everyone to have an early night, because it's going to be a long day tomorrow. I also want everyone to bring wellington boots and raincoats. Let's be prepared for what the weather throws at us." He dismissed the two detective constables before making his way home, at a reasonable hour for a change.

Inspector Rupert still had one more task to perform. He drove out to Wheatfield Villa to inform the Fosters of his intention. The housemaid ushered him into the hallway. He stood waiting for one or both of the Fosters to appear. However, it was Cynthia Foster who ventured downstairs, in a skimpy bath towelling robe that barely covered her breasts, hips and upper thighs. She stopped on the stairs to give him a view of her shapely body and, breathing heavily, she sighed.

"What can I do for you, Inspector?" she asked in a sexy tone.

"I need to speak to your husband, Mrs. Foster. I have something to tell him," he said, looking up at the shapely woman, who rubbed her breasts in an attempt to dry them.

"Shall I call my solicitor, Mr. Rupert? Or am I safe with you." She smiled then descended the stairs. "I'm afraid my husband will not be back until tomorrow, due to the time he wasted with you. However, I don't mind wasting time; I have all the time in the world." She put her hands around his neck.

"Please, Mrs. Foster, be sensible and put a dressing gown, or clothes, on." He removed her embrace. "I'll wait here until you are dressed."

She tutted and walked back upstairs, giving him more than an eyeful of her swinging hips.

A short time later she appeared in a dressing gown, and ushered him into the lounge.

"So what's so important that you have to call at this hour, Inspector?" She sat down and crossed her legs before lighting a cigarette.

"Nothing important, Mrs. Foster, it's just that we intend to search your garden, beginning tomorrow morning. I hope the machinery doesn't wake you," he said with a wry smile.

"I don't believe your crowd, Inspector. First false accusations, against my husband, then false arrest, and now this! My husband will not be happy. I'm sure you can understand why. I will phone him and our lawyer, who will raise an objection in the courts."

"That is your prerogative, Mrs. Foster. However, I can say that you, your husband and the solicitor will waste time since a warrant has already been granted." He stood up. "There is one thing I can't understand, Mrs. Foster: why your husband plays around when he has a good-looking woman like you to warm his bed." It was the wrong thing to say.

She rose from the couch quickly, untying the robe and letting it fall to the floor.

"Do you find me attractive, Inspector? Would you like to warm my bed tonight?" She tried to approach him.

Inspector Rupert bolted for the door then turned. "Just tell your husband of our intentions, Mrs. Foster." He was glad to feel the warm air on his face as he moved across the gravel to the police car. He puffed out his cheeks at the thought of what might have happened, if he didn't have to go home to a waiting wife.

It was the morning after the encounter with Mrs. Foster. The mist was slowly burning off to reveal the sunrise.

The excavator had been unloaded and the work force were standing by to receive instructions.

The foreman approached as Inspector Rupert and the team drove into the courtyard.

"We have a problem, Inspector; the owner will not allow us to venture any further. He has threatened us with court action."

"Ah, so he is at home then." He had no sooner spoken the words when the villa door flew open. "You're not going any further, Rupert. There is no way you are digging up my orchard garden, so take your arse of my property." He stood with arms folded in front of the excavator, as another figure appeared in the doorway. It was, as he expected, Simkin.

The solicitor made his way down the steps. "You have stepped out of line for the last time, Rupert. Now I'm ordering you to remove yourselves and the machinery from this property."

Inspector Rupert handed him a copy of the search warrant. "Too late, Simkin, as you can see the warrant has already been granted." He paused. "Now I'm warning you and your client that if you try to block our way, then I'll have you both arrested for trying to pervert the course of justice, attempting to block police officers in the course of their duty. Do I make myself clear?"

The solicitor looked at the warrant, then crumpled it into a ball, before putting a hand around his client's shoulder and leading him back up the steps to another figure standing in the doorway. This time she was dressed. However, she gave him a sly wave and a smile before turning and disappearing indoors.

"Right, let's get this show on the road," he barked out the order to be heard above the excavator engine.

The photographer had taken snapshots of the orchard garden for future reference.

Each area was marked into squares, then prodded with sharp spikes, attempting to indicate which part of the orchard had previously been dug over.

The foreman gave the excavator operator the order where to dig, tracing the main drain from the house and pegging it out down to the boundary fence, before the real search could start to take place.

The day wore on. The workers were glad of the sunshine. However, they were informed that the weather forecast was not good for the rest of the week.

Two days later the search team were still digging, removing stones and turf, bottles and tin cans that had been left when the garden was backfilled originally. The digging was difficult due to the tree roots that had spread underground in the large orchard.

It was decided to bring in arc lights to allow the workers to keep digging as the light faded and before the operation was shut down for the night.

Ernest Foster stood in the kitchen door, arms folded, and that smug look on his face, as the work force finished for the night.

Inspector Rupert got a call from headquarters, asking how the search was progressing.

He knew that something had reached their ears, probably a complaint from Simkin the solicitor, who was keen to get the excavation stopped.

That was only the start of it. The phone calls got more frequent, and more questions were asked, and Inspector Rupert knew it was a race against time before they pulled the plug on the operation and closed it down. That was when he decided to split the work force into a day shift and a night shift, keeping a permanent dig on the go, night and day.

He was right. Approaching the end of the week, the word came through from headquarters to abandon the search. It came as no surprise to him, because the money allocation was exhausted. The search of the garden had been completed.

Inspector Rupert stood in the drizzle and arc light totally dejected. After all that work, absolutely nothing. He wiped a tear from his eye before walking down the garden to give the foreman instructions to shut down.

He stood looking into the darkness of the fields that surrounded the villa, knowing that Foster could have buried Molly Stacey anywhere out there. He stumbled on a piece of raised grass that hadn't been touched. He looked at the oblong area that had been prodded. "Why has this area not been searched, Alistair? "

"That area is concrete, Inspector. That's the septic tank of the house." The foreman said softly, knowing how much this search had meant to the Inspector who would now face the wrath of his bosses for wasting so much time and money on a project that came up with nothing.

"Explain, Alistair, what's a septic tank?"

The foreman looked surprised. "Follow me up to the villa, then I can explain it better, looking down the garden." They walked up the orchard to the villa. The foreman turned and pointed down the orchard, which looked eerie in the arc light. The night workers stood leaning on their shovels, awaiting further instruction.

"Look at the markers that have been laid down to mark the main drain from the villa that takes the toilet soil down into the oblong septic tank. All drainage ends up there, although the waste water from the kitchen goes into a grease box that traps the waste from the kitchen and allows only waste water to flow into the main drain." He paused, pointing to the rainwater downpipe. "All the rainwater coming off the roof also helps to keep the main drain clear, and the way the weather is tonight, there'll be plenty going into the tank, then overflowing out into the stream that runs past the boundary fence. Come, I'll show you where that is." They walked back down the garden.

Inspector Rupert stood tired and wet, peering at the overflow that had a steady flow coming from it.

"How often does this tank need emptying, Alistair?"

The foreman laughed. "That depends on how many people are in the house, how many times they use the toilet. So a couple of factors dictate how fast the waste in the tank fills up, and let's not forget the micro-bacteria that break down the waste in the tank. It's a natural process, but a very good system. They say you can drink the water that emerges from the septic tank overflow. I can get you a cup if you want to try, Inspector." He gave a chortled laugh before coughing.

"I'll take your word for it. I wonder when this tank was last emptied and cleaned?"

"You're not suggesting? No, never mind. I think you need to speak to the local plumber. He and his son do a lot of work emptying tanks. They have the pump and the hoses. They also keep records of who they work for, when the job was done, and how much it cost. That would be your best bet, Inspector."

"D.C. Bowman," he yelled up the orchard. "Fetch the local plumber and tell him to bring his equipment for cleaning septic tanks. If he's in his bed, get him up and out here immediately." He turned to the foreman. "Okay, Alistair, let's get the machine down here to uncover the grass and earth over the septic tank lid. Then we'll take it from there."

The excavator was promptly brought down the orchard, then began to scrape away the top layer of clods and earth. Eventually the whole of the concrete tank was exposed.

Their attempt to lift the lid was futile until the foreman attached a rope to the lifting handle, then the claw of the excavator. "Slowly," he yelled. "Slowly."

The lid of the tank began to lift out of its area. The excavator operator expertly swung the lid to one side, revealing the inside of the tank. Inspector Rupert's heart sank as he shone the beam of his torch into the four corners, finding nothing.

"Let's wait until the plumber gets here; it is a big tank," the foreman said, trying to give the Inspector a boost.

As plumbers do, they arrived in their own time, two hours later. The orchard took on an eerie sound as the wind rustled through the leaves and branches.

The plumber introduced himself and his son. They had carried the Hathaway pump down to the septic tank. "I don't know why you're emptying this tank, Inspector. We emptied this about five, perhaps six, years ago. I can give you a precise date in the morning." He walked up the orchard garden and out to the front of the villa to get hoses and fuel for the pump. On their return, the plumber quoted an hour to empty the tank. "I hope your boss realises that we're on triple time, it being Saturday morning, Inspector." He started to assemble and attach the suction hose.

"Just get on with it, Arkwright," the Inspector said softly. He was in no mood to discuss terms at this time of night, while standing in the wind and drizzle.

The pump was filled with fuel, then started up. It chugged and spluttered before it took hold and the soil waste began to pump into the stream.

"How long did you say this will take, Arkwright?" Inspector Rupert asked over the noise of the pump.

The plumber shone his torch into the septic tank. "Just over half full, I estimated an hour but perhaps a little more to reach the sump." He paused. Before giving an order to his son. "Go to the van and bring out the hose on the reel; that should be enough to give the tank a good clean when we reach the sump. You can connect it to the stand pipe fixed to the wall on the garage. We connected it there before." He wiped his hands on a rag.

The church bell tolled four, the peal was carried in the breeze and left a strange sound as the fourth strike ended.

Inspector Rupert checked his watch. "The bakery will be opening shortly, Bowman, so take a note of who wants what. I'll just have a hot drink." He handed the detective constable a five-pound note. "And I want change," he said grumpily, as the rain ran down his neck, soaking him through to his underwear.

He considered the reports of the few days spent in the orchard garden. Each report was like a stab in the heart that revealed nothing.

He listened to the church bell toll five. Bending down, he almost fell through the open lid into the tank, but for the plumber's quick reaction, catching him by the collar, then pulling him upright.

"Take it easy, Inspector. It takes time, and the pump won't be rushed," the plumber said with a smile. He looked at his watch. "Not long now."

Inspector Rupert kneeled down on the wet grass and shone his torch into the tank.

"Bring that arc light a little closer, Buckingham." He sounded excited. "There, take a look in the left-hand corner," he said as the light illuminated part of the tank.

"I can't see anything, sir," she said in a disappointed tone.

"Let me have another look." He shone the torch into the dark corner. "Bring that hose over here, Des. I want to put a light spray onto the object in the corner," he said to the plumber.

As he directed the spray onto what appeared to be ivory, like the tusk of an elephant, there was a mixture of joy and sadness in his voice. "It's a skull, Buckingham. Who it is I have no idea, but we need to get the pathologist here now."

As the pump emptied more of the tank, another skull appeared. Both seemed to be in a sitting position in each corner.

"Oh my god no please." He let the beam of the torch edge slowly towards two other skulls. It now became obvious that there were four skeletons in the tank, each sitting propped up against each corner, heads hung low, two large skeletons and two smaller. He hosed each one down with a fine spray. "I can guess who three of them are, but the fourth victim baffles me," he said getting to his feet. "At least we've found them, Buckingham, that's the important thing."

Bowman arrived with rolls and hot drinks. Inspector Rupert took the coffee and downed the contents in one large gulp. "Right, I want you to come with me, Buckingham. Let's get Foster out of his bed." He paused. "I'll wipe the smug smirk from the swine's face." He turned to Bowman who was chewing on a bacon roll. "You get yourself over to Wilfred Ponsonby's villa, and drag him out of bed if need be, tell him to bring wellington boots and protective clothing. You can give him a hint of what we've found; that should brighten up his morning."

Ernest Foster and the household were awakened by the constant pounding on the door. "Get dressed, Foster, you're under arrest for the murder of Molly Stacey. We explained to you before who she was. Then Marion Fletcher, a Scottish nurse who worked at the Hatfield general hospital. Then a young girl called Amanda Smith from the Stevenage Orphanage. You will be charged for all three murders, until we discover who the fourth victim is. Therefore you will be held in custody, on these charges." He hesitated. "Incest also springs to mind, Foster, so you can inform your solicitor that every charge will take place the day after tomorrow at ten a.m." He dragged the culprit from the couch. "When he's dressed, caution him, Buckingham, then cuff him, and take him to the station where I'll interview him later today."

He walked back out of the villa and down through the orchard garden to the septic tank. The plumber and his son had continued with the hose-down. The last of the sludge had drained into the sump. As the Hathaway pump sucked the remaining water from it, the dawn was breaking. Thankfully the wind had dropped and the rain had stopped.

He watched the pathologist stride down the orchard garden. "Okay, so you're Rupert," he said abruptly. "Your reputation goes before you, Inspector. Why this couldn't wait until later is beyond me, but I'm here now on double time so where are the bodies?" It was obvious D.C. Bowman had not advised the pathologist what was in store for him.

"In there, Ponsonby, all neatly propped up for your examination." Inspector Rupert smiled as he watched the pathologist lean towards the opening.

"You don't expect me to go in there, Rupert, for god's sake, man, bring the skeletons out and I'll examine them."

"This is a crime scene, Ponsonby, therefore I want the skeleton corpses examined in the tank. It has been hosed down, and we will get you protective clothing. However, if you refuse then we'll bring in our own forensics team who will obey my instruction, but if I do that, you as the pathologist will no longer be employed by the Hertfordshire constabulary, which means you'll lose your nice income and retainer." The Inspector smiled as Wilfred Ponsonby cursed below his breath when the plumber lowered a ladder into the septic tank.

Inspector Rupert left the rest to D.C. Bowman. "Make sure the orchard is put back together, Bowman, and ring the station when the four skeletons have been removed to the mortuary."

He was totally exhausted. Wet and cold he made his way to the police station, with one last task, and that was to question Foster about the fourth victim.

The interview was short. Ernest Foster refused to co-operate with the police, obviously using his solicitor's advice from before.

Inspector Rupert wasted no time on him. "Take him to the cells, Constable. I'll hold a proper interview when his lawyer is present." He thought that that was that, but when he stepped outside to make his way home, he was hit with a barrage of questions by the assembled press. He held up his hands in defence. "It's been a long night, ladies and gentlemen; however, I can confirm that we are holding a prominent business man in custody for the murder of three people, that we know of, and a fourth victim who we still have to identify and trace. There will be the usual press conference by my bosses who will keep you informed, but now it's bed time." He walked quickly to the car and drove away.

CHAPTER FIVE

Inspector Rupert felt as if he had slept for a week. It was Deborah who wakened him with breakfast in bed. "The station have been trying to contact you, darling, but I told them you needed to rest, so I hope I've done the right thing."

He looked at his watch. "I have an interview to conduct at ten, darling, so I'll leave the cooked breakfast and just have some toast with tea." He saw the look of disappointment on her face. "I'm sorry, but this is important," he said getting out of bed. She just shrugged and took the tray back into the kitchen.

Inspector Rupert finished his tea and toast, kissed his wife on the cheek, then made his way to the police station. There he was told that Simkin had spent a good two hours with his client.

"Damn," the D.I. said loudly. "I didn't want him anywhere near Foster until the interview. However, no matter, let's just get on with it."

Inspector Rupert apologised for being a few minutes late. He handed the solicitor the charge sheets and a copy of the pathologist report. "As you can see, Simkin, each victim had their skull cracked open, probably with a cricket bat, which we recovered from the boot of Mr. Foster's car that is at present being tested for hair at our forensic laboratory. We expect the results back some time today."

The charges against Ernest Foster were a formality. However, the Inspector pleaded with Foster to reveal the fourth victim but, like before, Foster sat quiet with arms folded.

"Very well, Mr. Foster, all I can say is it wouldn't have helped your case, but it might have eased your conscience. It is now up to the Crown Prosecution to determine when you will make your court appearance. My job is done for the moment, so as from now you will be taken to a maximum security prison to await your trial, and may god have mercy on your soul."

Ernest Foster was led away to the waiting prison transport. The solicitor stood for a moment. "If I can persuade my client to disclose the fourth victim, will you put in a word to the Crown Prosecution Service?"

"I'm sorry, Simkin. That will not make the slightest bit of difference, because he has three murders to contend with, and

I'm sure you know as well as me: your client is going to swing, and nothing in this world is going to change that." The solicitor gave a slight nod before walking out of the stuffy interview room, and he didn't look back.

Now it was back to work. The first thought that came to the Inspector's mind was the daughter of Jennifer Steadman, but after a check was made, it was discovered that Anne Steadman, Ernest Foster's daughter, was at St. Margaret's Finishing School for girls in York, so that closed down that avenue of inquiry. He sat for a while in the interview room, going over in his mind who the young victim could be. The orphanage would be a good place to start, although there were several doubts attached; surely one of the staff would have mentioned another missing girl when inquiries were made about Amanda Smith. However, that was for another day.

The time passed quickly, and Inspector Rupert was the talk of the new expanding town, in fact his name was synonymous with the Whitechapel ripper murders, in London, and soon became a household name connected to the "Septic tank murders".

After the press briefing he was pulled aside by Superintendent Crawley. "The Assistant Chief Constable wants to see you at headquarters, 14.00, Rupert and don't be late." There was a sound of jealousy in Crawley's voice.

There was not much conversation between him and Crawley. In fact, he regarded the Superintendent as a dangerous insect that should be crushed underfoot. "Crawley by name, Crawley by nature," he said quietly before going back to the shoebox office.

After tidying up the paperwork regarding the septic tank murders, he went out for a sandwich and coffee, then he made his way to headquarters in Stevenage

"Come in, Rupert, take a seat." The A.C.C. sounded friendly enough. "I have to inform you that we'll be moving to the new premises before the end of the month, now that the building is completed, I believe your wife will take up her place at the new secondary school, and with the new teachers college, the art school, and the Fountain precinct now completed, it certainly makes the future brighter, wouldn't you agree?"

Inspector Rupert was clever enough to know he hadn't been summoned to headquarters to discuss building completions. "I'm not sure what my wife has in mind, sir. Frankly I'd like to stay put, because we've moved twice already, and I'm not sure I want to move again, but I agree, the new town will be beneficial to the area."

The A.C.C. clasped his hands. "I have to congratulate you on your success in solving the tank murders, but that's not why I brought you here." He stood up and walked to the window, before turning to face the Inspector. "I have learned from Ernie the mole that you were going through the old missing persons roller index in your quest to close the septic tank case once and for all." He walked back to the desk and sat down.

"Ernie the mole, sir, can you explain?"

"Indeed I can Rupert. Ernie Forbes looks after our records in the basement with the rollers of yesteryear. However, those cases have been closed down, so don't waste time by opening up old wounds." He was making himself as clear as mud.

"Am I to understand that when it comes to missing persons cases that have not been solved, you're prepared to close down an investigation? I hardly think that's fair on the victims, or their families, if indeed they are victims. Would it not be better to keep those cases open to work on in our spare time, when we get a quiet spell in local crime, sir?"

"You're not listening to me, Rupert, forget those cases, because we have much more important issues to deal with, namely a psychopath across the channel, who shows no respect for any country, and is dropping agents into Britain as we speak. That, Rupert, is our top priority for now."

Inspector Rupert nodded in agreement. It was a dangerous time for the free world.

"What are your plans should we ever go to war, Rupert?"

"R.A.F. fighter squadron, sir, that would be my first choice, since I have a friend who has the same thoughts."

"I'm sorry to disappoint you, Rupert, but I think you'll find that you'd be retained for the home front, because the country still has to live with crime. Therefore I can't see the home office releasing you to fly an aeroplane when there is a risk of a growing black market, and the crime rate going up if a blackout is put in place. However, there is an alternative that I can't speak too much about, but I know that if war breaks out Neville Chamberlain will be replaced, but by whom? That is the question. Personally, I think Winston Churchill is preparing to argue the fact that Chamberlain should go after his empty 'Peace in our time' speech, when he waved the treaty paper Herr Hitler signed. That's the situation we find ourselves in, Rupert. Things are not healthy in Europe."

Inspector Rupert knew instinctively that he had been sounded out on what action he would take should war be declared. He waited until the Assistant Chief Constable stood up to shake his hand before he made his move.

It was a bright Autumn September morning. Once again the church bell was pealing to encourage people to congregate.

He, and his wife Deborah, had finished breakfast, and were getting the children ready to go to Mass.

It was then that the radio programme was interrupted. It was 11.15 on the 3rd of September 1939 when the prime minister began to speak. It was short and to the point.

"I have to inform the nation that several demands have been made to Herr Hitler to withdraw his troops from Poland. I have to inform you that no such undertaking has occurred, therefore this country is at war with Germany."

It took all of five minutes for the broadcast on the home service to end before the normal programme resumed. Deborah looked at her husband.

"I'm sorry, dear, you and the children will have to go to church without me. I have a duty to perform at H.Q. now that the balloon has gone up."

Deborah nodded her understanding but said nothing.

"I'm not convinced that I want to be kept on the home front. I'm sure there are older capable men that are able to police the county, able to perform their duty, so why me?"

Deborah ignored him, and continued to get the children ready. She watched her husband leave without so much as a goodbye.

Inspector Rupert was amazed at just how quickly things had been turned on their head. It was on his mind to request permission to apply to a fighter squadron in the R.A.F. He stopped at a call box on his way to Stevenage. He called Colin Freeman, sure that his friend would have heard the news, but there was no answer so he pressed button B to get his money back. "I'll do it from headquarters," he said looking into the small mirror in the phone kiosk, and parting his hair with his comb.

There was not much activity at H.Q. Just the usual orders that could have been relayed by phone. He phoned Colin again. Still no reply so he went up to the Assistant Chief Constable's office. Obviously no one was as keen as he was; the door was locked and the office looked empty. He spoke to the desk sergeant on the way out. "I take it you and the rest have heard the news this morning, Sergeant."

"Yes, sir, that's why they've all gone to the town hall to talk things out with the town mayor. I should go there if you have anything to say." The sergeant continued with his work.

Inspector Rupert drove to the town hall and was directed to the boardroom.

"Ah, Rupert the very man," the Assistant Chief Constable said, holding a glass of champagne.

Inspector Rupert looked at him. "What's the celebration, sir, haven't you heard the news?"

"Don't be ridiculous, man, of course I've heard the news, that's why we are here." He sipped the champagne with his pinkie held aloft. "It's business as usual, Rupert, although we will work with the air raid wardens, and home guard units in the county. You'll get your written orders in due course. In the meantime it's just a matter of waiting to see what Herr Hitler has planned."

Inspector Rupert couldn't believe his ears. It was a waste of his family time. He could have been at church with his wife and children. "There is one thing I want to ask, sir."

The A.C.C. drained his champagne flute and reached for another from the waiter's tray.

"I want to make a request that I be excused from duty, sir. I feel my place is with a fighter squadron, helping to protect us from the enemy."

"Your place is here in Hertfordshire, Rupert, helping to protect the community. Is that clear?" His order sounded slurred. "Thankfully work on the new town will cease, far too much pilfering." He paused. "Have you sorted that out yet? I never got a report. Make it a priority, Rupert. We can't allow those thieves to continue robbing people."

Inspector Rupert agreed, for the sake of agreeing, then made his way home.

Each day was much like the day before, boring. In fact it was impossible to think that there was a war, the newspapers and cinema Pathé news reels called it the phoney war, and it was true: nothing was happening apart from troop movement and the British expeditionary force that had been sent to France. However, things were to change as Hitler began his plans for invading the British isles. Operation Sea Lion was underway, as the Luftwaffe began bombing the radar stations and airfields along the south coast of England. Things were bad, with the radar stations knocked out and the airfields being under constant bombardment, the Hurricanes and Spitfires could not land because of the bomb craters, having to be diverted to another airfield for landing, only to find that they were in dire straits, the same as everyone else.

It was a stroke of luck that a German bomber pilot dropped his bombs on London, by mistake, which made Winston Churchill furious. He, in response, ordered bombs to be dropped on Berlin. That saved Britain from disaster, because Hitler, in his rage, said he would flatten every city in the U.K. and that turned his attention away from the airfields and radar installations along the south coast, which gave them breathing space to repair the damage and intercept the bombers on their return from the bombing of London and other cities. Inspector Rupert felt completely left out of the war.

There were other things to occupy Inspector Rupert's mind. The moving of headquarters from Stevenage to the new town of Welwyn Garden City. Boring, but necessary, he assisted with the operation.

Moving into a large freshly decorated office gave him a slight boost, although the work was still boring. Most of it consisted of servicemen returning on leave, to find their wives shacked up with the lodger or lover. This led to a punch up, with windows and ornaments being smashed, and arrests made for breach of the peace.

This was something that any constable could deal with, and Inspector Rupert made it known that his resources were wasted on such trivial matters, and would be better spent in the Air Force.

That was when his life would change forever.

It was September 1940; the Battle of Britain was raging in the skies above the southern counties. It was a twist of fate that encouraged the Inspector to look at his present position.

The devastating news that his dear friend Colin Freeman had been killed on the 15th of September 1940, not in action, but by sheer stubbornness. He had paid no heed to the ground crew, who insisted that he allow the aircraft to cool down. Being Colin, he was keen to get back up in the air to intercept the enemy. So, after much discussion, the Spitfire was refuelled and re-armed, ready for take-off. Witnesses came forward to say that Squadron Leader Freeman's aeroplane simply blew up in mid-air probably due to overheating, which the ground crew confirmed to be the likely cause.

Amadeus and Deborah attended a memorial service in London. His friend's body had never been recovered from the English channel. The parents of Squadron Leader Colin Freeman approached Amadeus and told him that their son had bestowed his worldly goods on his dear friend Amadeus Rupert, which included £50,000, his Morgan sports convertible and his three-bedroom mansion apartment in Mayfair. There was also Colin's shares in his parents' jewellers' business which had grown considerably throughout England.

Amadeus explained to Mr. and Mrs. Freeman that he cared little about what Colin had left him. He would gladly trade it, and the world, if his dear friend were to appear on his doorstep any time in the future. That was never going to happen.

Now he found himself a very rich police inspector, who put his wealth aside to concentrate on the job he loved. And that was policing, despite the boring parts, he knew that things would improve.

It was just when he started to get over his friend's death, he received more devastating news. An air raid in Coventry had resulted in his mother's death; the bungalow had taken a direct hit. There was nothing left to bury. Once again he attended a memorial service in the bombed-out city of Coventry, where the ancient cathedral had been totally destroyed.

On his return to Welwyn Garden City, he went straight up to the fifth floor, bypassing the Assistant Chief Constable's office, going right to the top brass.

"I'm sorry to barge in on you, sir," he said to the Chief Constable, who was amazed at the sudden intrusion. "As you know, I have gone through a very traumatic period in my life." He stopped speaking.

"Yes, Rupert, I have heard, and you have the sympathy of me and the entire police force, but what gives you the right to come into my office without an appointment?"

"To be frank, sir, I'm sick and tired of all this flummery, having to carry out mediocre tasks, then sitting in my office twiddling my thumbs. Therefore I have taken the decision to put my cards on the table." He paused for breath. "I want your permission to apply to leave the force on military grounds. That way when the war is over I can resume my position and rank. It has happened in other police forces in the country, so I reserve the right to make that request again, sir."

"I can understand your frustrations, Rupert, but we still have an important part to play in the war effort—"

Inspector Rupert knew what was coming so he stopped the Chief in his tracks. "The decision is made, sir. My mind is made up that if you refuse me, then you will leave me no alternative but to resign. However, be sure of this." He hesitated. "When

I go, I will not be going quietly, all the cutbacks that are taking place are understandable, but to refuse to conduct an inquiry into the missing teenagers is unforgivable and a dereliction of police duty has occurred which you are answerable for." He looked at the astounded C.C.

"I hope you're not trying to blackmail me, Rupert. That could have very grave consequences on your career." He stood up and approached the Inspector. "I can understand your grief and your reasons to get back at the enemy, Rupert. Therefore on these grounds I'm willing to submit authorisation to apply for whatever force you wish to join, and I wish you all the luck in the world. Now if you don't mind."

"Thank you, sir, you will not regret your decision." He saluted and made his way out of the Chief Constable's office.

The very first thing he did when reaching his own office was to telephone the Royal Air Force recruiting station and arrange a medical. Then he began to sort out his in tray.

The days and weeks passed before he got word to report to his local G.P. in Hatfield. It was there he got the devastating news that he would not be accepted into fighter squadron because he was colour blind. "Surely with so much going on, the country and Royal Air Force have dispersed with all that red tape, Doctor?" he bleated.

"I don't make the rules, Mr. Rupert, and there are certain standards to be maintained, no matter how drastic things become." He took the stethoscope from his neck and went to his personal diary. "There is a an offshoot of the Air Force called Coastal Command, who aren't as stringent with the rules, and need pilots immediately, so I have a number here which you can try. The only draw back is that you would be based on the west coast of Scotland, helping to protect the incoming Atlantic convoys." He paused to flick over the pages. "Here we are, a place called Oban, in Argyllshire. What their training schedule is, I have no idea. Your best course of action would be to call this number; it puts you straight through to their operations department at Ganavan Sands outside the town." He handed a dejected Amadeus the results of his medical and the Scottish telephone number.

"Thanks for your help, Doctor. I'll keep this in mind." He waved the piece of paper before exiting the surgery. However, he was not finished. He telephoned the recruiting and training station at Padgate Camp, Warrington, explaining that he had flying experience, and was physically fit except for the slight impedance of colour blindness. Sadly, after speaking to the recruiting officer, he was turned down.

The last resort if he wanted to fly was Coastal Command. He dialled the number, only to be put on hold. "Sorry, sir the lines are busy at the moment, if you would like to try again later," the operator said in a quiet Scottish accent.

"Thanks for your trouble," he said in a despondent tone, replacing the receiver.

He felt as if he was at a loose end. However, never one to be beaten, he dialled the number again, and got an immediate response. "Coastal Command, Flight Lieutenant Tenby speaking."

Inspector Rupert gave his name, and answered the questions that were fired at him.

"No it's a mild form of colour blindness, but unfortunately it affects my application to be a fighter pilot." Amadeus was hopeful.

"Yes everybody wants to be a Spitfire pilot these days," the voice said in a droll. "Very well, if you can report to the base next Monday, then we can get a closer look at you, and decide what to do with you." The line terminated. Amadeus felt lifted after everything he had been through. He made his way home since things were quiet in the station and beyond. He decided to meet his wife from the primary school, and give her the hopeful news.

"That's wonderful, darling, when do you report?"

He explained everything that had been said and done with the medical and phone calls.

"There is word that the children are being evacuated to farms in the countryside. I never thought that would happen," she said softly. "Now there is talk of the Welwyn primary school being shut down as well as the primary in the new town, and that might make me redundant unless I'm prepared to travel." She paused. "Let's wait and see." They sauntered to the bungalow on the outskirts of the village.

"In the course of my duties, I have noticed that there is a private development due for completion in the new town. However, work has ceased due to the war effort, but now we have the money, it might be worth considering a bigger house, since the children are growing up, and will need a room of their own," he said trying to make conversation.

"Yes, that might be worth thinking about after the war," Deborah said in a non-committing voice. "Let's get you organised for your departure on Monday." She opened the house gate and walked quickly to the front door of the bungalow.

"We could always build an extension if you don't want to move, darling," he said understanding her reluctance to move again.

"Let's just leave it for now, Amadeus," she said, irritated by the conversation.

The week went by very quickly. Amadeus boarded the train that would take him from Welwyn Garden City to Euston station in London, where he would catch the overnight sleeper direct to Oban, on the west coast of Scotland.

Deborah said a tearful goodbye at the new town station, since she still had her classes to take. It reminded her of the tearful goodbye she had suffered after the train had pulled out of Bournemouth, so many years ago. But it seemed as if it was only yesterday she had spent most of the journey back to Paddington Station, London, with her friend Veronica handing her the box of tissues. She gave a slight smile as the last carriage disappeared around the bend in the track, and Amadeus who was still waving disappeared from sight.

CHAPTER SIX

The train north was crowded with troops sleeping in the corridors. He stood in his compartment after breakfast admiring the scenery of the Scottish lochs. The steam engines struggled to pull the coaches up Glen Ogle on the Callander line. Finally reaching the Glencruitten summit and gaining speed towards his destination, Amadeus looked down on the town of Oban. A golf course lay below, as the brakes began to screech. The whistle sounded, warning the station of its approach. He looked at the snow-capped mountains and hills that lay across the Firth of Lorn.

Ships of every shape and size were anchored in the firth, many lying deep in the water, ready to unload their vital cargo, while other markings on the vessels showed they had been unloaded and ready to make that hazardous crossing back across the Atlantic Ocean to the United States for more precious war material. Amadeus took his suitcase from the rack, as the two steam engines shuddered then came to a halt alongside the station platform. They both blew off steam simultaneously, as if they were relieved to be released from the burden of the tedious journey pulling fourteen coaches from London Euston to the Scottish town.

He was met by an enthusiastic flight sergeant who took his case. "This way, sir, I have a car waiting." They walked along the platform. "Give me a minute, sir, I need cigarettes." He walked over to the Menzies bookstall, then ordered twenty Players and a box of matches. The car was parked beside a small central garden, where the local Bluebird bus service was waiting. "I'll take you to your room at the Marine Hotel, then we can drive out to the base after lunch, to meet the boss," the flight sergeant said, lighting a cigarette.

Amadeus was only half listening, as he admired the town's quaint small bay, with its distillery that dated back to 1793. "What on earth is that perched up above the town?"

"That's McCaig's Tower, built to commemorate Mr. McCaig's family. He was a very rich eccentric merchant banker with money to burn. During the period after the coming of the railway, many of the big hotels had been completed, that led to a kind of recession in the town, among the stonemasons especially. So work was started on the tower to give the stonemasons and workers an income. You could say it was built for two reasons." He paused. "There was supposed to be a third tier on top, but unfortunately McCaig the banker died and his money was formed into a trust for the upkeep of the building that we admire today."

"You should have been a tour guide, Sergeant," Amadeus said appreciating his first historical lesson, as the car parked outside the Marine Hotel on the Corran Esplanade. "This is where you will stay during your time with us, sir."

Amadeus wondered how the Sergeant was so sure things would turn out fine for him, or that he would be accepted into Coastal Command.

It was a pleasant drive along the coastal road by Dunollie Castle, the stronghold of the clan MacDougall. It looked as if it had featured in many battles, with many of the curtain walls destroyed, probably by cannon fire in days of old.

They were stopped at the gate by a sentry who asked for their pass. "This gentleman has just arrived to take up his duties, so has no pass at the moment."

"Wait!" The sentry barked the order as he walked to the sentry box and wound a telephone handle. After a brief moment he lifted the barrier and allowed them to proceed.

"I go through this procedure at least three times a day, yet this gorilla still insists on me showing my pass." The flight sergeant laughed.

Amadeus looked at the set-up as they drove into the base. A beautiful crescent moon beach looking out to the isles of Lismore and Mull. There were three Catalina and two Lysander aircraft flying boats parked on the concrete area by a slipway where the aeroplanes were winched from the clear water. "There are another two Cats out on patrol; some of those are going through maintenance but they're wonderful kites, able to do the job they were designed to do: seek out U boats and kill the buggers. Oops sorry, sir, come on, I'll introduce you to the base commander."

They climbed a few steps that led into the granite building. A tall figure was standing, with field glasses watching the convoys that were moving about in the Firth of Lorn. "Mr. Amadeus Rupert just arrived from London, sir."

The commander ignored him for a moment. "Find out what that silly bugger on the Braer ship is up to, Flight, and bring me some tea please."

"Sorry, Mr. Rupert, there's a captain that is supposed to be going to Dunstaffnage boom-protected pier to unload." He gave a smile. "Right, my name is Alexander Stevenson, commander of this base. I understand that you have some flying experience with Tiger Moths. As you can see we have the twin-winged Catalina that handles well in all weathers, and believe me we get all weathers on this coast, so be prepared." He told Amadeus to follow him through to the small office where he would question him further. "So you would have no objections to taking off this afternoon on a training flight."

"None whatsoever, sir, I'm looking forward to becoming part of the service."

"Alright, I'll arrange for an aircraft to be put in the water. Be ready for take-off at 14.30." The Commander poured the tea. "We retain and take our discipline very seriously, Rupert. We do a very important job trying to protect the convoys as they approach the Sound of Mull." He stood up and pointed at a mountain. "Ben More, a great beacon to bring you home but, as we have learned to our cost, a very dangerous mountain, that can appear out of the mist and clouds to a catastrophic ending. So listen to your instructor on your test flight." The introduction and talk was over as Amadeus made his way to be kitted out in flying jacket and boots. The rest of the afternoon was spent at the rudder, flying to landmarks, then out into the Atlantic to search for a kill.

Amadeus found the different aeroplanes easy to handle, and after a few successes, hunting down submarines and sending them to a watery grave, became part of successful operations and was rapidly promoted to flight lieutenant. He soon understood what the commander had told him when he first arrived for his interview: how the weather could change so quickly from a breeze into a howling gale, especially in winter. There were two things he liked about Coastal Command: there was no night flying, and the Marine Hotel was comfortable with good food and clean beds. They even did your laundry, which gave Amadeus spare time to explore the small town

The views from McCaig's tower were spectacular, then on another day he would often go up to Pulpit Hill and view the town from a different angle, looking north-eastward towards the mountains of Glen Coe and Lochaber. So in some respects it was quite an easy life, hunting the submarine menace. There were many times he disobeyed an order and would land the seaplane close to a ship that was on fire, picking up survivors, covered in oil, both friend and foe alike. Always telling his superiors that a captured submarine crew could give them valuable information, which was not the case, but he felt good about rescuing a human being from the icy waters of the Atlantic, until he was threatened by dismissal if he continued to put his crew and aircraft at risk. That brought his daredevil pranks to an abrupt end. He had a good life here; he had made friends with many locals, who drank in the Bridge End pub and lounge. Deborah came to visit him when she could, sadly without the children who had been evacuated. However, they made the most of their time in the Station Hotel opposite the bus stands and railway station.

Everything was fine until she had to go back to her teaching job in Letchworth New Town. It was not practical for her to be travelling so far without a mode of transport, having to rely on a limited bus service, leaving the house for work before eight, and not getting home before six, sometimes having to rely on friends to rescue her if she missed the last bus to Welwyn. "I really am at my wits' end, Amadeus," she said as they lay naked together without much action from her husband, who seemed to be asleep as she spoke. She wasn't sure if he was genuinely asleep, or just ignoring her moans. She gave him a shake. "I need your advice, darling, so please listen." She leaned on her elbow. "Now that the Americans have entered the war, they have renovated the old secondary school in Welwyn. It is truly magnificent. The typing pool have access to American goods in their shops on the ground floor. They're recruiting staff for typing and secretarial work, so what do you think, should I apply?"

"You do what you think is right, Deborah. Now go to sleep, darling, I have an early flight tomorrow." He turned over and was fast asleep before she could explain in detail what the job entailed.

"Bloody typical of you, Rupert, you always get your evil way, then turn away from me." She pulled the covers over her and lay awake in frustration.

Their time together wasn't wasted completely; they took bus trips to the surrounding villages, visiting Boom Town, the prefab village built for the war effort at Dunstaffnage Castle, where they say it was warmer to spend time outdoors in the snowy winter, than stay in the concrete blocks they called houses.

Amadeus got her a pass to visit the Coastal Command base, showing her the different aircraft. Although it was supposed to be hush hush, he took her on board and explained where they patrolled and what their function was. Deborah was not in the least bit interested. "I just wish you were a little closer to home, Amadeus. This journey is far too long for such a short time together, wouldn't you agree?"

Amadeus lifted a map. "And this is the Corrievrechan whirlpool, very noisy when the tides turn."

She stepped down out of the aircraft. "Don't forget I leave for London tonight, darling. Let's go back to my room where we can say our goodbyes in private."

"Sorry, darling, I have work to do, so I'll get the flight sergeant to take you back to town, then I'll come in to see you off. I really have enjoyed your company, it stopped me from becoming a monk." He smiled at the disappointed look on his wife's face.

"Very well, Amadeus, if your work comes first, so be it. I'll see you at 19.00, that is if you can drag yourself from your work." She walked quickly to the staff car without so much as an embrace. She turned to wave, but Amadeus had already gone indoors. "Tell me, Flight Sergeant, has my husband a mistress in Oban, he's not telling me about?"

"Flight Lieutenant Rupert having a mistress? Never, Mrs, Rupert, of that I am sure. Simply because he is so involved in his work, he wouldn't have the time. So you can rest easy on that subject. In fact I was surprised he took the time off too bring you north for a walk." He smiled. "Have a good trip back to London, come and see us again." He got out smartly and opened the car door before shaking her hand.

Amadeus phoned her the following day, to make sure she had arrived home safely. The conversation was short and to the point. "I love you, Amadeus," she said softly before hanging up.

He made his way up to his room on the second floor. He still marvelled at the views, looking over Oban bay towards Kerrera, the island that sheltered Oban bay, the Morven hills and the Isle of Mull. Despite the fact that there were splendid views from the seaplane on a flight path, there was always a different colour and hue in the mountains and hills when the glorious sunsets painted the sky. Sometimes he wondered if there really was a war.

He got himself ready for the afternoon flight. Making sure his uniform was smartly pressed with razor-creased trousers, he followed his batman to the waiting taxi. Sometimes the air ministry used MacDougall's taxi, the only one that served the town, at times when the staff car was tied up with other duties. Reliable and punctual, it was always a pleasurable drive, with light conversation on the way out to the Ganavan Coastal Command base.

There was one thing Amadeus was aware of, and that was the uncertainty of spotting a submarine. Sometimes it was days, weeks before an attack could take place, and more often than not the U boat captain would dive before the seaplane got within striking distance. However, Flight Lieutenant Rupert had notched up a number of kills in the time he had been at the Ganavan base, more and more submarine kills, much to the pleasure of his superior officers.

He always made sure that his superiors knew it was his crew, including those on the ground doing the repairs, but especially his navigator that should be given a mention, and the credit. That went down well with the ground crew and the other crews who very seldom were rewarded for their daring attacks and never had the luck to be around when a submarine was on the surface recharging its batteries, and the submariners were having a welcome break from the diesel fumes below deck, often taking in the fresh air or a quick dip in the cold refreshing salt water of the North Atlantic Ocean. That was when Flight Lieutenant Rupert got lucky, catching them with their pants down, so to speak.

Letters from home, that sometimes took weeks to arrive, sounded much the same as the last. The one he opened first had a heavily perfumed envelope. He sniffed it before opening. He read it carefully before sniffing the envelope again. It was so unlike his wife to wear perfume for any occasion. However, the more he read, the more he began to understand why the heavy odour.

The primary schools had been closed. The large secondary school had been converted into offices for the American Air Force personnel. This had been suggested to him before. However, it came as a surprise to find that his wife Deborah had passed her interview and was now part of the typing pool, with all the perks that the American shops could bestow on them. She went on to say how much she was enjoying the job, how the pay was better than her teaching salary, with shorter working hours in a four day week, lots of overtime if you wanted it, depending on aircraft losses, and the parents in the United States that had to be informed. There were many condolence letters to write and be sent.

Amadeus read how the children were enjoying their time on the farms, helping the war effort. He gave the letter a kiss, then placed it against the family photograph on the bedside cabinet.

It was on one of these relaxation days that he picked up the *Daily Express* newspaper. The front page was all about the German cities that had been bombed by the bomber strike force, how Britain was able to strike back, getting more and better aircraft. He opened the paper and spotted an advert. *Experienced pilots and navigators wanted for new bomber squadrons, in a new bomber force called Bomber Command, training can be given. Please telephone this number for an interview.* Amadeus immediately wrote down the number.

It was only right that he should speak to the base commander before doing anything. That would have to wait until tomorrow, so he walked into the town centre and had lunch in the Royal Hotel in Argyll square. Afterwards he walked around the corner for a pint of orange and lemonade, having a game of dominoes for good measure, but losing to the experienced sharks at the table. He was sure some dropped their double six into their pint of Guinness when the game came to a spot count. The money soon disappeared deep into an empty pocket. He never questioned, or checked the dominoes box.

He arrived at the base early and made an appointment to see the base commander.

"Come in, Flight, take a seat, what's all the urgency about?"

"I spotted an advert in the *Daily Express* yesterday; it spoke of the need for bomber pilots and navigators. However, I want your blessing before I make my application."

"I always knew you were unhappy here, Rupert, too far from home perhaps." He stood up and looked out of the window.

"I'm not unhappy here, sir. It's just that I feel I can do more for the Air Force by hitting the enemy hard. If I can't knock them out in their factories, I can just as easy knock them out in their beds."

"Quite," the commander said turning to face him. "The reason they need pilots is that there is a new aircraft coming off the assembly line faster than they can recruit. It's called the Avro Lancaster, a four-engined heavy bomber that can carry a massive payload." He clasped his hands behind his back. "We'll miss you, Flight, you've been a shining example to everyone on the base. However, you're right: these new bomber squadrons are to be renamed and called Bomber Command, under Air Marshal Harris." He walked forward and shook Flight Lieutenant Rupert's hand. "It's a dangerous undertaking you've chosen, Rupert. All I can say is good luck, and be sure to come back after a mission." He lifted his finger. "I don't think your slight colour blindness will affect your application. However, I'll give you a reference letter to give to your Wing Commander. That should smooth your path to being accepted. Come and see me before you go." The Commander gave him a nod, in expression to leave.

"Thank you, sir. I'll leave here with fond memories and they will remain in my thoughts forever." He saluted then marched smartly out of the office. "Whoopee!" He jumped into the air as he walked towards the Catalina to prepare for his flight duty.

When he returned from his sortie, he phoned his wife to inform her of the good news. He found it strange that there was no reply; Deborah never ventured out at night, even when he was in the police force. He rubbed his chin replacing the receiver.

He finally contacted her the following morning before she went to work.

"Sorry, darling, I was at the pub, now that I am part of the quiz team." She paused. "That's great news, at least you will be a little closer to home. I must get off; there's a briefing this morning, bye." The line purred. He replaced the receiver, with a shake of his head.

It was two weeks before he was summoned to the training base at Padgate Camp, Warrington. The overnight sleeper passed through Warrington, so it was a short distance by taxi to the camp. He was taken for a medical, then met with the Wing Commander who would be his tutor for the next six weeks. "Flying Catalina and Lysander aircraft is entirely different to flying the Lancaster: you have more of a crew to consider and, as you can imagine, the aircraft is much heavier to get off the ground. However, I have all confidence in your ability." He read the reference letter. "You seem to have been quite a celebrity in Scotland, Rupert, but that goes for nothing here; you obey the rules the same as everybody else. Work hard and listen to the lectures, then perhaps you can retain your present rank of flight lieutenant. Lectures begin at 09.00 tomorrow."

"Thank you, sir. I won't let you down, I am truly keen on learning how to fly the Lancaster bomber plane."

"Don't call it a plane, Rupert, it's an aeroplane. I can see it will take time to knock out the lackadaisical things you inherited from Coastal Command in Scotland. That will be all."

Amadeus saluted before walking out into the rain. He watched in awe as the Lancaster bombers were taking off and returning from their operations, some of them battered and badly damaged, having difficulty coming into land.

A W.A.F. spoke softly, "This way, Mr. Rupert, I'll show you to your quarters." She marched smartly ahead of him. She looked quite nice in her Woman's Air Force uniform.

He was about to say so when she spoke, "Breakfast at 08.00, lunch when the lectures are finished for the morning, then dinner at 18.00, any questions? Good," she said before he had a chance to respond.

He settled in quickly, passing his first exam with high marks. The flying was not a problem; he was soon taking off and landing with concrete blocks replacing the bomb load. Although the Lancaster needed more speed and a longer runway before it lifted into the skies, the controls were basically the same as he was used to.

There had been little time for family life, although his letters were more frequent, and he would phone home, occasionally finding his wife was out at some quiz or a book club.

He had too much on his mind to be concerned with his wife's quiz nights and book clubs.

CHAPTER SEVEN

Deborah Rupert had become a quiz team captain. She selected who would sit in the contest. Often travelling to other pubs in the county, she would be the stalwart behind the team. It was her birthday, and after the quiz was over she sat with her newfound friends, enjoying herself. A large gin and tonic was brought to her table. "Compliments of Major Presley," the waitress said with a devilish smile.

Deborah had heard the name before. It was the major that held the interview for the job in the typing pool. She lifted the glass as she gazed at the smartly dressed man in his uniform. "Cheers, Major," she said loudly above the chatter of the crowded pub. He lifted his glass in response. Deborah went back to her conversation, as the drinks kept coming.

"Time, ladies and gentlemen please," the pub landlord said loudly.

Deborah was determined to finish her drink before she attempted to stand up. It was a struggle until she felt a firm hand grab her elbow. "Let me help you, ma'am," the Major said in his American drawl. "Now please allow me the honour of escorting you home."

Deborah wanted to say "No thank you" but couldn't get the words out.

The Major collected their jackets from the cloakroom. They stepped out into the fresh air. Deborah gave a slight stagger, so she clung onto the Major for support.

It was a beautiful moonlit night as the sauntered in the moonlight shadows. The stars shone brightly as they talked about the quiz night and her birthday, avoiding any conversation about work.

The stood talking at the bungalow gate. "Well. Goodnight ma'am, it's been a real pleasure." He gave her a quick kiss on the cheek.

"It's my birthday and I need company, so will you join me for a night cap?" Her voice was slightly slurred.

"Nothing would give me more pleasure ma'am." They walked into the bungalow, where Deborah took his jacket then poured two large gin and tonics. "Happy birthday, Deborah," he said, clinking their glasses together. They sat on the couch staring into the log fire embers.

"It must get lonely, with your husband away, and the children evacuated. Just as well you keep yourself active and in fine trim." He looked at her eyes shining in the firelight.

"Yes, I have my friends who take care of me. I've also found a new passion in jogging, usually at weekends."

"Yes I've noticed you in the town, and have to say, you keep your body in fine shape."

"What about you, Major, do you not find it lonely, being so far from home?"

"Please, call me Lester, I only want my rank mentioned when we are at work. As for loneliness, yes it can get that way sometimes." He gave her a smile, before putting his arm around her shoulder and drawing her towards him. "Here we are, two members of the lonely hearts club," he said softly looking into her tear-filled eyes.

She laid her head on his shoulder. He tilted it up gently, wiping away the tears with his shirt sleeve. They looked at each other before their lips met, gently. Their tongues collided in a moment of passion. Deborah pulled away instantly, and got up to switch on the radio. It was a futile attempt to delay the inevitable. She took his hand and lifted him from the couch. "I want to dance, Lester; it's been so long since I danced with anybody."

The Major smiled as he embraced her, kissing her neck on both sides, slowly letting them come cheek to cheek before their kissing became frantic and their tongues met again. He held her close before unbuttoning her blouse. He massaged the fabric of her brassiere, undoing the hook before letting it drop to the floor. He heard her gasp as he massaged her hard erect, flexible nipples, then he kissed each in turn. Deborah began to undo his shirt and tie, then unbuckled his belt. His trousers fell into a heap before he stepped out of them. He held her beautiful breasts against his forested hairy chest. She moaned as the kisses got more tender. He unclipped her skirt, letting it fall onto the floor. He held her buttocks when she stepped out of the garment.

She felt his hardness press against her, and she could not resist her moaning then, as she orgasmed. She pulled down his Y fronts, taking his large thick manhood in her hand while they swayed to the music. He pulled down her suspender belt and lace pants. She lifted her leg in turn allowing him to remove her silk stockings.

Now they were completely naked. Deborah had never experienced such an erotic moment as she took Lester by the hand and led him to the bedroom, where he expertly used his touch, making her orgasm again and again, something else she had never experienced, as he continued the foreplay, then entering her gently before they fell into a steady rhythm, demanding each other before they climaxed loudly together.

Their lovemaking went on all night until Deborah finally fell back exhausted as the dawn chorus began to sing. Her last thought before she fell asleep, was how caring Lester had been in every aspect of his lovemaking. How tender his touches and his ability to come back to a full and hard erection so quickly after his ejaculation that she lost count of how many times she had orgasmed. Those thoughts sent her into a deep sleep, and when she woke at mid-day Lester was gone. She lay thinking of her experience, as she began to think of her husband. Was it the alcohol last night, or was it something she had found lacking in the past? She didn't answer that question, but got up to have a shower and remove the juices and semen from her aching vagina.

As she let the warm water cascade over her body, she swore that this must never happen again. It would be difficult to avoid Major Lester Presley, should he make any more advances, but that was how it would be, because she was a married woman with a husband and children, a responsible position that she wasn't prepared to jeopardise. She put on her bath robe, then removed the semen-stained sheets that covered every part of the king-size bed.

Much as she wanted to, she could not erase the memory of Major Presley from her thoughts. There were nights when she longed for his company, and would begin to massage her clitoris before coming in a loud moan.

She was so glad when Amadeus was coming home; she knew it could never be as good as that night with Lester Presley, but she would go through the motions like she always had, and according to many of her married friends, felt the same way, giggling as they discussed their husbands' sexual failures. She suspected that some of her married friends had also been involved with some American airman, at some time or another, but that subject was never entered into their conversation.

Amadeus never talked about his flying missions, "it's different" is all he would say, but she was proud of him when he announced he had been made a squadron leader with eight bombers on his wing.

Deborah was always afraid that word would leak out about her infidelity. There were nights in the pub when she and her husband were there, with the Major sitting at the bar, it was an awkward situation. However, the Major turned out to be a gentleman, and the soul of discretion itself. There were times she caught him looking at her and she would give a slight nod, and a brief smile, hoping that she wasn't sending out the wrong message, but the Major seemed to have taken the hint, and never approached her again.

The war dragged on, her husband came and went. Life was becoming a bore for Deborah Rupert. She decided to take a short holiday in the Lake District before returning to her work in the typing pool.

She had been back only a few days when a telegram appeared. She opened it with trembling hands. She knew what it contained. It was something she had always expected, and dreaded, but it didn't make the news any easier to take. It was from Bomber Command.

"We are deeply sorry to inform you that Squadron Leader Amadeus Rupert was shot down over Germany, missing presumed killed in action."

This was just like the letters she had sent to families whose husband, son, nephew or any other relation had been lost in action for the American Air Force. She crumpled it into a ball and threw it at the wall, before she collapsed with the shock.

It was her step-mum who was banging at the door. "Deborah are you alright, darling?" She continued her knocking loudly, until Deborah lifted herself from the floor and staggered to the door.

"It's Amadeus," she said choking as the tears rolled down her cheeks. Her step-mum phoned the doctor immediately, as Deborah began to shake uncontrollably before she collapsed again.

The next thing she knew was that she was lying in bed. The doctor had been the day before when she got the news, and had given her a sedative that made her sleep. Her friend Veronica was feeding her soup as her step-mum arranged the bed covers. "I'll tend to her now, Veronica, thanks for coming." She took the soup bowl from her.

"I'll come back in a day or two, so chin up and hope it's not all bad." Veronica gave her a kiss on the cheek before going away.

"My job, Sam. Has anyone told the American office?" Deborah could hardly get the words out.

"Relax, Deborah, all that has been taken care of, and they understand your grief."

Deborah just lay back down wanting to die.

"Come now, you have two children to look after. What would they do if they had to face life without you?" Samantha paused. "The doctor is coming in this afternoon, to give you another sedative. You gave us quite a scare, darling, and you must face the fact that Amadeus may have survived. Hopefully we'll hear from the War Office what the situation is." She disappeared into the kitchen with the soup bowl.

Deborah recovered slowly from the shock,; hearing of her husband's death left an indelible mark on her. She felt totally ashamed at having deceived him. Now she suffered remorse.

The weeks passed slowly. Eventually, a visitor called. She opened the door to see the Major, standing with a bunch of flowers, and chocolates. "I'm sorry I haven't called sooner, Deborah, but you know how hectic things are. However, I'm glad to see you back on your feet." He handed her the offerings and was about to go, until Deborah invited him in for a tea or coffee. He gladly accepted a coffee.

"I appreciate you calling, Lester. I'm in need of company at the moment."

He gave her a smile. "I've been thinking of your position in the typing pool—"

He was interrupted. "I hope to be signed off by the doctor this week," she said in a panic, not wanting to lose her job.

"Don't worry, your job is safe. However, I have been giving it a great deal of thought, and it would not be right to have you sending out letters of condolences, especially now you are recovering. Therefore I'm willing to offer you the job of my personal secretary. It comes with higher wages, more free time and shorter working hours, but there is a downside to the proposal." He paused to drink his coffee. "You need to be on call twenty-four hours a day in case things take a turn for the worse. You would also need to accompany me to the War Office in London, usually once a month, depending on reports. Basically that is it. I should add, there are no strings attached, if you get my meaning. What do you think of the proposal? "

"Delighted, Lester, sorry, I meant to say, Major."

It was the first time she had smiled in weeks.

"Okay, start on Monday next if you feel up to it." He got up quickly. "Must dash, lots to do today." He gave her a hug and a slight peck on the cheek, before making his way out to the Jeep. Deborah stood at the door and waved him goodbye.

The offer of the new job certainly gave her a boost, she began to feel better already.

This was to be a new beginning for her; working as a personal secretary could have its benefits, with more time off, and better wages.

Being close to the Major was good company, especially when they were visiting the War Office in London. As time went by she knew that it was only a matter of time before they became lovers, only this time it was a full-blown love affair. Lester showed her positions and oral sex that she had only dreamed about. They did not care who saw them holding hands in public. The Major would often call her into his office to take dictation, and everything else he had to offer. They just could not keep their hands off one another, something Deborah had experienced in her early marriage to Amadeus Rupert.

What they did not know was the fact that Squadron Leader Rupert had landed the burning Lancaster bomber in a lake, which meant that he and his crew were safe, and taken into captivity. But for Squadron Leader Rupert and his bomb aimer, there would be unseen problems, when interrogated.

Squadron Leader Rupert was separated when captured. He was taken for special treatment. The Germans had developed a hatred towards bomber crews, especially bomb aimers and pilots. They took their wrath out on them, simply because of the propaganda that circulated after a school or a hospital was hit, which Goebbels made the most of in his fanatical speeches that were always exaggerated.

It was fortunate that the Scottish colonel in the prisoner of war camp was prepared for such an event, and Squadron Leader Rupert's identity papers were rapidly switched, because it was not uncommon for pilots to be taken out and shot on the whims and orders of the camp commandant, who was a fanatical Nazi at the best of times.

Amadeus simply disappeared, not sending word home of his internment, and it was to be a very long war, surviving on Red Cross food parcels, but keeping himself physically fit by jogging around the camp. Little did he know that his wife was having a love affair, spending weekends at country hotels, where she and Lester Presley seldom got out of bed.

It came as a complete surprise to Lester when Deborah revealed she was pregnant.

"How could you be so stupid, Deborah?" he said aggressively. "You always used your contraceptive coil when we made love, why on earth did you take it out?"

"Because, come what may, I wanted your baby. The war is coming to an end, and you have always reminded me that you would be going home to the States. I just wanted something to remind me of you."

"Wouldn't a picture have been better." He started to undress her. "I've been keeping this as a going away present but I think now is the time." He took a tube of Vaseline from his bedside cabinet, rubbing the contents onto his penis, then squirting some onto her anus. "You'll enjoy this, darling, I've always wanted to put my penis up your marvelous rear."

Deborah didn't know what to expect, but went along with her lover's demands.

The pain was excruciating as he thrust his large penis into her passage. She screamed and wailed, begging him to stop, but Lester continued with his pleasure until he finally erupted in a loud moan. Deborah was relieved when she felt the warm semen fill her. She quickly but tentatively made for the shower, she got no relief from the pain, so she ran a bath that helped her immensely.

Lester brought her a glass of wine. "The first time is always the worst, darling. It gets much easier the more we do it."

Deborah refused the wine. "There won't be a next time, Lester. I did not enjoy it one bit," she said, annoyed with herself for letting it happen. However, it did happen again, as she relented to his persistence. It was to become another one of their fantastic positions and it was she who would turn her buttocks up towards him, and enjoy the pleasure it gave her.

There was no position they had not experienced. It was almost as if their lovemaking had increased; where they found the time was anyone's guess.

It was on a lovemaking weekend away that they heard the news that the war was over.

Lester sprang out of bed. "We need to get back to Welwyn, darling. I will probably be recalled to the United States."

Deborah rubbed her tummy that was showing signs of swelling. "Come back to bed, honey. This could be our last tryst together."

He couldn't resist the good-looking woman who lay with her legs wide apart. They spent the afternoon in rapture. They departed the hotel in the early evening, arriving in Welwyn just as the sun was setting. The Major dropped her off at the bungalow before making his way to the office. He was greeted by the guard on duty. "We have been looking for you, sir. Great news." He paused. "We're homeward bound tomorrow morning; the sergeants will take over the tidying up and dispersal of the staff. We take off at 05.00. You have to destroy the secret papers that have accumulated over the past four years, sir. I'll assist you in taking them to the incinerator."

The Major nodded. "Has anyone informed my wife?" he asked sternly.

"No, sir, we thought we would leave that to you." The guard saluted as the Major walked into the compound.

There was so little time left to do what he had to do. He hastily packed all his clothes into the cases. Then telephoned Deborah, explaining that his country was still at war with Japan and his orders were to return to the United States immediately.

She pleaded with him to come over and stay the night.

"Don't be ridiculous, Deborah; I'm far too busy. Sergeant Maldon will give you instructions on what to do. All I can say is goodbye. It's been lots of fun, honey. You English certainly know how to pleasure a man." The line went dead.

Deborah tried to redial, but without success. Tears welled in her eyes. It was the first time in their affair that she felt used. She poured herself a stiff gin and tonic, then sat down to cry. For her the party was over, the only consolation in all this was the children would be coming home, and the local primary school would be reopening. It was something to look forward to, and help bring some normality back into her life, at least until the baby was born.

CHAPTER EIGHT

The troops were returning from far-off shores. There was so much happening that made it difficult to keep up with her school classes. The children seemed to be much less disciplined than before. Deborah, as well as the other teachers, blamed the evacuation for their misbehaviour, having to punish them and help them to behave like normal children did before the war; there was just so much lack of discipline nowadays.

She was finding it hard to concentrate due to her condition. She was five months gone, and knew she would have to give up work when it became impossible to move about freely. She waited for her children at the school gate before taking their hands and walking home. Her dad usually collected them but he had his own duties to perform at the new secondary school in Welwyn Garden City where he taught.

She was glad to get indoors, to put her feet up, and when the children went to their room to do their lessons.

The doorbell rang, and she made her way lethargically to answer it.

She stood for a moment totally dumbstruck. She had to look again at the handsome muscular man standing in front of her. She rubbed her eyes, thinking she was seeing a ghost. "Amadeus," she blurted the name out before collapsing onto the floor. She was rushed to the Hatfield general hospital where she was placed in intensive care.

Amadeus Rupert stared at his wife through the glass window. She had tubes coming out of every orifice, the oxygen mask placed over her nose and mouth reminded him of his time with Bomber Command.

The children had been taken by Samantha and her dad, who said they could stay with them until their mother got better. It was for the best.

Amadeus stood looking at his wife. He couldn't understand her unconscious state. A nurse offered him a cup of tea, which he refused. "The doctor will be along shortly, Mr. Rupert. It would be better if you waited in here." She opened a door to a small room with two chairs.

He took her advice, then said he would have that tea after all if the offer still stood.

"Certainly, take a seat, I'll bring one through." A short time later she appeared with a sweet mug of tea. "I hope you take milk and sugar," she said smiling.

Amadeus nodded. "My wife, is she in any danger, Nurse?" he asked taking the mug from her.

"The doctor will explain everything. Meanwhile, take your tea while it's hot." She turned and walked out of the room.

Amadeus had finished his tea when Doctor Richards appeared. "Your wife has had a very lucky escape, Mr. Rupert. I'm sorry to inform you it was saving her or the baby, and the decision was taken to save her, because there is no reason why you and Mrs. Rupert cannot have more children in time."

"What?" Amadeus screwed up his face.

"Yes it was a difficult decision to make. However, we'll keep her in the intensive care for the time being, at least until she recovers consciousness. Perhaps in a week or two we will move her into the recovery ward, where you can sit and talk."

Amadeus thanked him for his concern. There were so many questions he wanted to ask, but decided to keep quiet for the moment, because he found it very hard to digest and take in what the doctor had just told him.

His thoughts were of mixed emotions when he left the hospital: what was his wife up to in his absence? It was obvious she had been having extramarital affairs, but with whom?

She was not well enough to be questioned at the moment. However, he had an appointment with the Chief Constable for reinstatement back into the Hertfordshire constabulary, and he would use his experience and subterfuge of the force to discover who her lover was.

It didn't take long to find out his name.

Inspector Rupert cursed the man. He didn't expect his wife to sit brooding at home every night, but this was different.

Amadeus was a proud man, and could hear the whispers of the gossipmongers when he entered the shops.

The visits to the hospital became less frequent. He had stopped visiting during the day, and went over to the hospital every alternate night, if he felt like it.

It was the children who he felt for. "When is Mummy coming home?" April would ask with tears in her eyes, when he took them out on a free Saturday.

That was when he made the decision to send them to boarding school. It had always been the plan before the war, but now they were that bit older and had been away from home during the evacuation, it was time to put it into action, to prevent them knowing what was to come. There was also the gossipmongers and their children. He knew that children could be just as cruel as their parents, so Amadeus took the final decision to send his son Colin to the Buxton Grammar School for boys in Derbyshire, while April would be sent to St. Margaret's Academy for girls in York.

Amadeus took the time to drive to each school when the children were enrolled. It was the least he could do, while his wife slowly recovered from her miscarriage. She was in the recovery ward for months as an infection had been found in her womb.

Amadeus knew that now was not the time for recriminations, that could wait until she felt stronger and in full recovery, but Amadeus knew it was a subject that was not going to disappear and would have to be talked about to get to the truth.

He had settled down into the police work that seemed to be never-ending.

Victoria Buckingham had returned from Portsmouth where she had served as a W.R.E.N. in the naval dockyard.

The sad news was that Donald Bowman had been killed when he parachuted into Arnhem, to capture the Arnhem bridge. That was supposed to shorten the war, but history would turn that on its head, because it turned out to be a total disaster when ten thousand troops were dropped into Holland and only two thousand came out unscathed.

"I have some good news for you, D.C. Buckingham. I made a request, and the promotion we talked about before the war has finally come through, and your rank is now detective sergeant. How does that sound?"

"Thank you, sir, I had intended to bring it up, but now I'm just so glad it has happened."

"I want you to keep a sharp lookout for Donald's replacement. It'll be a hard task for someone to fill, but I'm sure once we get things back to normal, there will be somebody out there." He was about to leave. "Yes, Buckingham, what is it?"

She was about to ask how his wife was, but hesitated knowing the gossip that was circulating around the station and the town. "Nothing that can't keep for now, sir," she said, changing the subject. "What do you want me to do, sir, is there anything on the go?" she asked with a smile.

"I'm not sure yet. I'm wanted upstairs to meet with Superintendent Crawley so something is in the air. I can smell it." He paused. "There is one thing you can do at the moment." He rubbed his chin. "Go down to the basement and ask Ernie the mole to dig out the unsolved rotary card system. I had a bad feeling back in thirty-eight about it and was told in no uncertain terms by the C.C. to ignore it, because of the septic tank murder inquiry that was on the go at the time. However, I was going through the wall safe and discovered an index roller that had a few names listed on it, but I' m sure there's more to it than meets the eye, so you do that now, and we'll meet in the canteen for a coffee and chinwag to catch up on what you've found." Inspector Rupert stood up and prepared to climb the stairs to the Superintendent's office.

"Right, Rupert, take a seat." It was not an invitation, but an order spoken harshly by the Superintendent.

Inspector Rupert looked at the tired face, the Crawley who had aged before his time. Was it the war? He didn't want to know, so sat down as ordered.

"You are the detective we need to examine a missing persons case, after your success with the septic tank murders, the Chief

Constable has insisted you are the man for the job, despite my protests. I don't like you, Rupert. You think just because you served in the Metropolitan Police and the Bomber Command that it makes you a cut above everyone else. Well let me tell you, Inspector, that is not the case with me. I know you and your kind, so I'll be watching you, just waiting for you to slip up, then I can take my doubts in you upstairs." He paused. "How is your wife?" he asked with a smirk on his face.

"Recovering, sir." Inspector Rupert kept his composure. "What was I summoned up here for sir, or have you forgotten?" Inspector Rupert was playing the mind game.

"No I haven't bloody forgotten, Rupert. I have been instructed to tell you that two young teenage girls have been reported missing, one from Hatfield and the other from Stevenage. They did not come home from school in Stevenage, and Hatfield." The Superintendent hesitated. "Both are thirteen years old. The first to be reported is Cynthia Wood who went missing on the 8th of November, the other is Alison Brent, on the 8th of September. The Brent girl is a bit of a tearaway, and could simply have taken off to London, like so many teenagers do, but Cynthia Wood is a home-loving girl, and that raises a concern." Superintendent Crawley leaned back folding his arms behind his head. "Let's not drag this out, Rupert, we don't enjoy each other's company, that much. Certainly not as much as your wife and the American major." He gave another grin.

Once again Inspector Rupert managed to keep his temper in check. He wanted to break Crawley's scrawny neck, but he simply screwed up his face.

"That means Cynthia Wood was reported missing two weeks ago and, worse still, is the fact Alison Brent was reported missing fourteen weeks ago." He stood up. "Why has this investigation been so slow to get off the ground? I wanted to open up the missing persons cases before the war, and was told to drop it. Well, I'm not so sure I want to drop it now, because I think we have a psychopath, even a serial killer, on the loose, that has been around for a long time, killing women and young girls."

Inspector Rupert paced the room. "How do I explain this to the newspapers? You know what they're like, sir." He watched the Superintendent squirm in his seat.

"You keep the newspapers out of this until those girls are found, Rupert; is that clearly understood?"

"You know I can't guarantee that, sir. Once they get a sniff, they're like bloodhounds. I wonder how many heads will roll if this gets out. Strewth, I hate to contemplate the outcome." Inspector Rupert had to turn away and make for the door before Crawley could recover his composure.

However, he did hear the loud voice call, "Rupert" as he descended the stairs two at a time until he reached the ground floor. He made his way to the canteen for a coffee. Detective Sergeant Buckingham sat waiting for him with arms folded before getting up and joining him at the counter.

They settled down with their coffee and cake. "It's worse than I imagined, Buckingham. A missing persons case that's fourteen weeks old and another two weeks ago." He paused. "I have a nasty gut feeling about this, Sergeant, pray tell me some good news."

"There is none, sir. Ernie the mole gave me three missing persons files that are quite thick. He also gave me the index rollers dating back to 1934, and he wants them back in the correct order." D.S. Buckingham looked over the rim of her cup. "You could be right, sir, I think there is something brewing." She sipped her coffee. "How is creepy this morning sir?" she asked with a smile.

"Now, now, Sergeant, don't forget his rank, but it looked as if he had just crawled out from below the woodpile." They both laughed out loud, turning heads in the canteen.

After their morning coffee they went to the Inspector's office. "I've been thinking about a replacement for D.C. Bowman, sir: a keen young constable, much like Donald was, and he has a sharp brain, so I think he's worth considering."

"Name?" Inspector Rupert asked quickly.

"Derek Bradley, sir, shall I ask him to report to you, when he comes off the early shift?"

"Yes, do that, Buckingham, but don't ask him, you order him, use your power of rank, Sergeant." He looked at her consternation.

"Yes, sir, I might as well start where I mean to finish. However, back to the missing girls, what now, sir?"

"We need photographs of the two girls, so you go over to Hatfield and question the parents, who just might remember something. I will go to Stevenage to question Alison Brent's parents."

They returned to the unused incident room. It was like opening the door to a place in history that was never ever going to be erased from their memory: the empty information board, the empty seats and dusty tables. Detective Sergeant Buckingham pinned the photographs up onto the board. "Derek Bradley is waiting in the canteen, sir, shall I order him in to speak to you?" She smiled.

"Do that, Sergeant. I might as well get it over with sooner rather than later."

She noticed since her return to duty that Inspector Rupert's attitude had changed. Gone was the soft-spoken, understanding man that she knew before the war. She noticed that Inspector Rupert was more aggressive, more cynical in his approach to lower-ranking officers. She dismissed it as a difficult time for him, and walked out to fetch the young constable.

Introductions were made and Derek Bradley was now a detective constable, in the Hertfordshire police force.

Inspector Rupert tapped the information board. "This girl, Alison Brent, has a court order placed on her for truancy from her school, so it is not the best of starts I was hoping for. But Cynthia Wood is much different; she was an obedient, home-loving girl, so tomorrow you will take Bradley over to Hatfield School and question the teachers, while I go to Stevenage to carry out the same. We'll finish today by examining the roller index cards and files that P.C. Ernie Forbes the mole gave us, so plenty to do before we go home."

Inspector Rupert was about to call it a day, when D.C. Bradley spoke out. "Take a look at this card, sir; it just might interest you."

Inspector Rupert got up and walked to the table and lifted the index card. He studied it with interest. Another teenage girl, aged fifteen from the village of Stapleford, was reported missing on the 8th of October 1944. Her name was Linda Symonds. She attended the Letchworth secondary school, and was never seen again after leaving school to make her way home. Inspector Rupert studied the card and noticed the date. There was a coincidence, and it was something he did not like, and that was a coincidence.

"A change of plan for me tomorrow, I will go to Stapleford Village to question the mother of Linda Symonds. I'll go to Letchworth School to question the teachers, then I'll make my way down to Stevenage, to question the teachers about Alison Brent, so I might be a little late back. However, after the pair of you have questioned the Hatfield teachers, come back here and go through these index rollers very carefully, as it might be worthwhile. We can also have a look at the files again, just to go over the reports on each girl, although I don't recall seeing Linda Symonds' name mentioned." He paused and rubbed his chin. "Hand me the files, Sergeant. I want to go through them again." He thumbed through the pages. "Why is Linda Symonds listed in the index roller system, yet there is no mention of her in these files? Now there's a conundrum that needs looking into." He looked at his watch. "Goodness is that the time? Okay let's call it a day."

He made his way to the fish and chip shop before heading over to the Hatfield general hospital. Deborah was still in a coma in intensive care, so he stood for a moment looking at her through the window. The doctor came up beside him. "It might help if you spoke to her, Mr. Rupert. However, we will need to gown you, and give you a face mask."

"No problem, Doctor; I was used to wearing an oxygen mask as a bomber pilot. So show me where to go."

After being kitted out he entered the intensive care room, and spoke softly, uttering her name. He was sure he saw her finger move as an alarm sounded. The nursing sister came in and switched it off. "Nothing to worry about, Mr. Rupert, but

I think you should leave now." He hadn't realised it, but he had been in the room for nearly thirty minutes.

After he discarded the gown, overshoes and mask he made his way home to Welwyn.

He sat with an estate agent's brochure, looking at future developments in the new town of Welwyn Garden City, that was expanding day by day now that work had resumed. There was one villa that caught his eye and he pondered over it as he sipped his wine.

5 Oakland Avenue fascinated him, with plenty of rooms, a dining room, a large lounge and kitchen. The most important thing was the privacy, with pastures to the rear of the villa, and oak trees on the horizon. That sounded ideal, so he took a mental note to visit the villa, and if it was the way it was described in the brochure he would purchase it. It would give his wife a nice surprise when she was able to sit up. After another glass of wine he retired for the night, and wakened as usual with the screams of airmen who had left their intercom switch on as their burning bombers fell from the sky. He woke up in a cold sweat with the blankets lying on the floor.

This was a secret he kept close to his chest. He even kept it from his doctor, refusing to get medical help, while each night was a nightmare.

He was up early next morning, and after a shower, he made his way to work, where he ate a full English breakfast in the canteen. He was well on his way to Stapleford Village before the canteen began to fill with the early shift.

He visited the parents of Linda Symonds, only to find that her father had been killed in Holland, the same conflict as Donald Bowman. So, after a cup of tea, he took the photo of the pretty young teenager while handing Mrs. Symonds his card. "Telephone me night or day," he said loudly. "Something might spring to mind." He made his way to the school, where he also drew a blank.

"Linda was not the kind of girl to go off to London, Inspector. In fact she had a bright future ahead of her, a very intelligent girl," the headmaster said without any hesitation.

Inspector Rupert made his way down to Stevenage to go through the same routine. The only difference between Linda Symonds and Alison Brent was, that Alison was a wild one, who encouraged boys to the school bike shed, and even flirted with teachers, and older men in Stevenage. "Her probation officer could give you more information on her than we could." The teacher paused. "There is one factor that might be of use, Inspector." She paused and placed her hand on the desk. "Alison used to get picked up in a van from school, not every afternoon, but quite regular."

"What kind of van, and what colour?" he asked quickly.

"Oh, Inspector how do I know what type of van? As for the colour, it was a dark colour, perhaps dark blue or even black, but who was paying attention in those days with so much going on. However, I once got a glimpse of the driver, who was much older than Alison: grey sideburns, sharp features. Oh, another thing, there was writing on the side of the van, I can't remember what it said."

Inspector Rupert handed her a card. "Phone me if anything comes to mind." He made his way out into the foggy late afternoon, to drive back to Welwyn Garden City.

Sergeant Buckingham was still in the incident room when he arrived.

"This is not looking too good, sir. While you were away, I used some spare time to scroll through the index cards like you suggested." She had laid out separate cards on the desk. "These are the more recent names of missing persons. However, look at the dates, they all fall in around the 8th of each month. I have checked the lunar calendar, just in case there was a connection, but that has turned up fruitless, because there was no moon, full, half or quarter at that time, so I think we can rule out a werewolf, but there is a connection somewhere that we are not aware of yet." She slid each card towards him. "I've also instructed Ernie the mole to dig a little deeper into his files, hoping he might uncover something that could prove useful." She looked closely at the cards on the table.

"The visit to the parents and schools of Alison Brent and Linda Symonds have turned up fruitless. However, one teacher did say that Linda Brent was being picked up from school occasionally, by an older man, in a dark-coloured van." He caught the Sergeant's look. "Yes, I know what you're thinking, Sergeant, but at least it tells us that someone, who was not her parents, was picking her up from school." He rubbed his chin. "These names you have taken from the rotary card index could prove useful, so get them listed with ages, names, and addresses and get them put up on the information board. I have a job for you, D.C. Bradley." He paused as Sergeant Buckingham took a note of the new names on the cards. "I want you to look through the telephone directory and list down all firms that make household deliveries. When you've finished Hatfield, go on to the other towns in the county. This will take time, I know, but I have a hunch that this van with the writing on its side could be the breakthrough we need. Don't forget builders' merchants and kitchen replacement firms." Inspector Rupert rubbed his chin, stood for a moment then went to the top floor.

The secretary gave him a look.

"Is the Chief Constable free? It's very important I see him."

The secretary went through the usual question. "Do you have an appointment, Inspector?"

"You're the secretary. You know I haven't," he said firmly.

"Just a moment." She lifted the telephone, pressed a button and spoke in a whisper. "Okay, sir, I'll tell him." Replacing the phone she said, "I'm afraid the Chief Constable is busy, so please make an appointment." She lifted the desk diary.

Inspector Rupert ignored her and barged into the Chief's office unannounced, followed by an irate secretary. "I'm sorry, sir, he just ignored me."

"What's the meaning of this, Rupert? Have you no respect, man?" The C.C. was rising off his chair in anger.

"I'm truly sorry, sir, but this can't wait," he said in earnest walking towards the desk.

"Thank you, Lucy, that will be all for now," the C.C. said softly to his secretary. He looked at the Inspector. "This better be good, Rupert," he said in an angry voice.

"It's regarding the two missing girls, sir. My sergeant has been doing a little digging, and come up with more missing teenagers who I have not had a chance to study yet." He paused. "If you think back to 1937 into 1938, you took the decision back then to shelve the missing persons at that time. Once again I haven't checked if the names that have appeared are the ones you discarded, but I do remember quite clearly how you blamed budgets." He hesitated. "I spoke to Superintendent Crawley about this issue, and he gave me the same answer that you gave back then, that the septic tank murders were more important. However, I now believe this investigation just might come back to haunt you, and I will tell you now what I said to the Superintendent, that if the press were to hear of these missing persons cases that were shelved and have now raised their heads again, then there could be severe repercussions for you and the Hertfordshire force." He paused. "That is not why I am here, sir. It is my belief we have a serial killer on the loose, who has been around for some time. Let's say as far back as the late thirties, perhaps before, I don't know, but this is turning out to be a manhunt for a psychopath."

"You can't go to the papers with this, Rupert. What proof do you have? None." The last word was delivered loudly.

"You barge into my office, with ifs and buts and maybes, Rupert. That is not good enough." He pointed his finger. "You tread very carefully with this investigation, Rupert. I don't forget or forgive easily, and I don't suffer fools gladly, now get out."

"Don't worry, sir, I'll try to keep the skeletons locked in the cupboard as long as I can."

He left the Chief Constable stuttering, as he always did when he got annoyed or excited.

He stopped at the secretary's desk on the way out. "Tell me truthfully, Lucy, does the Chief ever stutter when he's whispering sweet nothings in your ear?" He gave her a smile before bounding along the corridor, down the stairs and back to his office on the ground floor.

He had hoped that the conversation with the C.C. could have been more constructive, but at least the point was made about the dereliction of duty by senior officers at that time.

CHAPTER NINE

A night visit to the hospital found that his wife had improved, and although still in intensive care she managed a short wave before lying down again.

He touched the glass window before exiting the hospital. This was one diversion he didn't need right now, as the investigation was beginning to gain momentum.

There were other interruptions that he didn't need, but decided to go ahead with it anyway.

He had been offered a police house in Welwyn Garden City but turned it down, knowing that if he was ever out of the job, he would be out of the house as well.

The dream house was 5 Oakland Avenue, in the suburbs of the new town, with a view that looked out across meadows to two large oak trees that spread their branches on the horizon. The villa consisted of twin garages, three double en suite rooms, a separate bathroom with a double walk-in shower, a bath and twin wash hand basins, a water closet. A large fitted kitchen, large lounge, and a modest-sized dining room that could sit eight persons. He could well afford the luxury, because of the money he had inherited from his dead friend, and his wealthy step-parents, so he alone took the decision to purchase it, while his wife was still in hospital. If anything it would be better for her, with a room on the ground floor, to help her recovery when she regained her strength and was allowed home. He left the removals to a respected removal firm in the area. The furniture and décor was chosen by an interior designer. The first piece of furniture to be sent to the dump was the double bed, which Amadeus had misgivings about. He did wait to discuss the sale or lease of their bungalow in Old Welwyn, which the overgrown village was now called.

Amadeus watched as his wife slowly returned to reasonable health. However, there were issues that would have to be addressed sooner rather than later, but now was not a good time.

Inspector Rupert stood looking out of the window of his spacious bright, air-conditioned and central-heated office. His thoughts were interrupted as Sergeant Buckingham entered.

"Sorry for the delay, sir, the typist was busy with other work. I've left the list with her anyway."

The Inspector nodded. "What about those extra officers, Buckingham? We'll need them to do good old-fashioned police work."

"All ready and waiting in the incident room, sir, raring to go." She smiled.

"Has D.S. Bradley got anything yet? We need those company listings desperately."

"Patience, sir, the directory is rather thick, but I'll speed him up," she said, taking the heat out of the situation. Inspector Rupert knew how clever she was at changing the subject before he could reprimand her.

"Okay, let's see who we've got to help us." They walked to the incident room. The crowd of police officers stood to attention as they entered. "Please be seated," the Inspector said as he walked to the information board. "Before I begin explaining the current investigation, there are a few points I want to put to you all." He looked at each officer that was seated. "I'm sure most of you will have heard of my reputation by now. However, for the benefit of those officers joining us from other stations, there are two very important things that I demand from you. The first is punctuality, the other is smartness, a tie will be worn at all times. Sergeant Buckingham will advise you on other qualities I expect from an officer working in my team, such as politeness and respect when knocking on doors. We need the public's help with this; therefore it is important that you approach these neighbours in the right frame of mind." He looked at the Sergeant. "Buckingham will split you into sections. Hatfield for the Cynthia Wood section, Stevenage for the Alison Brent section and the most recent that has come to light is Linda Symonds in Stapleford Village. That particular area might be more productive, since villages tend to notice strangers in the area. However, the main question is who the older man is? What type of dark-coloured van with writing on the side? Those questions are important, so if you do find anything of interest, I will be in Stevenage at the probation officer's office. There is a possibility she has had other girls on her books that have disappeared." He paused. "Okay. Chop, chop, time for good old-fashioned policing."

The assembled officers remained seated as they were allocated their various destinations by Sergeant Buckingham.

Inspector Rupert made his way to Stevenage to speak to the probation officer, only this time he had an appointment. He already had the woman typecast as an ageing spinster with brogues and a tweed skirt, thick stockings and a twin set, a tweed jacket and her grey hair set in a bun with Kirby grips supporting it.

How presumptuous and wrong he was. He was shown into an office by an older woman and asked to take a seat. He was about to start his questioning when a door opened behind him. He turned to see a young woman appear, nothing like what he expected.

"Inspector Rupert, Miss Sutton," the older woman said before taking her leave.

"Call me Barbara," the young woman said introducing herself and shaking his hand.

"But you're a—"

"A probation officer," she said with a radiant smile on a face that could launch a thousand ships.

"You're much younger than I expected, Barbara. However, let's begin." He studied the woman for a moment. "We have a missing girl who is, or was, on your house calls. Her name was Alison Brent, by all accounts a bit of a tearaway. But we know quite a lot about her, with information received from other sources." He paused. "The reason I'm here is to find out if you have any other girls on your books who have gone missing recently, or if you have any records of girls from the past, dating back to 1936 for example." He clasped his hands awaiting a response.

"The early ones are before my time, Inspector. I would need time to delve into our records. Another girl does spring to mind, though, Linda Symonds, who was caught stealing sweets and cigarettes from her local newsagent and tobacconist shop. She was placed on a short period of probation, which I believe has run its course." Barbara Sutton got up and went to a filing cabinet. She flicked through her records. "Here we are, Linda Symonds, yes. Her probationary period has expired, but I had no idea she had gone missing. There is a note in her file that her parents were concerned for her safety, but there is nothing mentioned from the courts, who normally pass information to our department if there is a need for house visits, or restrictions. That has not happened, so basically our work with Linda is at an end."

Inspector Rupert nodded his understanding. "At the moment we have three missing teenagers, and Linda Symonds is one of them. So again we have her on our radar, and to be frank, Barbara, I have concern for those girls' safety." He paused. "What do you say to joining me for lunch and we can talk over a bottle of wine?"

"I only drink Remy Martin Brandy," she said with a smile, "but not so early in the day, so wine will suffice."

"Me too, Barbara," he said getting up quickly just in case she changed her mind. There was not much to say about the missing girls, nothing that Inspector Rupert did not know already. Therefore the conversation was relaxed as they discovered things about each other.

When it was time for him to drive back to Welwyn Garden City, he took her hand. "We must do this again sometime, perhaps when you have gone through your older files."

"I'd like that very much, Amadeus."

He kissed her lightly on the cheek and got a whiff of her perfume that made the peck last a little longer than intended. However, he noticed that she didn't withdraw her body from his embrace.

"I'll phone you if anything comes to light."

"Phone me anyway," he said before paying the restaurant bill, then making his way to the police car. He sat watching her shapely legs bend as she pulled herself into her car.

He was in a joyful mood as he drove back to the police station. He thought about his audacity, asking a beautiful woman to join him for lunch, especially a professional who could have information on the case. His mind returned to the roller card system that had a large capital S marked in the corner, which meant solved. There were others which he paid little attention to at the time because he did not know what the lettering meant, but now he did. The large capital M meant missing followed by a capital U meaning unsolved. It was time to take a closer look at those cards in the roller index system. Even the cards that Sergeant Buckingham had separated from the system must have some bearing on the case.

It was the first thing he attended to on his return to the incident room. What he did notice was that there was a substantial gap between the time when Linda Symonds was reported missing and Cynthia Wood and Alison Brent: over a year in fact. So, if it was a serial killer, then why the delay? Could he have been in prison for another offence, perhaps in hospital? Inspector Rupert scratched his head in thought. Now that he was studying the roller index system a pattern started to emerge. He looked at the information board at the list of new names Sergeant Buckingham had pulled from the rotary index system. He looked at the printed list again, ignoring the three most recent names.

The first one that took his attention was a fifteen-year-old from Hatfield, called Zoe Brooke, who was last seen getting into a van outside her school gate in February 1944. An older teenager called Sandra Phillips, aged eighteen, from St. Albans, was reported missing in March 1944, last seen talking to an older man outside the factory where she worked. Then there was a break in the pattern. A shoe shop assistant, Felicity Roach, aged thirty from the town of Ware, who was reported missing when she failed to turn up for work at the end of March 1933.

Inspector Rupert realised that this serial killer was not particular about age, and probably used the blackout to murder and bury his victims. He was aware that he now had a serious crime on his hands that could take years to solve unless he got a lucky break, and lucky breaks were few and far between in detective work. Breaks came with hard work. So he decided to inform the team about the massive task ahead. It was something he would have to take to the Chief Constable, in time, but not until he had the investigation so far underway that even the C.C. with all his power would be unable to stop it.

His wife was now in full recovery. However, there was a time, when she was still in the recovery room, that as he sat by her bed, the nurse daubing the patient's sweating forehead with a cold compress, Deborah sat bolt upright and yelled for Lester to hold her before she collapsed back down, as the nurse tried to soothe her and place the head back on the pillow before tidying the white sheets.

It was the final humiliation for him when the nurse said quite innocently, "It's best you leave now, Lester, your wife needs to rest."

He walked out of the recovery room in a daze, walking past Deborah's step-mum and her dad sitting awaiting information. He really had nothing to say to them, knowing it was not their fault. He never heard the shout from Samantha, asking what the matter was, that was explained to him when they came calling later that night.

Amadeus knew in that brief moment in the recovery room that his marriage to Deborah was over. There was no way back for the couple who at one time had fallen head over heels for each other, claiming love at first sight. Now it was a total disaster.

He explained to Barbara that things had not turned out in his marriage the way he would have wanted, but she had sympathy for him and was an expert listener, giving advice on how he should handle Deborah: not to throw her out of his life completely, because they still had two children to consider. There was also the trauma of what his wife had gone through. "Give her a chance to recover, and regain her health and fitness, before embarking on the tete-a-tete that has to come eventually."

Amadeus nodded in agreement. "I hope that will not interfere with our relationship?" he asked anxiously.

"Why should it, Amadeus? We are intelligent, responsible people. Let things cool down before you question her about Lester Presley, who, by all accounts, wanted someone to warm his bed while he was away from his wife and family in the United States. Should we blame the war?" Barbara shook her head. "There were many men and woman in exactly the same situation that managed to remain faithful, despite the separations." She turned on her side and went to sleep.

He took the decision to follow Barbara's advice, it would be a tricky situation living in the same house with the woman he now despised but, to please his newfound partner, he would go along with it for now.

Amadeus lay awake, remembering his time with the Metropolitan Police in London: how his old inspector treated each case methodically and with skill. That in most cases the woman and girls listed as missing were in fact shacked up with some silver-tongued devil who eventually had them on the game and acted as their pimp. He couldn't explain why, but this was different. So when he heard Barbara snore, he got out of bed, dressed and drove back to Welwyn Garden City to be on hand when his wife got home from hospital. He didn't feel quite so bad after the advice that Barbara had given him. However, it would be separate beds, and rooms, for the time being.

A housekeeper had been employed to help with the cleaning and cooking of meals, so there was little conversation, when Mrs. McGinty was present. She was a very good employee, who came with excellent references; a very good cook; and did all her own baking. Better still, there was always a breakfast on the table in the morning and a hot meal in the evening, something Inspector Rupert had missed for years. He would often joke that if it wasn't for the works canteen he would have starved to death.

There were other aspects of his life that had changed. He had taken Barbara's advice and seen a councillor about his nightmares, and, despite Deborah's frailties, she was always there sitting on his bed to sponge and dry him, which he often told her he did not need her help with. Living in the same home was not working for either of them, especially when Barbara came to the villa for the weekend. Passing each other on the stairs without a word was putting an extra strain on their present situation.

He decided to have it out with her, but used the soft approach that Barbara had advised him to. Although, Amadeus was an expert at putting things across to other people and therefore found it no problem to have it out with Deborah, but he used a cunning trick, inviting her to lunch at the Fountain lounge bar.

They ordered lunch before Amadeus began to speak. "I have something very important to say to you, Deborah, so I want you to listen very carefully." He paused. "I'm glad that you have recovered from your miscarriage, and that is what I need to talk to you about." He paused again." I know about your affair with Lester Presley, the American major. I won't hide the fact that it sickens me to think how far you have fallen in my esteem." She was about to speak, but he held up his hand. "Please let me finish, I need to get this sorted in order that I can clear my head, because I have lots of work to be getting on with, and I really don't need any distractions." He took a sip of his beer. "First things first, as you know, I have found myself another woman. It wasn't meant to be like this, but with Barbara staying over at weekends, it has become impossible for you and her to be in the same house." He hesitated. "That is why I want you out, I'm quite prepared to help you find another place."

There was a tear in Deborah's eye. "Believe me, Amadeus, I would have given anything to have gone through what you and I have gone through." She gave a wry smile. "Let's just call it the fortunes of war. When I didn't got word that you were alive, I just wanted to die. It was Lester Presley that helped me get over the difficulties I was going through and, in time, I fell in love with him, but never ever forgot you. I realise now that I was duped, by a man who just needed a bed partner, but I'm a big girl and can handle that quite easily." She cut her roast beef before continuing. "I'll be out of your hair, as soon as I let my dad know the situation. I can live with them until I find something, and I already have a place in mind, so I don't want you to concern yourself, because while recovering in hospital I had already made up my mind to leave you. That was even before I found out about your probation officer." She took a potato into her mouth, and chewed on it before talking. "All I can say is that I am glad that we have had this out, because I was trying to find a way of telling you of my intentions, and you have just made it easy for me. I will finish this conversation by saying how much I did love you. I wish you all the best for your future life, whichever way it goes, though I am sad I can never be a part of it."

Deborah remained perfectly calm as Amadeus told her about his luck, putting a burning bomber down on the German lake, how his identity was changed for survival reasons, how there was no chance of giving his own identity away to a German camp commandant whose parents had been killed in a bombing raid on Berlin.

Both tried to maintain an ounce of decorum, as they ate their lunch, then Amadeus fetched the coffee from the bar.

"Everything alright, sir?" the landlord asked smiling.

"Just a family problem that had to be cleared up," Amadeus said taking the coffee cups.

"I meant the food, sir. Did you enjoy the roast beef lunch?"

Amadeus smiled at his misinterpretation. "Yes, very tasty thank you."

They were interrupted by an ageing woman with lots of makeup, bright-coloured clothes that dated from the roaring twenties and a bright red lipstick, her double string of pearls, large gypsy-ringed earrings and bangles that hung loosely on both wrists indicating the era she still lived in. "Please ignore them, sir. Eccentric, but very good customers," the landlord said with a large grin, before walking over to serve the quiet old gentleman accompanying her.

"My word what a beautiful woman you have on your arm; those high cheek bones would thrill any film director." The woman went on quickly, "Do you know I played alongside Lawrence Olivier at the Talk of the Town, London, and again with him at the Shakespeare theatre in Stratford on Avon."

She turned in a way that demonstrated her acting skills in days of old, then walked back to her stool where the old man who Amadeus assumed was her husband ordered two large schooners of dry sherry then said, "Sit down, darling, and stop making a nuisance of yourself."

Amadeus simply raised his eyebrows before returning to his seat, now realising that Deborah had gone. He drank his coffee, paid the bill, and took his leave with a slight wave from the actress.

He made his way up to the Oakland villa to find that Deborah was loading her car.

"Dad will put these ornaments in his garage for now. I want nothing else from the house except my clothes, which I will collect later. Just one more thing, Amadeus, we have to consider the children and the finance, which I hope can remain amicable in the settlement, so you will be hearing from my lawyer in due course." She started up the car then drove away, much to the surprise of her astounded husband, who hadn't expected this so soon.

The incident room was full of chatter when the Inspector entered. Eventually it became quiet, as the Inspector began to speak. "I'll ask how you got on with your door-to-door on Friday and Saturday, but in the meantime let me tell you of our new missing persons discovery, spread over a wide area of the county." Inspector Rupert went on to name the other girls, and older woman. "This break in dates and ages must mean something. I have mixed feelings about this case, part of me wants those persons to be alive, while another part of me tells a different story because I think this woman and these young teenage girls are dead." He pointed at the information board. "This means extra work, because we have to go through the same procedure as with our first three missing persons. Once again I'll leave it to Sergeant Buckingham to allocate your addresses to visit, only this time, after interviewing the parents, I want you to make inquiries like you did on Friday and Saturday, by questioning the neighbours as well." He paused. "You'll notice that a definite pattern has emerged, which makes me convinced there is a serial killer roaming around this county. So I would not make any plans for free time until we have this psycho safely locked up." He paused pointing at the board, then turning to face the team. "To save everybody talking at the one time, I want you to stick your hand up if you have anything to say, no matter how trivial it may seem, just spit it out."

A woman police officer raised her hand. "There's a point I'd like to make, sir. After speaking to a neighbour, it drew my attention to the fact that all our three victims were, or are, blonde. The neighbour went on to say that a dark green-coloured van was responsible for Cynthia Wood's abduction, not when she was collected from her school, as we thought, but one weekend, from outside her house, which means that her family must have known the driver of the van, someone delivering food for instance." She sat down.

"Well done, Constable. Yes, we had taken note of the fact that all three girls were blonde, and knew their abductor, but that's what I am looking for from the team: get personal and sympathetic with the parents of our new victims. Please note I've said victims. However, there's no need to alarm anyone until we have concrete evidence. I want an officer allocated to visit the schools of the new missing girls: talk to teachers, talk to friends, find out if they were dating anybody. He or she can drive over to Ware and talk to the shoe shop staff. There is always a chance they might come up with something."

He turned to D.C. Bradley. "What about you Detective Constable, have you anything to offer?"

"Nothing at the moment, sir, I'm studying a revised edition of the directory, since a lot of listed companies folded before, during and after the war."

Inspector Rupert spoke to the assembly. "If anyone comes up with anything, I'll be in my office or the basement, going through old records."

He left D.S. Buckingham to arrange the details, before deciding to take on the task of the schools and the Ware shoe shop.

Inspector Rupert made his way into the dimly lit basement, going through old records again, before ascending to his office, taking the index rollers from the wall safe to cross-reference them with the files.

A tap at the door interrupted him. "Sorry to disturb you, sir," the desk sergeant said as he entered the Inspector's office. "There's been a development. Whether it's connected to the missing persons case, I don't know, but the caller has said that her dog has just dug up two skeletal remains, in a shallow grave." The Sergeant looked at his notes. "In Parson's Wood, sir, on Hatfield Heath."

"Get me a car, Sergeant, and get hold of Sergeant Buckingham."

"She's gone to Ware, sir, and has other inquiries to make."

"No matter, Sergeant, mobilise the forensics team, and contact Wilfred Ponsonby, the pathologist in Hatfield. Tell him I'll meet him at the crime scene."

Inspector Rupert was alive with excitement as he drove to Parson's Wood, then up onto the heath where a crowd of walkers and joggers had stopped to find out what the commotion was about in such a quiet spot. At least the police officers who were first on the scene had the sense to cordon off the grave.

"Get those onlookers moved on." He barked out the order so a number of them left without the police clearing the area. "Where the hell is Ponsonby?" he asked sharply, looking into the disturbed grave.

The forensic team complete with photographer began to dress in their protective attire, then began work, slowly revealing the two remains.

Word had reached Inspector Rupert that Wilfred Ponsonby was working on a corpse in the mortuary, and would be available until after lunch.

"Lunch my arse," Inspector Rupert yelled above the wind. "Somebody get down there and pull him out of the mortuary by the scruff of his neck before I really lose control and arrest the useless git for wasting police time."

Ponsonby the pathologist arrived with a scowl on his face.

"Sorry, Ponsonby, did I disturb your game of golf, or your luncheon appointment?" Inspector Rupert was slightly agitated at the time the pathologist had taken to travel the short distance from the Hatfield mortuary, if that was where he had come from. He pointed towards the clearing where the forensic team were still brushing away the earth from the partially clothed remains.

The wind rustled in the trees and mist swirled around the clearing as Inspector Rupert led the way to the crime scene.

"You're becoming a real pain, Rupert, the kind of officer I don't like to be associated with. You're a bad omen, Rupert, everywhere you go. I sometimes wonder if you've taken on this case just to be noticed. Although I have to admit, it is a better location than the last one."

A constable lifted the security tape to allow the pathologist to enter. "Why is this crowd of amateurs disturbing the grave before I've had the chance to examine the corpses?" the pathologist asked bluntly.

"If we hadn't cleaned the earth from the bodies, you wouldn't be able to examine them, would you?" the face-covered forensic officer said, quickly beginning to brush earth from his protective suit.

Inspector Rupert stifled a laugh. "Get on with it, Ponsonby, I haven't got all day," he said with a smile.

The pathologist began to work on one skeleton then the other. "Certainly two corpses buried at different times, the bottom one is a male, judging by the size of the skull. The top corpse is female, young, what looks like remains of blonde hair, but I'll know more when I get them on the slab at the mortuary." He looked up at the Inspector, and added, "Where I'll have much better working conditions." He climbed out of the grave.

"Your sure the bottom remains are that of a male, any hint on the age of the victim?" There was more pleading in the Inspector's voice.

Wilfred Ponsonby smiled. "You haven't changed, Rupert, always looking for answers before they're even out of the ground.

However, let's just say the bottom corpse is a male aged around mid-thirties to forties. The top corpse, her clothing still partially intact..." He paused. "These are only estimates, Rupert. But a young girl, let's just say a teenager at the moment, because the acidic soil has played havoc with the victims."

"Thank you, Wilfred, one more question, how long have they been in the ground?"

"I couldn't possibly say at the moment." Ponsonby gave another smile.

"A guess, Wilfred. That would suffice." Inspector Rupert used that pleading tone again.

"I don't guess, Rupert, I leave that to your crowd, and please don't try to patronise me with your detective tricks. You'll have my report in two to three days, after I've finished with my other work."

"Not good enough, Ponsonby, I need those reports as soon as you've finished with them on the slab, as you so coarsely put it. Therefore I'll expect word from you tomorrow, better still today. I'll come over to the morgue and collect the information myself, that should please you no end." He watched as the pathologist walked out of the clearing and into the surrounding overgrown path leading from the wood.

He, took another look at the shallow grave before the corpses were removed by the pathology handlers and taken to the waiting transport.

"Whoever buried them must have known of this clearing, sir, and must have had some difficulty getting the bodies through the undergrowth. Burying the first body would have been hard digging, because of the tree roots, though opening up the ground to bury the second body would not have been so much of a problem. He must have been a fit man to carry the bodies from the wood path to the clearing, sir," a young constable said.

"Any other suggestions, Constable?" the Inspector replied quickly.

"Sorry, sir, but there is one thing I noticed, and that is the bottom corpse had a uniform, tattered but still recognisable as having been one of the forces, which tells me he was attached to some regiment during the war, perhaps home on leave. The smaller corpse has been put in the ground much more recently, you can tell by the state of her dress, where the acidic soil has not worked so quickly on her remains." The young constable picked up his shovel and was about to walk away.

"Just a minute, Constable, state your name and mother station that you are attached to." Inspector Rupert watched the constable come to attention.

"Constable Boris Weatherspoon, attached to the Hatfield police station, sir."

"Okay, Weatherspoon, how would you like to be seconded to the police at Welwyn Garden City? I could do with a bright young man in the team. I'll arrange to have you transferred, and elevated in rank to detective constable, how does that sound?"

"I'd like that very much, sir, thank you."

"Very well, report to the incident room tomorrow morning 08.00 and don't be late. Meanwhile you can assist the forensic team unearthing the rest of the remains. I have a job for you which I will explain tomorrow."

Inspector Rupert walked along the path to the car. He looked carefully at the tangled foliage, and removed a piece of cotton that was caught in a thorn, placing it in a forensic bag. He now understood what young Constable Weatherspoon had said about how awkward it would be to carry the corpses to the clearing, through the overgrown path.

"But was the path overgrown at the time?" he asked himself. Was there another approach to the crime scene? There were now lots of questions floating around in his head. He couldn't help thinking about the male corpse. Who was he? Why the two corpses in the one grave? Who was the teenager lying on top of the male corpse?

His immediate thought was to question Mrs. Wood again. There were doubts creeping into his head about the statement she had given the visiting constables. This time he would do the questioning.

The woman opened the door, aware that this was a senior police officer.

"Inspector Rupert of the Hertfordshire constabulary, madam. I take it you are Mrs. Tina Wood?" He watched the woman nod as he showed his warrant card. "I wonder if I could have a quick word? It was my team officer that questioned you before, but certain things have come to light that need to be explained." The Inspector edged his way into the house. "It's really your husband I wish to speak to, perhaps you can tell me where he works, so I can pay him a visit?"

The dark-eyed woman hesitated for a moment. "My husband John never came home from the war, Inspector. Lying dead somewhere in France, killed in a covert operation. The bloody War Office and government never responded to my letters."

"So John never returned?" He sat thinking for a moment. "What year was this, and what regiment was he in?" He saw her hesitation. "I'm not interested in anything else, Tina. We can always check it out with the War Department and war graves commission, if he was killed in action. However, this way is quicker."

Again she hesitated before speaking. "John came home on leave prior to going back to his special forces unit. That was in 1943 when he left after a bust-up with one of our neighbours, who was also home on leave, but my neighbour was killed in the D day landings. John found out about our short affair, during his home leave, and gave the neighbour a good hiding. That was the last time I saw my husband. I never had another man to this day."

Inspector Rupert knew she was lying about her sex life and would prove it in time.

"Tell me more about your daughter Cynthia. Was she fond of your husband? Were they close, perhaps confiding in each other? She would have been twelve years old when she last saw her father." He looked at the photographs on the mantelpiece. "Is that John and Cynthia? It looks like it was taken on Brighton pier."

"Yes that picture was taken just before John joined up, happy times, Inspector." She paused. "I'm sorry, would you like a tea or coffee, perhaps a gin. I'm afraid that's all I have to offer. Times are a bit hard at the moment due to rationing."

"No thanks, Mrs. Wood, I have lots to be getting on with. However, I would like to take the photo of the pair together. I promise it will be returned intact."

He watched the woman rise and remove the photograph from the frame.

"Can you tell me where your husband John was employed before he went off to war, Mrs. Wood? If you could also tell me what he did in his place of employment?"

"My husband was a skilled cabinet maker, Inspector. He did private work for the big houses in England, that is before the Americans arrived with their prepacked furniture. My John loathed the work; he was a wood turner at a lathe, then became a machine operator that carved out the furniture, ready for packing. We needed the money so he stuck it out for the family's sake. I knew how much he longed to use his skills. He was threatened with the sack by Wood Press Mills if he continued doing private work; that was a good income which dried up." She turned to face him. "It's been a very trying time, Inspector." She hesitated for a moment. "There's one thing that John had on his mind, Inspector, something he said had to be done, something sordid, but alas he never disclosed what it was."

"Was this while he was working at the factory, or when he came home on leave?"

"Definitely when he came home on leave. He was very agitated. I remember it well."

"Just one more thing, did Cynthia ever hint that she was fed up with life at school, or even here at home? It must have been quite a blow to find out her father hadn't returned from the war. She would have needed comforting. So was there any special friend, an elderly man, a relation for instance, that would pick her up from school, especially if the weather was bad? The reason I ask this is because we have a middle-aged man driving a dark green van on our radar, and if Cynthia was being collected from school by such a person then we would be very interested."

"Your constable asked all of those questions before, Inspector," she said replacing the empty frame back on the mantlepiece.

"Okay, thanks for your time, Mrs. Wood. I'll be in touch should anything arise, and I'm sure you'll contact me, if you think of anything relevant to your daughter's disappearance."

Inspector Rupert was clear in his mind that he would be visiting the tired-looking woman before the week was out.

CHAPTER TEN

Inspector Rupert went through the process of having Constable Weatherspoon transferred. He decided now would be a good time to go to the fifth floor, with the information on the index roller system having revealed another three females, missing in suspicious circumstances. The skeleton corpses found in Parson's Wood could help to secure a large budget. He also had the threat of the press, he found it strange that they hadn't contacted him after the discovery of the latest victims.

The secretary never acknowledged he was standing there. Inspector Rupert tapped the door, then walked into the Chief Constable's office.

"I know, sir, I'm out of line but when you hear what I have to say then I'm sure you will forgive the intrusion again."

"You're becoming a pest, Rupert," the C.C. said getting out of his chair.

"Funny, that's what Wilfred Ponsonby said at the graveside this morning." The sentence was beautifully inserted.

"Grave side, Rupert?"

"Yes, sir, two skeletons uncovered, a male in his mid-to-late thirties, and a young teenage girl, found buried in the same grave." He knew he had the Chief's full attention.

"I'm not drawing any conclusions yet, sir. However, I'm positive the young girl is that of Cynthia Wood, one of our original missing persons." He watched the C.C. cringe before sitting down. "As for the press, well, I'm trying to keep a lid on things at the moment, until we trace who the second corpse is." Inspector Rupert lied about the press knowing it would have a profound affect on his boss.

He went on to tell the Chief about the other missing persons. "As I tried to explain to you already, sir, this is big, and I believe as time goes on it will escalate. Therefore I've taken on extra uniforms to assist in the house-to-house: nothing that will knock your budget sky high." Again Inspector Rupert knew this would have an affect on his boss. "You know the figures better than me, sir. However, I personally would not be putting a cap on it at this stage; the press would crucify you, and I won't be able to help you, sir."

"Quite, Rupert, but I need to be informed the minute this breaks in the press."

The pow-wow was over after Inspector Rupert went into the other missing persons. He left the Chief Constable's office with a spring in his step. He stopped at the secretary's desk on the way by and simply rubbed the side of his nose, insinuating that he knew her secret.

Her face blushed as Inspector Rupert smiled then walked away along the corridor and downstairs to the incident room.

He was in a jovial mood as the other officers began to appear after their door-to-door inquiries. There were a couple still out working. However, rather than waste time, he decided to tell the assembled team about the developments this morning, and inform Sergeant Buckingham of a new recruit to the detective team.

He leaned on the desk and spoke candidly to the team. "I'm sure as time goes by you'll come across a pathologist called Wilfred Ponsonby, from the Hatfield mortuary." He paused. "Don't underestimate the pathologist, or any pathologist for that matter; they are very intelligent men and women who do a very nasty job, which I could not do." He smiled before speaking again. "This morning's find reminded of a time I was with the Met in London, and we were invited to a pathologist's gathering. A question was asked, what do you call a group of pathologists? You know, like a herd of cattle, a flock of sheep, a lamentation of swans. We never did find out what a bunch of pathologists were called."

"A body, sir, a body of pathologists," a voice said in response.

Inspector Rupert could not hide his appreciation. "Well done, Jenkins, that fits Ponsonby to a tee, which brings me to tell you about the two golfers in the clubhouse, standing at the bar drinking. The pathologist apologises to the club captain. 'I really should not be drinking with you full-time members in this bar because I'm a country member.' The captain of the golf club replies, 'Yes I remember'."

There were a few titters from those that got the joke while the majority just flicked the pages of their notebooks.

"Right, Buckingham, fun's over. How did it go with the shoe shop in Ware?"

"Nothing much, sir, remember it was a while ago. However, this dark van seems to be popping up again, no definite description, but the van was dark green, with writing on the side."

"John Wood," the Inspector said quickly. "Nothing to do with the van, Buckingham."

Sergeant Buckingham shook her head. "Who's John Wood when he's at home sir?"

"John Wood, I think, is the male skeleton in the grave at Parson's Wood. I've checked with the war graves commission, three John Woods are dead and buried: one in the Burmese jungle, another in Italy, the last in Holland, but John Wood from Hatfield never returned to his regiment, and, according to the War Department, he was listed as a deserter, which Mrs. Tina Wood never disclosed. Now why would that be?"

"Shame, sir, or perhaps the War Department never chased it up. However, surely the police in Hatfield would have been instructed to serve an arrest warrant, if it ever got that far?"

"I don't think they need to look any further, Sergeant, but let's wait with bated breath to see what our pathologist comes up with. So if there's nothing else to report, I'm going to treat myself to a large gin and tonic." He paused. "Just one thing, Sergeant, the young constable joining us in the morning, give him instruction on sealing a crime scene. He did a good job over in Parson's Wood, but instruct him in procedure, informing the forensic team and the pathologist. He alone will be responsible for making sure the crime scene is secure."

"Are you expecting more graves to appear, sir?"

"I hope not, Sergeant, I truly hope not," the Inspector said softly, before walking out of the incident room.

The walk down to the Fountain lounge bar did not take long. He was greeted by the ageing actress, who threw open her arms in encouragement as if on stage. "Why, if it isn't Romeo himself," she said walking towards him. "Oh if only you and I were younger, we could do so much treading the boards." She threw open her arms again.

"If you were younger, madam, I would charge you with smoking dope." Inspector Rupert smelled the sweet aroma on her clothes, and watched her facial features change. Her husband ordered her to her perch. "Sit down, Alexis darling, I've ordered another schooner of dry sherry."

"Oh you are a sweet one, my precious." They sat eyeing Amadeus, remembering his appearance out of the blue some time ago with a beautiful woman on his arm.

Amadeus caught the landlord's attention.

"Good evening again, Inspector. Ah word goes around you know…" the landlord said, as if it explained everything. "I'm John, by the way, my partner Dot is in the back cooking, what can I get you?"

"A large gin and tonic, John, and set one up for the old couple at the end of the bar." He paused. "Tell me, John, do they always sit in exactly the same place?"

Every day and every night," John said pouring his drink. "I'll be honest with you. They don't seem to be affected by the alcohol they consume, although I do keep a close eye on them, but they are very good customers as I told you. She was a well-known actress, and her husband's a retired naval commander, who fought at the battle of Jutland on the 31st of May 1916, which he doesn't talk about, but Alexis makes sure Dot and I are reminded, of his exploits, and anyone else that cares to listen. That's why the regulars never sit on the stools at the bar." John gave a smile. "Do you want anything to eat?"

"No thanks, John, I'll just stick to my drink. Besides, my housekeeper always has a hot meal for me." He knew he had said to much, but John was polite enough not to say anything more, and went to serve another customer.

The old couple were listening in to the conversation, so Amadeus finished his drink then went home to an empty house.

The incident room was busy and noisy as the team talked about their home visits.

"Thank you, please settle down now, and let me explain the situation." He pointed at the information board. "This is a photograph of the victim I believe was buried in Parson's Wood. He's the husband of Tina Wood, and the father of the missing teenager, Cynthia." He paused. "I await the pathologist's report. However, I also believe the corpse that lay on top of John Wood is, in fact, his daughter Cynthia, who is listed as a missing person. Here we have a recent photograph taken at a guide camp, and this is Cynthia and her dad taken on the pier at Brighton. I've also been informed that John Wood had something sinister on his mind. He knew something that was never disclosed. However, there was a disagreement between John Wood and his employer, due to the fact that he was a skilled cabinet maker, making top-class furniture for those that could afford it, and getting paid handsomely for his skills, which his American employer did not agree with his doing outside of his work for them. So now we have father and daughter, buried in the same shallow grave. My thanks go to P.C. Weatherspoon, who advised me that someone must have known the area, and buried Cynthia's corpse in an already-dug-up spot."

Inspector Rupert pointed at the information board. "Apparently the company John Wood worked for was requisitioned by the War Office to make pots and pans for the armed forces until they started making furniture again, to replace the damaged furniture. I understand the name of the operation has changed, but it's something we must check out." He addressed P.C. Bradley. "You've been responsible for tracing factories, and companies that move and deliver goods, so what have you come up with, Bradley?"

"A lot, sir, I'm having them typed out for your inspection, there's a lot around the industrial part of Hatfield that was replaced after the bombing."

"Okay, have that list on my desk before lunch." He asked again for anything that could be useful to the investigation.

Sergeant Buckingham spoke up. "I think you should be aware, sir, that a number of missing persons have gone without being solved. Between 1904 and 1926 each case was marked in bold red letters. N.F.A.R. which means no further action required." She paused. "Granted the First World War was on the go, which would have taken men and women away from the police investigation at the time, but after that, sir, other cases were abandoned between 1934 to 1938. N.F.A.R. then a lull, sir, that's what makes it so frustrating."

"Yes, Sergeant, I can understand your frustrations. However, let's work with what we have at the moment, then work back if the need arises."

"Fine, sir, if that's what you want," Buckingham said sharply.

"You don't sound convinced at my decision, Sergeant." He gave her a disapproving look.

"It's not that, sir, but I really do think we should keep an open mind. Not so much on the oldest dates of missing persons, but let's see what the other index rollers reveal, because I believe there are more recent cases as well. We already have dates going back to 1933, and now with this murder of John Wood in 1943, it makes me ponder, what else will turn up in the coming weeks, or months? We've hardly started the investigation and we have a teenage body, buried in her father's grave. What next? I ask myself."

"Alright, Sergeant, I take your point and will bear it in mind. However, it's time to pay our dear friend Ponsonby a visit; that should please him no end." Inspector Rupert was about to leave. "On second thoughts, Sergeant, you stay here and go through those other index roller cards that the mole gave you. If any other names appear, get a copy printed out and put up on the information board." He had finished talking and made his way over to the Hatfield mortuary.

"Good morning, Wilfred, what have you got for me on this fine morning?" he said smiling.

"Go away, Rupert, I'm not in the best of moods, because I have been up half the night working on those corpses."

"Excellent, Ponsonby, I admire dedication in one's work." He removed his head from between the spacing slats, then entered the mortuary through the thick plastic sheeting, and walked towards the examination slab. "I can give you information on the two corpses, Wilfred."

"That will not be necessary, Inspector. The male corpse had a wallet in his pocket, with his regimental number. He also had his identity disc around his neck. He has been in the ground for three years, perhaps a little longer. The uniform was not in a good state, but the insignias on the shoulders told me more about the corpse. 'Who dares wins.' That is a special forces insignia, so the male corpse is that of John Wood." He paused and ordered his assistant to bring the teenage girl from the freezer. "This was a bit of a mystery, Inspector, but I put two and two together when I discovered a bracelet which was engraved, 'To C.W. from Dad.' Therefore I assumed it must be John Wood's daughter, but note that is only an assumption. It is for you to trace who she is."

Inspector Rupert nodded. "Your assumption is right, Wilfred; that is Cynthia Wood."

"Now there is a beneficial factor, with this girl. She was buried face down on top of her father. This helped to preserve the front torso from the acidic earth. The other fact is her stomach contents were still intact, which told me that she had not been in the ground that long, perhaps four months maximum. I still have some more work to do on her." He placed a bowl in front of the Inspector. "There you are, Rupert, good old-fashioned fish and chips."

The Inspector put his hand up to cover his face, then once the bowl had been removed, he spoke, "That is all very well, Ponsonby, but you've not told me how they were killed."

"You really are an impatient man, Rupert. In all my years in pathology, I've never met anyone like you." Ponsonby ordered the assistant to replace the body cover and put the remains back in the freezer, then said, "The man was drugged, then severely hit on the back of the head with a heavy blunt wooden club, like a cricket bat, or something similar. However, that's not what killed him; he died from suffocation. John Wood was still alive when he went into the ground, drugged but alive."

Inspector Rupert gasped. "You're telling me that John Wood choked to death with the soil that buried him?"

"Well done, Rupert, you're coming on. Yes that is how John Wood died." He paused. "Now the girl, she was already dead when she was buried, strangled with a tie, a red and blue tie. There were still fibres left on the neck." He leaned on the slab. "She had been sexually assaulted, traces of semen were found in her vagina, but let me point out that there was no internal bruising on her vagina walls, like you would normally find if there was a struggle. Therefore Cynthia Wood, if that is who she is, was a willing partner in the sex act." The pathologist took off his thick green gown. "You'll have my report this afternoon Rupert, but we have covered everything."

"Yes, Wilfred, I'm in your debt. Just one thing, if I could have the bracelet, I can show her mother. That's my next port of call. The part I hate most about this job is breaking the bad news." He paused. "If I could use your phone, because this next part needs a woman's touch so I'll get a woman police constable from the Hatfield station to meet me at Mrs. Wood's house."

The arrangement was made. A young woman police constable met him at the address. "I hope you're good at making tea, Constable. This woman is in for quite a shock; that's why I need you close at hand." They walked up the garden path and knocked on the door. Mrs. Tina Wood broke down, instinctively knowing the reason for their visit.

After breaking the sad news to Mrs. Wood, showing her the silver bracelet, it was suggested that the W.P.C. would keep her company until a relation arrived to console her.

Rupert made his way back to the Welwyn police station, walking straight into the incident room. "Well, Sergeant, have you come up with anything interesting?" he asked abruptly.

"Indeed I have, sir." She ignored his foul mood. "Take a look at this list I've compiled from all the index card roller system." She handed him the printed list, and waited for his reaction.

The Inspector looked at the list. "Strewth, Sergeant, all these names and dates are reported missing persons. Why has this never been followed up? Surely someone during the war years would have noticed that those girls were missing and should have recognised that something serious was going on. Okay, get a copy made and put it up on the information board. Now we have a lot more work tracing those girls, which means more door knocking and school visits." He handed her back the list. "According to Ponsonby, John Wood and his daughter Cynthia were both murdered, which means it's not a missing person any more, we're dealing with two murders: one that occurred three years ago, and the other more recently, four months ago, which corresponds with the time Cynthia Wood was reported missing." The Inspector tapped the information board with his pen. "I now fear for our other two teenage missing persons, Buckingham. And our shoe shop assistant, let's not forget her just because she was older, and the case dates back to 1933."

Sergeant Buckingham nodded. "I'll get this copied and put up before our team arrive back."

"Yes do that, and change Cynthia Woods' listing from missing person to murder, a murder inquiry, so that the team can see what we face in the future." He paused. "Has P.C. Bradley finished with that company directory yet? I wonder if we, or he, have wasted too much time on that particular subject." He shook his head. "Let me know if he comes across anything useful, Sergeant, I'll be in my office."

He sorted out his in tray, with the other offences that had piled up over a period. Most, like before, could be handled by the uniformed officers.

He dropped his pencil onto the floor, and scrambled beneath the desk to retrieve it. He could not believe his eyes. Looking at the label that had been stapled onto the underside of the bottom drawer. *Wood Press Mills, Hatfield 1945*. He reached for the pencil then walked down the corridor to the desk sergeant on duty. "I need a police constable to accompany me to Hatfield, Sergeant, have you anybody spare?"

"Yes, W.P.C. Stapleton is in the canteen on her tea break. She's due out shortly so I'll fetch her for you, sir."

"I'll be in the compound, Sergeant." Inspector Rupert could not believe his luck at spotting the name of the factory that John

Wood had worked at before going off to war. He felt a little disappointed with himself for not following up the name Mrs. Tina Wood had given him on his first visit to question her. It mattered not; he was following it up now as W.P.C. Stapleton jumped behind the wheel and began to drive over to Hatfield.

She drove into the factory yard and parked in the space marked *Chairman*.

The Inspector smiled, but said nothing, as they got out of the police car and entered the reception area. "I want to speak to the manager," he said abruptly, before showing his warrant card.

"Do you have an appointment, Inspector? Mr. Dick is a busy man," the receptionist said in a squeaky voice.

"I don't make appointments, dear, so get him on the phone now, before I get upset."

The receptionist lifted the phone. "Sorry to disturb you, Mr. Dick, but there are two police officers wanting to talk to you." She listened to the reply. "I don't know what it's about, Mr. Dick."

Inspector Rupert snatched the telephone from her hand. "Listen, Dick, this is a murder inquiry. Now get your arse out here and take us somewhere we can talk or I'll arrest you for wasting police time." He slammed the telephone back onto its cradle.

The receptionist sat with her mouth wide open as the factory manager appeared almost immediately. "What can I do for you? I'm extremely busy, Inspector."

"Just a few questions, Mr. Dick, it won't take long. Is there somewhere we can talk in private, or will I ask the questions out here?"

"That won't be necessary, come through to my office," he said, slightly put out by the Inspector's approach. "Tea or coffee?" he asked, trying to remain calm.

"No thank you, Mr. Dick, I'm a busy man myself, so let's start with John Wood, who worked in this factory before going off to war."

"John, yes I remember him, a very fine craftsman if I remember. He could have made a factory foreman, if he hadn't fallen out with the chairman at the time, over something petty, if my memory serves me correctly, to do with extra work he was doing and using the company machinery on his dinner hour."

"This chairman, is he available today?" the Inspector asked quickly.

"Oh no, Mr. Davidson senior retired in 1939. The factory went back into full operation after the war. His son Eric sits in judgement now, Inspector. He is a busy man."

"So it was the chairman John Wood fell out with, not a fellow worker on the factory floor. I might need to speak to the retired chairman, Mr. Dick."

"You can't do that, Inspector, unless you have a direct line to god, because Mr. Davidson senior died seven weeks ago."

Inspector Rupert nodded. "I notice by your lapel badge that your Christian name is Fredrick, you won't mind if I call you Fredrick." Inspector Rupert was trying the friendly approach, as he watched the manager relax.

"I've been called worse, Inspector, but most people just call me Fred, or Freddie, I prefer Freddie to be honest, it's more friendly."

"Indeed Freddie, much better than Mr. Dick." He paused for a moment. "So John Wood was a likeable character, just like you, Freddie. What about his daughter, did you ever come into contact with her?" he asked quickly changing the subject.

"I met her once, Inspector. We didn't encourage family members to enter through the factory gate, not that we suspected them of stealing, but with so much traffic in the yard, it would be an accident waiting to happen."

"Talking of transport, Freddie, I noticed when we pulled into the yard that a few box vans parked in the loading bays are bright yellow, have they always been that colour?"

"Yes, as far as I can remember, bright and cheerful and cheap; that's our slogan."

"Yes, very apt, for the furniture you produce." The Inspector moved in his chair. "How did you deal with complaints, Freddie? Surely with so much distribution there must have been a lot."

"Certainly not, Inspector, there would be the odd part missing from the prepack boxes, like a hinge or a packet of screws, but they were delivered personally by me. Keep the customer satisfied. That was my motto, and the chairman's motto for a successful business."

"Ah so you actually visited the place where the prepack furniture was delivered?"

"I don't like the direction this interview is taking, Inspector, perhaps I should call the company solicitor before I say any more."

"I'm still waiting for an answer to my question, Mr. Dick, so while I'm waiting I'll ask another; did you ever help assemble the prepack furniture for your customers."

"The answer to that is yes, but very occasionally. We tried to encourage the purchaser to seek help from a neighbour, a friend or a relation, but some of the older people didn't have that luxury." He lifted the phone and began to dial a number.

"No need to call your solicitor, Freddie. What are you afraid of?" Inspector Rupert stood up. "There are two thing you can do for me, the first is a list of your employees at Wood Press Mills, dating back to 1939, before, if possible, but that date will suffice for now, and please include your delivery drivers in that request." He watched the manager cringe. "The second request is all your delivery notes dating back to the same period. I might need your help to go further back if the need arises."

"Are you insane, Inspector? Do you not realise what a logistical nightmare you're trying to involve this company in?" He attempted to lift the telephone again to dial his boss, until Inspector Rupert grabbed his hand.

"Tell your boss I want those requests on my desk at the end of play on Friday. It shouldn't be too difficult if you keep your records in order like the mole."

This baffled the manager who continued his telephone call.

"Thanks for your time, Mr. Dick. No doubt I'll be seeing you again. Oh, just one more thing, don't leave the town without informing the Hatfield police or myself at headquarters." He gave the woman police constable a slight move of the head to indicate they were leaving.

"You certainly put the frighteners on Freddie, sir. Did you see his hand shake as he lifted the phone for the second time?"

Inspector Rupert smiled. "Okay, Stapleton, let's get back to the incident room. I need to see the complete list of missing persons."

"One thing I noticed about Fredrick Dick, is that when you mentioned Cynthia Wood, he wanted the floor to open up and swallow him."

"Very observant, Stapleton, but one thing you'll learn about C.I.D. work is never to jump to conclusions based on the way people react."

The drive back to Welwyn Garden City was pleasant enough, with light conversation.

Inspector Rupert went to the incident room. "Right, Sergeant Buckingham, let's see your complete printed list." As he read down it he could not believe what he was witnessing. "How many in total, Sergeant?" he asked softly.

"Excluding the three girls we have on our radar, there are thirteen, as you can see. So put the other three on the list, that gives us sixteen in total, then we still have John Wood to contend with." Sergeant Buckingham paused. "Things are not looking good, sir. It's like you said, a pattern has emerged. Shall I get copies made for the rest of the team?"

"Not yet, Sergeant. I want you to run a check on a Fredrick Dick, who is the manager of Wood Press Mills in Hatfield. He's hiding something; I'm sure of it. In the meantime I'll take the list to my office and study it. Get somebody to bring me a cup of tea, I think I'm going to need it."

He picked up the pathology report. There was nothing to add except the approximate height of the victims. There was another thing the pathologist had failed to mention and that was the gold band wedding ring on John Woods' finger, with the engraving *T.W. – J.W. 1930*.

That could wait for another day. He was more interested in the names and dates that jumped up and hit him like a cricket ball. He started with the most recent:

Cynthia Wood aged fifteen, Hatfield, reported missing, October 8th 1945.

Linda Symonds aged twelve, Stapleford Village, reported missing, 8th September 1945.

Alison Brent aged thirteen, Stevenage Orphanage, reported missing, 8th May 1945.

Beverley Strang aged fourteen, Hertford, reported missing, 20th April 1945.

Janet Findlay aged fourteen, Hemel Hempstead, reported missing, 8th April 1945.

Sandra Phillips aged eighteen, St. Albans, reported missing, 8th October 1945.

Inspector Rupert sat staring into space when the tea was delivered. Then he continued reading the list.

Lesley Hood aged twelve, Hoddesdon, reported missing, 9th December 1944.

Emma Miller aged twelve, Leighton Buzzard, reported missing, 11th October 1944.

Zoe Brooke aged nineteen, Hatfield, reported missing, 4th October 1944.

Inspector Rupert sat drinking his tea. He noticed the substantial break, and wondered if this was what Sergeant Buckingham had spoken about.

Maria Reynolds aged thirteen, Buntingford, reported missing, 16th March 1943.

Nicole Fenwick aged sixteen, Stevenage, reported missing, 12th February, 1942.

Jane Riley aged thirty, Letchworth Garden City, reported missing, 5th November 1942.

Polly Aniston aged fifteen, Harlow, reported missing, 22nd August, 1940.

Elizabeth Fry aged twenty-eight, Luton, reported missing 9th July 1938.

Sophie Black, aged???? from Bishop Stortford, reported missing???? 1938

Felicity Roach aged thirty, Ware, reported missing, 3rd December 1933.

Inspector Rupert finished his tea, and made the decision to go to the top floor with this.

He did not know quite what to make of it. However, he did know that someone in the Hertfordshire constabulary had fucked up big time. Two or three names was serious enough, but sixteen names and John Woods' murder was too much for him to take in.

He summoned Sergeant Buckingham to his office.

"You have done a good job, Sergeant. I never quite took on board the seriousness of this list. I did say that there would be trouble ahead, but this…" He waved the list at her. "This is dynamite, Sergeant. God help us if the papers get hold of this. I think the best course of action is to take it to the top floor. The Chief Constable has a lot of explaining to do, and whoever was following up the cases on those women and girls." He looked at the Sergeant. "I need to be sure that this is all the missing persons from the thirties before we go upstairs with it."

"Yes, sir, it's all the missing persons that were listed on the index card rotary. However, I will say this." She sighed. "There is a possibility that other names have been discarded from 1933 to 1938 and perhaps before, and perhaps even after these dates. Just look at the breaks in missing persons from 1938 onwards into the early forties; why did that happen? I believe that this serial killer has killed more than what we have listed, sir."

"So you do think we are searching for a psychopath, which will turn this investigation into a man hunt?"

Sergeant Buckingham raised her eyebrows as she always did when about to make a comment. "Yes, sir, we definitely have a serial killer on the loose, of that I am certain."

"Very well, Sergeant, let's take this upstairs and find out what the Chief Constable makes of it, and don't be surprised if it becomes a shouting match." They took the lift.

Inspector Rupert walked smartly along the corridor, with Sergeant Buckingham in tow. He stopped at the office of the secretary to the Chief Constable. "I'll give you the opportunity, Lucy, to inform the boss I need to speak to him urgently, and please inform him it's in his best interest that he gives me five minutes of his precious time."

She didn't use the telephone, but got up quickly. Tapping the door, she entered the Chief Constable's office through the connecting door, appearing shortly through the main door.

"Five minutes, Inspector," was all she said before sitting down and going back to her typing.

"Thank you for seeing us so quickly, sir, I have something very important to tell you."

"Well, Rupert get on with it," the C.C. said clasping his hands.

"First let me introduce Sergeant Buckingham, a very talented officer." Inspector Rupert let the Sergeant sit down. "If you remember the last time we spoke, sir, we had discovered two bodies buried in Parson's Wood on Hatfield Heath, and we also had another three missing persons. Well, thanks to Sergeant Buckingham's tenacity, she compiled this list from the old system of index roller cards, that she got from Ernie the mole in the basement." He held the list in his hand before continuing, "I'm sorry I have to say this, sir, but there has been a severe breakdown in communication between the officers in the upper floors. These names on the list now date back to 1933 and 1938. There is a possibility that other names were not put in the index system, but let's leave that for now, because most of the names on this list are dated when they were reported missing, and that means, sir, it was under your watch, both as Assistant Chief Constable, and your present position, sir. I really can't fathom out how all those girls and women were swept under the carpet and forgotten about."

"Give me the list, Rupert, and stop throwing accusations around the room that you can not substantiate."

"That's the trouble, sir, you can quite clearly see the dates, and I don't know if you were ever informed of what was going on back then, but I'm sure an investigation will discover the truth."

The C.C. pursed his lips as he read the list of names. "There was a missing person back in 1933 as I recall, because I had just been given the job as assistant to the Chief Constable at the time, but that case was solved when the woman appeared back from her fling in London. As for those other names…" He hesitated. "They mean nothing to me. If anything like this had crossed my desk, I would have insisted on a full-scale man hunt."

"I have to insist, sir, that according to our investigation, Felicity Roach did not return to her job in Ware, and nothing else was heard of her. Therefore I have to ask, sir, who was the senior officer leading the 1933 missing person case? And if you did not know anything about this then I'll have to dig a little deeper to find out who was in charge of these other reports, although I already know who it was, sir."

"That's easy to answer, Inspector. I remember he was a sergeant back in 1933, and the only senior officer available, because for most of those other dates, he was kept back for the home front. His name is Superintendent Robert Crawley, who, if my memory serves me correctly, was made up to Inspector, Chief Inspector, and now holding his present rank."

The C.C. waved the paper in the air. "This is serious, Rupert. I could lose my job if this came out, even although I am an innocent party in all this."

"I won't mislead you, sir, this will come out when those other victims are found. Notice how I call them victims, because I know those girls are dead and we have a serial killer on the loose. I'm doing my best to keep the two murders away from the newspapers, but when they get a whiff of this list, well, all I can say is it'll open up more than a can of worms sir, which incidentally puts Superintendent Crawley right to the top of my suspect list." Inspector Rupert watched the Chief Constable draw the handkerchief across his brow.

"You can leave Superintendent Crawley to me, Inspector. Now what's this I hear about you upsetting the staff of Wood Press Mills, grabbing phones from their hands and demanding that they produce evidence by next Friday? Their chairman is going mental, and you parked a police car in his clearly marked parking bay."

"I was just following up a routine inquiry, sir, part of the ongoing investigation, which could have a bearing on the list you are holding. Just keep that, sir, we have copies in the incident room." He turned and walked to the door. "I may need to call in officers from another force, sir. I'm sure you'll have no objections."

They walked down the stairs to the incident room.

"What do you think, sir? Are the Chief Constable and Superintendent Crawley mixed up in this scandal, or was it just overlooked because of the missing person in 1933, therefore no pressure was put on Inspector Crawley at the time?"

"What do I think, Sergeant? I think you may well be right, but you have to agree that there has been a severe lack of policing, no matter what."

Sergeant Buckingham screwed up her face and shook her head. "I'm not convinced, sir, and it's something that can't be proved, because it would first of all have to go through the officer at the bar, whoever that was, because over a period of time he or she could have just thrown it in the bin. Irresponsible I know, but after the bar officer received the phone call, did they pass the information onto the senior officer, Inspector Crawley? I'm sure his lawyer would have something to say on that score." She pointed at the list of names.

"I've been talking to W.P.C. Stapleton, sir; she told me about the interview with Fredrick Dick, and I noticed it wasn't mentioned upstairs a few minutes ago." She tapped the information board. "Apart from 1938, those employees delivering the goods for Wood Press Mills were women, because all the younger men would have been drafted for war. The older men would have been taken for home duties like the home guard, or the air raid wardens, the fire service and special policemen. That's why I joined the police, because my dad was a special policeman in Stevenage. However, the point is this: look closely at the employees when you get the information from the manager of the Wood Press Mills. I think you'll find that the deliveries were made by women, and I find it hard to believe that a woman has committed these atrocities, because I, like you, now believe those young girls and women are dead, but involvement by senior officers…" She shook her head. "I just can't buy that, sir."

Inspector Rupert pondered over what Buckingham had just said. "Let's wait to see what Mr. Dick comes up with. Meanwhile we have a load of other work to keep us busy this week. We can always keep ourselves available should anything turn up, because I'm sure there's a link somewhere with the Wood Press Mills, but we just need to be patient for now."

He tapped the photograph of John and his daughter Cynthia. "Send someone over to the Hatfield mortuary to retrieve John Wood's wedding band. We'll need it for evidence when we catch this psychopath. That bugger Ponsonby has us running after him; he should have mentioned it when he gave us the bracelet."

Sergeant Buckingham ignored the moaning. "Give me a few minutes, sir. I'll go down to the basement to see if Ernie Forbes has any files on the 1933 missing persons case. Because there's no information on the roller card index, of that I'm sure."

"Very well, Sergeant, then we can attend to the car thefts and a break-in at some squire's mansion. Something those in uniform should be dealing with."

He went to the canteen for a pot of tea and a slice of Madeira cake.

Sergeant Buckingham joined him. "Nothing, sir, Ernie assured me that if there was paperwork on the missing person he would have it filed in the year it was reported. So if she turned up, more than likely the paperwork would have been incinerated."

After their tea, they made their way to separate addresses in the new town, to question the likely suspects.

After a tiresome afternoon, he went home to find a letter behind the door. He knew the postmark. Things had become strained between Barbara Sutton and himself. Their romance had hit the buffers when she refused to travel to the football with him every Saturday. There was also her travelling up and down from Stevenage at weekends, when she should be visiting those who had a court order placed on them and failed to attend their interviews. The letter was complimentary, saying how much she had enjoyed his company, but the affair would have to end. He picked up the phone and dialled her office to reach her answering service. He tried her home number and got no answer. He left it until later when he was sure she would be home, but alas met with the same result. He was determined to speak to her, and tried constantly the next day, but there was no joyful response like before, so he finally accepted that their time together had simmered, but left a message with her answering service to say that if she needed anything or changed her mind then he would always be available for her. There was no reply to his constant calls, so eventually as the week dragged on, he gave up trying.

Inspector Rupert was in a foul mood when he and Sergeant Buckingham drove over to the Wood Press Mills factory in Hatfield.

The Sergeant said nothing on the way, knowing that any form of conversation would be rebuffed. They parked in the chairman's parking bay and made their way to reception.

The woman was expecting him. "Mr. Dick will see you now, Inspector." This was a different receptionist from his last visit.

The manager appeared almost instantly.

"I saw your car drive up, Inspector, please come through." He showed them to a chair.

"This is our company lawyer Mr. Simkin. We have barristers in London should the need arise." He gave a discreet smile.

"I've had dealings with Mr. Simkin before, Freddie. Do you need a solicitor present, a guilty conscience perhaps?"

"Mr. Simkin just happens to be here on other business, Inspector, and no, I do not have a guilty conscience."

"You do realise that I have given up my leisure time today to chase up the requests I made to you last Monday. So why did you not hand in those requests yesterday?" The Inspector raised his voice.

"I don't think you realise exactly the work that has been put in to get your requests attended to, Inspector. We have thousands of delivery notes every week going through the gates for delivery. However, the employee listings were not too bad because from 1939 to 1945 all our delivery drivers were women, with a few exceptions, covering holidays, and sickness." He stood up and walked to his filing cabinet. "This is what you are looking for, but I'm afraid the delivery notes will take a little longer, unless you are prepared to lock me up for not making sure every piece of paper is given to you." He looked at the Inspector. "No, I thought not, my boss has had it out with your boss, Rupert, so don't come in here trying to throw your weight around. Tea?" he asked with a smile.

Inspector Rupert snatched the employees list and spoke harshly, "I understand the logistics concerned, Dick, but this is a murder inquiry, so please put in some overtime and get those notes over to me as soon as possible." He stood up. "Just because you had female drivers working for you during the war, it does not detract from your statement, the last time I was here, that you did visit houses to assist the maidens in distress, and it was there you befriended the daughters. I don't have a search warrant, so it would be handy if you have any personal desk diaries that must be kept for reference. Therefore it would be appreciated if you could make them available when you hand in your delivery notes." Inspector Rupert paused. "If you fail me, Mr. Dick, I'll organise a search warrant and go through this factory like a dose of salts, which would mean loss of production, especially when the factory has to be shut down for safety measures. However, thanks for this, but don't forget the warning."

They made their way quickly to the car leaving the manager speechless. Now was not the time to make matters worse by intimidating Mr. Dick any further. They sat discussing the meeting.

"It doesn't help when you speak to an individual like that, sir, especially in front of the company solicitor. He's now hostile towards the police, and that doesn't help our cause. I would like to suggest that I go back indoors and apologise for your outburst, which I think was unwarranted."

"You don't have to apologise for me, Sergeant. I know what I'm doing," he said huffily.

"Then let me telephone Mr. Dick, with a soft voice and diplomacy, when we get back to the station, and say that I'll come over personally to pick up the rest of the information we need."

"Very well, Sergeant. In the meantime you can drop me at the Fountain lounge. I've had it up to here with it today."

Amadeus wearily climbed onto the barstool. The two elders perched in their favourite position gave him a wave.

"Busy day, Inspector?" John the landlord asked matter-of-factly.

"Frustrating, John, give me a large gin and soda, and what's this Inspector nonsense? I don't recall ever discussing my work with you."

John gave a short laugh and handed him the *Hatfield Herald* newspaper.

"Two bodies discovered in Parson's Wood, no comment from police despite being discovered over a week ago. Not a bad photograph, it makes you look younger."

"Just keep them coming, John. I'll tell you when I'm finished. That remark from the *Herald* just about sums up my day." He took a large swallow of the gin and soda, then smiled. "Are you and Dot looking for any bar staff by chance?"

They both burst into fits of laughter that even made the elders at the end of the bar look up. "I used to be famous like that, Inspector," the ageing actress said loudly. "Every newspaper every day, a photo on the front page." She waved her arms. "How wonderful it was back then."

"Be quiet, darling, have another sherry," the Commander said embarrassed.

Amadeus and John just looked at each other and again gave out hoots of laughter.

"Okay, John, one more then I'm off home," he said after his fifth. He walked tentatively up the avenue, and into the villa. There was no roaring fire in the black grate. He switched on the light and trudged through to the kitchen. The dirty plates and pots from Friday's dinner and Sunday's breakfast were still piled up in the sink. The toast rack was still on the table. He began to tidy the table, emptying the toast into the bin, before going to work on the dirty dishes and pots.

It was then that he decided he needed a full-time housekeeper. He would offer Mrs. McGinty the job on a full-time basis, and live in would be preferable. There were times he missed his ex-wife, who would leave a note. *Gone to visit Dad, Chinese takeaway in the oven.*

He finished the cleaning up, then went upstairs to bed. He definitely needed a full-time housekeeper, that was his last thought before he turned over and went to sleep.

CHAPTER ELEVEN

Monday morning came around far too quickly. Amadeus put it to Mrs. McGinty that he needed a full-time housekeeper, live in preferably but would consider her position, as long as she worked the seven days. "I certainly need the money, Mr. Rupert. However, I would need some form of guarantee before I moved in, because my sister would be left on her own."

"You've been loyal to my family, Mrs. McGinty, so I'll give you any written guarantee you require. There would also be an increase in wages."

"The only thing I would ask is a Sunday off, to visit my sister. We go to church together. However, I would have your meals cooked just ready to put in the oven, and I need to know how much you'll deduct from my wages for food and keep.

"There would be no deductions from your wages, what you earn is what you keep."

"In that case, when I do the shopping I'll inform my sister of my new hours. I'm sure she'll be very pleased." The middle-aged woman smiled as she laid out his cooked breakfast. "This actually suits us better, Mr. Rupert. She'll have the house to herself again."

After his hearty breakfast, he made his way down the avenue with a spring in his step. All his gaiety was to change when he entered his office and saw the four large boxes, tied with string, sitting piled on his desk.

The door opened and Sergeant Buckingham walked in looking pleased with herself.

"I told you that a little diplomacy would help. Mr. Dick very kindly had them delivered yesterday afternoon. So I came in to receive them, and the good news is, there are approximately another twenty boxes to come, give or take, because during the war years, production halved. You'll notice I left them intact for you to open, sir," she said with a radiant smile.

"We can't study them here, Buckingham, arrange for the tables to be pushed together in the incident room, then we can share the load between the officers on duty." He lifted one box. "How many are invoices and how many are delivery notes?"

"Three boxes of delivery notes and one of invoices, all placed in date order, so it shouldn't take too long to match them together."

"Okay, you arrange that after we get the reports from the door knockers who were interviewing some of the older cases on the list."

They sat and listened to the same broken record. Nothing of any value was revealed to help solve the list, except for the fact that the parents of those girls had moved away, or passed away.

"Alright, some of you will remain in the incident room, while the others carry on with your door-to-door inquiries." He thought that the reports were finished until a young P.C. stood up.

"Just before you start, sir, there is something which caught my attention, in regards to Linda Symonds from Stapleford Village. According to our earlier reports, both from her mother and her school, she was a good pupil, and a loving daughter. However, it now appears that Linda was placed on probation for shoplifting, hardly the crime of the century when you think of the hard times people went through."

"For god's sake, Fenwick, get to the point," the D.I. said, getting agitated.

"Well, sir, I did a little bit more digging because the Symonds family did not have transport, and it turned out that Linda's probation officer was visiting the girl on a regular basis, often picking her up from school and driving into the countryside. Don't worry, sir, it wasn't Barbara Sutton, but a probation officer called Dinah Tenby, who Barbara took over from, and by all accounts had lesbian tendencies. However, I can't prove that. What I can prove, after a visit to the current probation officer, is that Dinah Tenby destroyed all the files of her so-called professional visits to Linda Symonds, and my point is this: if she was able to destroy Linda's file then why not others, sir? Is there a list of other names that have been kept from us?"

The Inspector rubbed his chin. "Alright, Fenwick, you take a W.P.C. with you and question Barbara Sutton. My personal opinion is that Miss Sutton was not withholding anything. I think if there were files on other girls they would have been destroyed before the new probation officer took over, and if that is the case then Dinah Tenby has taken her secrets to her grave. But check it out anyway. Well done, Fenwick," he added.

He left the team to sort out the delivery notes. "Before I go, Sergeant, did Dick mention anything about his desk diaries? I think we need to get them and quick. I'll phone the factory and find out why he hasn't sent them with the boxes."

"I'll make it a point to phone him, sir. We don't want to break our renewed friendship, do we?"

Inspector Rupert could only smile, knowing exactly what the Sergeant meant.

"Very well, but give him a slight push by saying I'm not too happy about those diaries, and, if need be, I'll come and collect them myself. That should put the frighteners on him."

The team came up with nothing. A copy of the invoices were matched to a copy of the delivery notes, revealing that no delivery was made to any of the missing teenagers dating back to 1944. He felt thoroughly dejected. All he would have needed was a delivery to any of the girls whose addresses were on the list made by the Wood Press Mills. That would give him the excuse to bring in Mr. Dick for a more serious chat.

Sergeant Buckingham entered the office. "Nothing to report, sir. I've sent the team who were doing the sifting out to those delivery addresses, but it's only routine. I don't expect anything that will push us forward, sir. However, take a look at this plaster cast of a tyre imprint in the mud. All other vehicles have been cleared by our forensics except this one. A long wheelbase with a narrow gauge tyre, there can't be many box vans like that, sir, so I need your permission to go over to Wood Press Mills and discreetly try to match their fleet with this casting."

"I appreciate your enthusiasm, Sergeant, but let's try and keep it within the bounds of reality. Firstly, most if not all their vehicles will be out on deliveries, secondly there are hundreds of those vehicles on the road. I'm sorry but your time will be better spent here at the station."

"Alright, but I know those factories have a standard size for all their delivery vehicles. It's standard practice having their wheels and tyres all the same standard size."

"Very well, Sergeant, but don't go into their yard, just put a tail on one of their vehicles, and when it stops then do what you have to do."

He lifted the telephone. "Freddie, Inspector Rupert, no don't hang up just yet because I want to thank you for a speedy delivery. However, I have to ask, is that all the delivery notes and invoice copies concerning those dates?"

"Yes, Inspector, and my staff worked tirelessly all through Saturday boxing that damned paperwork. More expense in overtime payments."

"Yes I quite understand, Freddie; my bosses cringe at our overtime sheets." He paused. "I need the rest of those invoices and delivery notes. Oh, and don't forget the diaries; we need them urgently. It will help take your name off our suspects list."

The call was terminated. "That bloody man is hiding something, Buckingham. However, that will save you making a phone call."

Inspector Rupert was experienced enough to know that sooner or later, the "high heid yins" upstairs would start asking about the operational costs again. He was clutching at straws, because nothing was giving him the breakthrough he so desperately needed, with two corpses in the mortuary, and no leads.

Sergeant Buckingham arrived back with news of the Wood Press Mills vehicle tyre check. "Negative, sir, their vans are certainly long based but their tyres and wheels are much broader, and therefore do not match the plaster cast taken at the crime scene in Parson's Wood." She paused. "I know you told me not to go into the factory yard, but I had to be sure that the employees' cars and the management were not the vehicles involved, so we can eliminate them from the inquiry."

Inspector Rupert sighed. Every time something hopeful appeared, it was like hitting a brick wall and each possible clue was wiped out and disappeared like snow off a dyke wall in springtime.

The case was practically at a dead end. The only saving grace was the other invoices and delivery notes with Dick's desk diaries. He did not hold out much hope, simply because there was no match found in the recent paperwork, and although he was never a pessimist, his resolve was beginning to wane.

"Head up, sir, and remember what you always drummed into us: a breakthrough will come. Cracks will appear in this serial killer's movements. I think he is running scared at the moment, since there have been no reports of any other missing persons."

"You're right, Buckingham, sometimes I feel I'm not doing enough. It's not that I'm incapable, but when a case drags on like this it really does bother me."

Worse was to come, the invoices and delivery notes dating back to 1938 revealed nothing. There were only three desk diaries to go through; the others had been destroyed in a bombing raid when the German Luftwaffe were after the Boeing aeroplane factories. He said nothing to Sergeant Buckingham, but was seriously considering throwing the towel in, and explaining to those upstairs that there was no chance of solving the recent missing persons, let alone solving the ones that dated back to 1938. He would insist they kept the murder cases open, though, because there was always the chance that the pathologist would come up with something. "Anything," he heard himself say.

"Sorry, sir, I didn't catch that?"

"Just continue with those diaries, Buckingham," he said harshly. "I need to do some serious thinking, so I'll be in the Fountain lounge should anybody want me."

He approached the bar. "A large brandy and soda please, Dot." He took the glass from her and swallowed the contents in a oner. "Same again, Dot," he said holding the brandy glass towards her.

"Have you had anything to eat, Amadeus Rupert?" she asked before pouring his second drink. "No, I thought not. Well, have those two sandwiches, they will help to soak up the alcohol. I can get John to make you something if you prefer a meal from the menu."

"Thanks, Dot, the sandwiches will suffice for now, because I have a full-time housekeeper who will have my dinner ready for me."

Dot commenced to pour his large brandy and opened his bottle of soda. "You make sure you eat your meals at regular intervals." She was not scolding him, but giving him some healthy, friendly advice. "I have heard on the grapevine that you have had personal problems with Deborah, no chance of a reconciliation?"

Amadeus did not like discussing his marital problems, especially in a bar with the two dinosaurs earwigging into people's conversations.

"That was finished months ago, Dot. A lot of water has flowed under the bridge since then, so I'd prefer if we dropped the subject." He swallowed his drink and ordered another. "One for the road, Dot," he said with a smile.

"If I had a pound in my pocket for every time I've heard that said, I wouldn't be standing behind this bar serving you morons, would I?"

"Do you speak to all your customers this way, Dot? I might have to consider changing my watering hole."

"Only to my friends, Amadeus. As for you changing your pub, well, I suppose I'd miss the excitement, but I'm sure I'd get over it." They both laughed loudly.

The next morning was a cold, wet, grey day. He drove down to the Welwyn Garden City police office, he had made his mind up, that the "high heid yins" should be made aware of the way things stood in the investigation. However, he was met by a jubilant Sergeant Buckingham. "I worked on after you left last night, sir, and guess what I came up with."

"I do not have time for guessing games, Buckingham. Please tell me you have some good news for a change."

"Better than that, sir, I've found a link between Fredrick Dick and three of the missing girls in his desk diaries for 1945 and 1944. Now he told us that he visited customers with missing parts, but what he did not tell us was that he visited the parents of Sandra Phillips in St. Albans and the parents of Janet Findlay in Hemel Hempstead in 1945 before the girls were reported missing. Now we move to 1944. The same scenario, sir, a visit to the parents of Emma Miller of Leighton Buzzard, again shortly before the twelve-year-old went missing. I know you don't believe in coincidences, sir, so what do you think?"

"Excellent, Sergeant, that gives us an excuse to bring him in for questioning on our home patch. Get a car ready, we'll drive over to pick him up. I'd also give his lawyer Simkin a call, just to keep things regular, in case we can bring a charge against our dear Freddie Dick." He wanted to give the Sergeant a hug but protocol prevailed.

They drove at a reasonable speed over to the Wood Press Mills in Hatfield. There was no procedure when they entered the reception area. They walked straight into Fredrick Dick's office.

"What is the meaning of this intrusion, Inspector? Can a man have no privacy?"

"On your feet, Mr. Dick, you're under arrest for the murders of John Wood and his daughter Cynthia Wood. There's a question mark about you visiting them. You have the right to remain silent, but anything you do say will be noted down and might be used in evidence against you."

"You're making a big mistake, Rupert, huge, massive. I need to contact my lawyer before you take me to the police station."

"No need, Mr. Dick, that has already been arranged. He'll be waiting for us at the station," Sergeant Buckingham said quietly.

The accused stood up and pressed a button on his phone. "Len, come through and take charge of things; the police have arrested me and are taking me in for questioning." He turned to Rupert. "Thank you, Inspector. I'm ready when you are." There was no need for handcuffs, Fredrick Dick went quietly out to the police car, constantly pleading his innocence.

"Yes, yes, Mr. Dick, we've heard it all before. Now sit quiet, there's a good gentleman."

He was taken directly to the interview room where his lawyer Mr. Simkin was waiting patiently. "Have you telephoned London, Simkin?"

"All arranged, Freddie, your mother-in-law is on the train north as we speak."

"What's all this business with mother-in-laws, Simkin?"

"Oh did Freddie not tell you?" He gave a smirk of satisfaction. "His mother-in-law is a top London barrister who owns the law firm Peabody and Peabody. You must have heard of them when you were in the Metropolitan Police. Mrs. Peabody is on her way north to speak to the Chief Constable, and probably you."

"You are not being charged at the moment, Mr. Dick. However, we have the power to keep you in custody for thirty-six hours, while our investigation continues. Then we can apply for an extension to hold you in custody if the need arises."

"I must protest in the strongest terms, Inspector. My client has co-operated with you, even working overtime to get copies of invoices and delivery notes to you. That goes beyond a call to help the police. More important is the fact that he never knew Cynthia Wood, and only knew John Wood through work."

"How does he explain the fact that he visited the parents of three missing girls, with the excuse of supplying missing parts?" Inspector Rupert turned to Fredrick Dick. "Perhaps you would like to comment on those visitations, and why you never told us about it when questioned before."

"Yes, yes Mr, Dick, we've heard it all before, now sit quiet, there's a good gentleman.

"Ah, so you remember the dates now, Freddie." Inspector Rupert said quickly hoping to catch the suspect off guard.

"I am still confused, Inspector, but how can I deny them visits if they were written into my desk diaries? I'm sure that's where you got the link."

Inspector Rupert was under pressure from the top brass to solve the two murder cases or the investigation would be suspended in six weeks. He had been told from the top that the missing persons cases would have to be shelved and again listed as unsolved.

It was with great persuasion that he managed to keep the hounds at bay, and this arrest would help smooth the way to the top floor.

"Okay, Freddie, tell me how and why you killed the Woods? Well, we know how but why? Were you having an affair with his wife, or his daughter, when John Wood found out about it? What substance did you use to disarm him? You must have used a drug, because no one could get near John Wood, he was skilled in self defence. The pathologist report stated that a drug was administered by an alcoholic drink, probably in a hip flask. Cynthia was strangled and put in the ground three years later, so just come clean, Freddie, and admit that you killed John and Cynthia Wood. We know you did it Freddie, then you can tell us about the missing girls. It will help you in the long run."

"I'm sorry, Inspector, but my client does not, and will not, answer any of those ludicrous accusations, and I must warn you that you have made a false arrest."

"Come now, Simkin, there's too much linking your client to the missing girls, and the Woods. Therefore I intend to hold him in custody pending further investigation."

The solicitor stood up quickly. "All you have is circumstantial evidence, Inspector, nothing more. However, I can see that I have no influence in these proceedings, therefore I'll take my leave and let you face a much better adversary than me. Good day, Inspector." He lifted his briefcase and walked to the door. "I suggest you keep your afternoon free, after Mrs. Peabody has spoken to the Chief Constable." He gave a smile and departed.

The prisoner was taken back to the cells. "What do you think of that, Sergeant Buckingham?"

"He has a point, sir. What we have is circumstantial. Who is this barrister Peabody that has entered into the suspect's defence?"

"I came across her in my younger days with the Met." He paused. "She and her husband set up business together in London, and don't underestimate her, Sergeant; she's a crocodile." He gave a rueful smile. "While giving you that beautiful broad smile, she's plotting to roll you over and take you down to tenderise you before she destroys you in court. So be prepared. Meanwhile, have we received the other documents from the Wood Press Mills?"

"I'll check, sir," was all Sergeant Buckingham said, getting to her feet.

Inspector Rupert also got up and stretched. "We'll leave Mr. Dick to sweat. However, I did think he would crack, and save us time because the top brass are getting restless and want a speedy conclusion to the two murders. I think I've pushed the boat out because of them upstairs. I also know that all we have is circumstantial, but Mr. Dick and Wood Press Mills are connected to those murders and missing persons; that's why I'll put him under pressure when his barrister arrives. Use a sprat to catch a mackerel, so to speak."

"So you're not sure if Fredrick Dick is guilty, sir?"

Inspector Rupert knew which way the conversation was heading. "You go and find out if those documents have arrived. If not, chase them up again with your charm."

He sat in his office going over everything again and again. He was missing something, but could not put his finger on it. Suddenly the telephone rang. "Yes, sir, I'm busy, but it can wait."

He knew why he was being summoned to the fifth floor. It was obvious the barrister had arrived from London. He was shown immediately into the Chief Constable's office. The introductions were made.

It was the barrister, Mrs. Peabody, who spoke, "The same old Rupert, keen as mustard. I remember you from the good old days. I'm sure you remember me." She didn't allow the Inspector to answer. "What I am here to find out is why you are holding my son-in-law for murder when you have no concrete proof of evidence against him. I demand you release him immediately."

The Chief Constable spoke out at this point. "You might make demands like this in London, Mrs. Peabody, but you're in Hertfordshire, and we don't take kindly to people making demands on us. So if you allow Inspector Rupert to give his reasons for the arrest of Fredrick Dick, then we can decide what is best for you and your son-in-law."

Inspector Rupert was glad of the timely intrusion.

He went on to explain that Fredrick Dick had not been charged with murder, but was arrested on suspicion while the police made other investigations.

"As you are aware, Mrs. Peabody, we can hold Freddie for thirty-six hours, and more if the need arises." Inspector Rupert watched her expression change.

"Alright, but I will be timing you to the nearest minute, Rupert, and you can be sure, you will not be granted an extension that you so graciously put across with my son-in-law's first pet name, that does not work with me." She got up quickly, and shook the Chief Constable's hand. "Thank you, Lawrence I'll be in touch." She ignored the Inspector, but Inspector Rupert still remembered that crocodile smile.

"I'll be in touch if there are any other developments, Mrs. Peabody." Remembering his manners, he stood up and nodded.

She just gave him a scowl before walking out.

"Well, Rupert, you can see what we're up against. So are there any other suspects regarding this case? It seems to be dragging on forever."

"Apart from the arrest of Fredrick Dick, there's nothing new since the last time we spoke."

"Very well, keep me posted." He waved his hand indicating the meeting was over.

Inspector Rupert sat at his desk contemplating his next move. He read the drug report that had come across his desk. Welwyn Garden City had become a haven for drug pushers and drug users in the new town. A lot of money and resources were being used in that direction. He hated drug use, it was becoming an epidemic and the scourge of the country.

He shuffled the papers around feeling slightly bored, until the door tapped and Sergeant Buckingham appeared. "That's the last of the invoices and delivery notes, sir. It took a bit of gentle persuasion before the chairman released the documents, due to the fact you've arrested his factory manager." She gave a smile. "I threatened to lock him up in the damp basement cell if he refused to co-operate, that seemed to do the trick, sir." She paused. "I have the team sorting them out in the incident room, just like the last lot, sir."

"Okay, Sergeant, I'll be through in a minute after I've studied and sorted out these drugs crimes." The afternoon was coming to a close when he made his way to the incident room

There were seven days left before the "high heid yins" were going to pull the plug on the missing persons cases, despite Inspector Rupert's pleadings.

After studying some of the paperwork spread across the tables he finally took the decision to call it a day. "Okay you've worked hard on all this paperwork, but as you can see, we still have boxes to go through tomorrow, so a clear head will be required by everybody, including you, Grimshaw." Who like Rupert's dead friend Colin Freeman was known as a party animal, which reminded him that Colin' s memorial service would be next month.

He discarded the thought of going for a quick one in the Fountain bar and made his way home to a lovely hot meal laid out by Mrs. McGinty, his housekeeper. He really did appreciate what she did for him, sometimes putting in more hours than she was paid to do. He knew there would be an extra bonus in her Christmas stocking, which seemed so far away.

Next morning he was up with the lark, then after breakfast walked down to the police station. He was met with bad news from the duty desk sergeant. "Another missing person reported this morning, sir, another thirteen-year-old girl, this time from Harlow. Her name is Janine Chearsley. Sergeant Buckingham is on her way over to interview the parents."

Inspector Rupert nodded, and tried hard to hide the disappointment in his face.

"Don't worry, sir, you will catch this monster," the desk sergeant said before returning to the desk ledger.

Inspector Rupert could not find the words to express his feelings. He just walked sombrely along the corridor to the office and closed the door. "What a bloody start, just what I needed," he said loudly, throwing his hat and coat over the chair, not bothering to hang it up, which was not his normal routine, having had R.A.F. discipline installed in him.

He sat for a while to take stock of the shock he was encountering. The door tapped and W.P.C. Stapleton put her head in with anticipation. "Sergeant Buckingham told me to remind you that all the boxes have been emptied and are ready for your inspection, sir."

"So soon, Stapleton?" he said abruptly.

"Yes, sir. She and a couple of the team came in early to set things in motion." She paused. "You will have heard the news, sir. That's why she's driven to Harlow to question the parents. She should be on her way back by now."

The door closed quietly, leaving Inspector Rupert to his thoughts. He got up quickly and went to the incident room. "Weatherspoon, I want you to go over to Wood Press Mills and find out if they have made a delivery to Harlow recently, and get back here as soon as possible." Once Weatherspoon had gone, Rupert said, "Okay now let's get a look at those invoices and delivery notes."

They were the same, different dates and addresses, once again when cross-referenced, some of them showed that Wood Press Mills had delivered at some time to that of the missing persons, except John and Cynthia Wood, and the shoe shop assistant who went missing in 1933. Was Felicity Roach a chance pickup? Was she actually part of this investigation? There was a huge age gap that did not fit the pattern. Felicity Roach was thirty years old while all the rest were teenagers, apart from Emma Miller from Leighton Buzzard, who was twelve, but Inspector Rupert suspected there were others who were not on the list of missing persons.

He looked at the delivery notes and invoices stapled together. "What is this C.O.D. marked up in the corner of some invoices, Bradley? Forget I asked the question; it's cash on delivery." He rubbed his chin. "I noticed another abbreviation, C.A.P. Any ideas, anyone?" He looked at P.C. Bradley. "Struck dumb, Bradley, lost your tongue?" He patted the constable on the back. "Sorry, son, it was just something to say."

"It could be clean and polish, sir," the young constable responded, "or another form of payment."

"Yes, it could be either of those things," Inspector Rupert said softly. "We have those other invoices and delivery notes, so dig out the ones that link to the addresses of the missing girls, to see if there is a C.O.D. mark on the invoices. We could also look at the other markings of C.A.P. to see if there is a link to the girls' home addresses as well."

There was little left to do except mark up the details of the recently reported teenager. He went back to his office to get his head into the drug crimes. The door knocked loudly and P.C. Weatherspoon entered with his report. "Nothing, sir, no delivery to Harlow, not ever."

"Okay, thank you, Weatherspoon, go and help out in the incident room."

No sooner had Weatherspoon disappeared than the door tapped lightly.

"Yes," he said loudly. "What is it, W.P.C. Lawson? Can't you see I'm busy?"

"Sorry, sir, I had an idea about the murder cases and the missing persons, but I'll come back when it's convenient."

Inspector Rupert beckoned her into the office, moving a chair for her to sit down. "Okay, Lawson, spit it out, and if it concerns old history you will be on school crossing patrol for the rest of the year."

The young police woman looked uneasy at the threat. "There are nights I've been kept awake thinking about the two murders and the missing persons cases. I know there is a link to Wood Press Mills, something we've missed, sir."

"Yes?" Inspector Rupert said in an agitated voice, bordering on a reprimand.

"Well, the more I thought about it, it made me think that I was concentrating far to much on Wood Press Mills and their vehicles, and also their staff, then when I heard you telling the team to concentrate on the invoices, it suddenly struck me." She hesitated. "The point is, sir, what if it was another company who made those C.O.D. deliveries, cash on delivery, sir, and the other marking in capitals is not clean or polish, but some method of payment, to an agency or something similar?"

The Inspector sprang to his feet. "You've cracked it, Lawson. How could I have been so stupid? It's just as you have said, Constable; I couldn't see past Wood Press Mills when we made the discovery about the invoices and delivery notes. I couldn't see the wood for the trees."

They made their way to the cell where Fredrick Dick was being held. The duty officer unlocked the cell door. Fredrick Dick was sitting on his bed eating his breakfast.

"Freddie, we've discovered something that might help set you free today."

"No more tricks, Rupert. I've been instructed not to speak to you, so sod off."

"Put that tray down for a moment and take a look at this invoice. You'll see cash on delivery clearly marked on the left side of the page, but what are the other capital letters in the right hand column?"

Fredrick Dick snatched the invoice and looked at it. "This C.A.P. lettering is for Crown Agency Payment. They deliver the goods and collect the money if the goods have not been prepaid. They then bring back the payments and we stamp the original invoice with C.A.P. which shows us that the money has been collected and the Crown Agency reimbursed for their delivery. Now my tea is getting cold so bugger off."

"Just one more thing, Freddie, who was the delivery driver? And where does this Crown Agency work from?"

"That's easy, Rupert, go to Hatfield Industrial Estate. You'll see their name up on the listed company boards that will direct you to their storage yard and warehouse. They also have an office in Stevenson street in Hatfield." He put down his breakfast tray. "You're not seriously suggesting that the Crown Agency are involved in all this pantomime Rupert? Eric Davidson is a well-respected businessman in Hertfordshire. Eric's dad ran the company. Sadly he passed away in 1936 and Eric took over. Nothing changed; they were a reputable firm, reliable and honest, never a penny short when they collected money. In fact Eric even did what I do, occasionally dropping off parts and helping women to assemble the flat packs, which can sometimes be difficult, especially if you live on your own." He stood up. "Eric Davidson is a happily married man, with two teenage daughters. So trust me, he is in no way connected to your murders or missing persons." He smiled. "You will have to excuse me. I have to freshen up before my mother-in-law arrives."

Inspector Rupert knocked on the door and waited until the duty officer came and unlocked it. "Tell your barrister that if things work out, you could be freed by the end of play today."

He and W.P.C. Lawson left the cell. "Okay, Lawson, get a hold of Sergeant Buckingham, with back up, and meet me at the Crown Agency office, Stevenson street in Hatfield. That's where we'll start, and another team can seal off the warehouse and yard. Nobody leaves the yard. However, we will allow vehicles to enter, but once in, they will have to wait on my approval to leave. Is that clear?"

"Yes, sir," she said, then went to find out where the Sergeant was.

Inspector Rupert sat waiting until the backup team arrived.

"Has the Crown Agency yard been sealed off, Sergeant?" he asked sharply as she stepped out of the patrol car.

"Yes, sir, everything is in place." She hesitated. "My word, but things have certainly taken a turn for the better. When did you realise it was an agency making the deliveries?"

"I didn't, Sergeant, it was young W.P.C. Lawson that drew my attention to the fact, which reminds me. Ask if she is interested in joining the C.I.D. She would make a very fine detective, just like you, Sergeant Buckingham."

She smiled, it was not very often the Inspector handed out compliments.

They marched into the agency office. "I want to speak to Eric Davidson. Can you ask him to come out into reception?" It was said in a tone to tell the receptionist that it wasn't a business call.

"I'm sorry but Mr. Davidson is out of the office. However, I expect him back soon. Who shall I say is calling on him?"

Inspector Rupert ignored her. "Get the police cars of sight and tell the backup to stand by, and react on my signal."

Sergeant Buckingham obeyed the order.

"While we're waiting, a cup of tea would go down a treat, then you can tell me all about yourself and the Crown Agency." Inspector Rupert sat on on the comfortable reception sofa and waited until the receptionist returned with W.P.C. Lawson in tow, carrying the tea tray.

"Excellent, Lawson, you play mummy while Mrs. Digby gives us a list of all the employees. She can also bring out the payment documents from Wood Press Mills."

"I'm sorry, Inspector, but I don't like your tone. Besides, all the employment records are kept at the distribution yard, and would need Mr. Davidson's authorisation." She hesitated before opening the large filing cabinet. "I hope you have a search warrant, Inspector?" She closed the filing cabinet again. "No, I'm sorry. I'm going to wait until my boss gets back. You can ask him for the documents you have requested." She sat down behind her typewriter and began to type.

Inspector Rupert looked at his watch, then again ten minutes later. He was becoming impatient. "Where did you say Mr. Davidson had gone to?"

"I didn't, Inspector. All I know is he had a few business calls to make when he left early this morning."

Inspector Rupert pursed his lips, then looked at his watch again. He finished his tepid tea as the door opened. A tanned-faced man stood in the entrance, in a light blue boiler suit with the Crown Agency logo printed on the breast pocket. The well-groomed silver hair told Inspector Rupert that this was not a manual worker.

"Mr. Davidson." He paused. "Mr. Eric Davidson?" he said quickly, catching the man by surprise.

"I am Mr. Davidson. However, I am very busy this morning, so please make an appointment with Mrs. Digby, my receptionist." He was about to enter a door marked *private* which Inspector Rupert assumed was Davidson's office.

"This is not a business or social call, Mr. Davidson." The back up team came into the reception. "Mr. Eric Davidson, you are under arrest for the murder of John and Cynthia Wood. You are also under arrest on suspicion of murdering fifteen teenagers whose names will be made clear when we formally charge you at Welwyn Garden Police Station. I must read you your rights at this stage. You have the right to remain silent, and anything you do say will be taken down and might be used in evidence when you make a court appearance, do you understand what I have just said?"

The accused nodded, as Mrs. Digby held her hand to her mouth and gasped before breaking down in tears.

"Before we take you in, there are certain documents we require. So to save us getting a search warrant and ripping your reception office apart, you can give Mrs. Digby permission to dig out what we need."

The accused nodded to the receptionist, then said, "Call my lawyer, Mrs. Digby."

That said, Eric Davidson was handcuffed and taken to Welwyn Garden City Police Station.

He was taken straight into the interview room, where he was informed of the charges that would be brought against him in the presence of his lawyer. He was handed a list of all the women and girls he was suspected of murdering. He was informed that he would also be formally charged in the presence of his lawyer, at a later date to be arranged, relating to the murder of John Wood.

CHAPTER TWELVE

"You have been read your rights, Mr. Davidson, so let me remind you in front of witnesses that you understood those rights earlier in your office. All I want from you at the moment is your name, address and place of employment." He watched the appointed lawyer flinch.

Inspector Rupert went on to ask the relevant questions. "All I can ask is why, Eric? You have a well-established business, a wife, two teenage children, and a nice house with money in the bank."

Eric Davidson began to speak of his own free will. "I never meant to kill my first victim, Inspector." The prisoner's eyes glazed over. "All I remember is, I went in to buy a decent pair of shoes because my work boots were killing me. A woman came over to serve me, then we got talking. I remember like it was just yesterday."

"Stop please, Eric. You don't have to say any more." Inspector Rupert looked at the young solicitor. Who sat speechless.

"I want to, Inspector," he began to froth at the mouth while smiling. His eyes were glazed when he began to speak. "I arranged to meet her after work, then we went to get a fish supper, before going to see some picture showing at the Odeon."

"This is Felicity Roach from Ware we are talking about here?" Inspector Rupert watched his reaction.

"Was that her name? A slut, Inspector. I was just newly married to my wife when this slut seduced me in her flat after the pictures."

"So after you had sex with her, you killed her. How did you kill her, Eric?"

"I remember she liked to be tied to the bedpost, that's when I strangled her."

Inspector Rupert couldn't believe it. This killer was confessing to murder but it was so neatly explained, almost as if it didn't matter, like an everyday occurrence.

"So you strangled Felicity Roach of Ware. How did you dispose of the body?"

"I put her in the back of the van and drove to the town dump in Hatfield, then cremated her in the incinerator. There was never any questions asked, because my father and I were frequent visitors to the town incinerator with rubbish from jobs we had done."

"Did it never frighten you that her remains would be discovered, like parts of her skull or bones?"

"At those temperatures, Inspector, I had no fear. When she went into the furnace, and I pressed the start button, she became ash, but I did take care to remove her jewellery, just in case it didn't melt, and was discovered by the men that cleaned the ash trays." He gave a creepy smile. "All very neat and tidy, no graves to dig, leaving telltale footprints, and getting your hands dirty. Some of them were quite hard work."

"Let's stick with the incinerator for now, Eric." Inspector Rupert had to pause. "How many more bodies on the list I gave you were cremated in this way?"

The serial killer studied the list. "I cremated seven in total."

"So you buried nine victims including Cynthia Wood?"

"Yes that will be about right, Inspector."

"Will you mark down which ones you cremated and where you buried the other victims, Eric? It could help you in the long run." Inspector Rupert knew that nothing could help Davidson's cause, but he wanted as much information as possible before the serial killer's company solicitor arrived.

"Some were buried so long ago that I might have difficulty remembering the locations. Besides those sluts should be left in the ground, and if god wants them he can cleanse them before he takes them to into heaven."

"Was it god's voice that told you to kill those girls, Eric?" Inspector Rupert had his fists clenched under the table, and found it took all his experience to stay calm and collected as this monster played tricks with him. "Don't worry, Eric, we'll help you remember where you buried them. Let's talk about John Wood and his daughter Cynthia; we've found their grave, but why bury the two in the same grave?"

"Ah yes I remember them well." He wiped the froth that had trickled down his chin. "The John Wood saga started back in 1943, if I recall the year." He paused. "Yes, definitely 1943, I went into the Hatfield railway station to buy a paper and cigarettes from the Menzies tobacconist and news agent. A young girl stood behind me waiting to be served. I hung back waiting for her, then offered her a bar of chocolate." He smiled. "Always a good way of introduction. I recognised the name when I questioned who her dad was. Oh, she was an innocent twelve-year-old at that time, a ripe little virgin ready for picking." The killer licked his lips. "We went out to the van and I asked if she wanted to go for a run out to the country. With the offer of more chocolate, she was almost persuaded when her friend who she was meeting appeared just as she opened the passenger door. I cursed the friend before I settled down, had a smoke while reading the paper. Suddenly the driver's door banged, and the brown-skinned man stood holding his kitbag. Lucky for me I had the driver's door locked as the stranger tried to force it open. I wound down the window and asked him what he thought he was doing. He laid his kit bag against the wheel arch and said rather loudly, 'That was my daughter you were speaking to just now. What did you want with her?'

"I had to think quick but kept my nerve. I calmly said that she and my daughter were going to the pictures, and we were waiting for Janice, my daughter, who had just arrived. That was a lie, but it worked. This seemed to calm him down, and we got talking. I put in quickly who I was and mentioned that he was a craftsman in furniture making. 'Not any more, Eric,' he said in response. I seized the chance and told him not to waste money on a taxi, that I was going in his direction, and offered him a lift which he gladly accepted. On the journey I told him about a slimy character that worked as a part-time labourer. I told him that his wife had taken Sean O'Leary in as a lodger, hinting that he was a womaniser, and that got John Wood into a temper. 'I'll fucking kill the both of them.' He had obviously been drinking on the train coming on leave. I told him to calm down, and have a drink, so I produced the good old hip flask of Scotch laced with a drug. I always had a plan B that had an instant effect. He offered to share the remaining liquid but I told him I had other deliveries to make, so he gulped down the remainder. I had to get rid of him so I drove up to Parson's Wood and began to dig his grave. The sod began to come round, so I cracked his skull open with the cricket bat I kept handy in the van, because I used to practice my batting in my spare time. I had always thought that I could play for the county cricket club, but that never happened." He wiped the saliva from his mouth. "After I cracked him over the head I dragged him through the undergrowth. I put him in the ground and buried him. I was sure I heard him moan as I shovelled the earth onto him. That, as they say, was that. If the nosey bastard had not intervened he might be alive today."

Inspector Rupert pursed his lips in disbelief. "Tell me about Cynthia," he said softly.

"I went to the railway station every Saturday at the same time, hoping to get a glimpse of Cynthia and her friend, but I gave up in the end. However, just by chance, I was eyeing up a possible victim at Hatfield Primary, when a girl appeared at the driver's door. 'Do you remember me?' the voice asked. 'Hatfield station three years ago. I recognised the van and I thought it was you,' she said, getting into the passenger seat. 'What about that drive out to the country you promised me?' I could not believe my luck, so we drove out to Parson's Wood where the vehicle is hidden from the road. She did what was necessary, and it became a regular sex tryst, which we both enjoyed until she told me that she had sex and slept with her mother's lover, Sean O' Leary. I couldn't stand the thought of her betraying me, especially with him. So I strangled her and buried her with her dad who lay thirty feet away every time we had sex in the back of the van. It certainly turned me on."

Inspector Rupert couldn't listen to any more crap from the psychopath. He unclenched his fists before standing up. He wanted to lean across the table and give the serial killer a severe slap, but kept his cool, realising that they would need his help in finding the missing girls. He signalled for the recorder to be switched off. The young appointed lawyer seemed to relax, but still said nothing.

"Have a word with your company solicitor when he arrives, Mr. Davidson. He will advise you to co-operate with the police, who can make a report to the Crown Prosecution Service. It's then up to them what prison you are sent to. Personally I think you'll be sent to a mental institution, but, as I have just said, that's not up to me. I'd have you strung up or shot like the wild animal that you are, if I could."

He had to get out of this man's company. "Go and release Fredrick Dick. I don't think he can assist us any more. If he had told us about the Crown Agency in the first place, we could have had this cleared up months ago. Time to go to the top floor with this. Tell Sergeant Buckingham to meet me in the incident room at 16.00 hours." He made his way out of the interview room and climbed the stairs to the Chief Constable's office.

When everything was explained, the Chief Constable could not hide his joy, slapping Inspector Rupert on the back in friendly gesture. "We'll have to call a press conference, Rupert. This is a feather in your cap when the promotions board meet." He hesitated. "And this information was given voluntarily?"

"Yes, sir, we brought in an appointed solicitor to witness what we did, and the killer was told that his rights were in no way impaired. I just think he wanted to be caught, to make a full confession, sir."

"Excellent, Rupert, keep me informed about the body searches. My word, this has saved us a fortune." With that remark, Inspector Rupert left the Chief Constable in rapture. He thanked him for his time, saluted, then turned and walked smartly out of the office.

He met up with Sergeant Buckingham in the incident room. She was removing the names of the girls that had been cremated in the incinerator.

"No need to continue with the Janine Chearsley case from Harlow. The stupid young girl went to London on a shopping trip, and decided to spend time with an aunt." She smiled. "You have been busy, sir, what a result. I knew you would get there in the end. It's going to be very quiet around here."

"Don't tempt fate, Sergeant, besides we still have to find those bodies." He checked the information board. "I think we should inform Mrs. Wood of the situation. I'm sure she will be pleased to know we have caught her husband and daughter's killer. You can do the talking when we get there." He tapped the information board with his pen. "While we're on the subject, let's not forget that all those girls' parents have got to be informed, regardless of how they died, and hopefully we can find their daughters' bodies, in order that they can give them a Christian burial. Right, we'll start with Mrs. Wood."

Inspector Rupert tapped the door lightly and it opened. He looked at Sergeant Buckingham when he heard the giggles coming from upstairs. They stepped into the hall and listened as the giggles turned to endearments, and the bed began to shake. They walked quietly up the stairs and stood on the landing, listening to the moans and squeals that were now becoming a loud panting and groaning. It was obvious the couple had reached their climax, so he opened he door to find Mrs. Tina Wood naked on top of a naked man.

He couldn't believe it, her family lying in the mortuary while she was having an affair with her lodger. He was sure it was Sean O'Leary on the bed.

"Both of you get dressed and come downstairs." It was said harshly.

They went down and waited in the lounge for the two lovers.

"I'm not here to judge, Mrs. Wood, but you could at least have waited until your husband and daughter were buried, and, if I can add, a good-looking woman like you could do better than getting mixed up with this layabout."

Sergeant Buckingham spoke loudly. "I'm sure you'll be pleased to hear that we've found your husband and daughter's killer. Therefore you can put them to rest when the pathologist releases their bodies for burial."

Inspector Rupert turned to the man slouched on the chair. "I know who you are, but for the record, what is your name?"

"None of your fucking business, I don't talk to pigs," O'Leary said with a smirk on his face. Opening a bottle of gin and taking a swig.

"Mr. O'Leary, I could take you over to the police station to continue this conversation, but it would be an insult to the other pigs, having someone like you contaminate their sty." Sergeant Buckingham laughed loudly. "We will be keeping a close eye on you O'Leary, and I'll make it a point to inform the unemployment centre that you're working part time for cash in hand."

Inspector Rupert tried to stifle a smile. "Okay, Sergeant, we've done what we came here to do. So we can go over to the mortuary and tell the pathologist the good news."

They left the house and made their way to the mortuary where Wilfred Ponsonby was up to his waist in blood and guts. "A hit and run, Rupert, way out of our league. What now? Can't you see I'm busy?"

Inspector Rupert covered his mouth.

"Getting squeamish, Rupert? Don't you go spewing on my clean floor. Give him a bowl, Sidney."

"I've come to inform you about our missing persons cases, and that we have caught the killer, so you won't need to keep the two Woods bodies any more."

"Well, well, Rupert, another victory for the police." He wiped the blood-stained knife on a rag. "I take it there will be more autopsies to be carried out. Which reminds me, you have outstanding chits to sign, in order that I get paid for my graveside attendances."

"Yes, we still have to find the burial sites. However, the serial killer has done you out of some payments, because he cremated seven of his victims."

The pathologist raised his bushy eyebrows.

"Don't worry yourself, Wilfred. There will be plenty of chits to be signed by the time I've finished." Inspector Rupert smiled. "I can sign them all at the one time, because I can see you are far to busy to be interrupted." He never heard the reply, he turned quickly and pushed through the thick hanging plastic.

The darkness was falling fast as they drove back to Welwyn Garden City Police Station. It was surrounded by reporters and photographers. As soon as they saw the car approach they jostled for position as the two officers stepped out of the car. The camera bulbs popped and flashed as the questions were fired at the Inspector.

"I have nothing more to add than what you already know, but I can confirm that we have a man in custody who is helping us with our inquiries. The Chief Constable will inform you of a press briefing in due course."

He turned and walked into the station only to be confronted by a very irate solicitor. "We need to talk, Inspector. I am not at all happy at you interrogating my client without me being present."

"Ah, I'm glad you're here; that will save me contacting you. I intend to charge your client on Thursday, after he has volunteered to help us find the missing girls. However, you can instruct him to help, that would be your common duty, so give your details to the desk sergeant and I'll see on Thursday at 10 a.m. sharp."

He did not give the solicitor a chance to recover. He hurried along the corridor to his office and closed the door quietly.

"Okay, Buckingham, can you remember the firm we used the last time we dug up that orchard garden?"

"Yes, sir, but a record will be kept in the typing office upstairs. I can remember how efficient they were, and it was an advert for landscape gardening that gave us the idea to use them: Alistair Sweeney and son, if I recall correctly. However, their name will be on their invoice. Shall I instruct them to begin excavation when Eric Davidson leads us to the grave sites?"

"I would hold back on that for the moment, Sergeant. I'm not convinced that our killer is telling the truth. Did you notice that during the revelation, he tried to divert our attention from John and Cynthia Wood's grave? I don't think that the clearing in Parson's Wood is the burial site for any of the other bodies, far too many tree roots for one thing, but I'm willing to hazard a guess that he's buried some or all of his other victims on Hatfield Heath. What we could do is start by using detectors, then we could peg off each section as we go. Perhaps two or three detectors, to speed things up, then we could call in the excavator company to dig if we get a result."

"Hatfield Heath, sir, do you realise how many acres the heath takes up?"

"Do you have a better suggestion, Sergeant?" he said abruptly.

"Not yet, sir, but Hatfield Heath could take years to cover. I suggest we give our killer the benefit of the doubt. Don't forget it was him who gave us the information we have in your office safe, sir."

"I agree, Sergeant, let's try to coax Davidson into helping us find the girls. That's a much more sensible approach." He stood up. "Time for some refreshment at the Fountain."

He tried to dodge the reporters who were still hanging around like vultures, and slipped quietly through the fire escape door at the side of the building, leaving the baying wolves in his wake. He had second thoughts about the Fountain lounge, far too close to the police station, and sooner or later one of the reporters would twig and come looking for him. So he went up Oakland Drive and cut through the lane that connected the drive with Oakland Avenue. He was glad to reach the safety of his villa.

Mrs. McGinty was busy in the kitchen. She scolded him for not eating his dinner the night before.

"You must eat, Mr. Rupert, otherwise you will end up with an ulcer."

He sat down to his favourite, homemade soup, and steak pie with all the trimmings. The morning brought the usual array of questions and suggestions. It was even suggested that they bring in a helicopter to view Hatfield Heath from the air.

"Please, let's keep it in the bounds of reality, children," Sergeant Buckingham said with a smile. "Besides, the Chief Constable would have a heart attack when he got the account placed on his desk."

"Thank you, Sergeant, I couldn't have put it better myself," Inspector Rupert said in earnest. "However, we have some spare time before we meet with Eric Davidson and his solicitor from Stevenage." He looked at the notes given to him by the desk sergeant. "A Mr. Butterworth, who by all accounts, sails close to the wind, and does not have a good reputation. But we'll cross that bridge when we meet him tomorrow morning."

He looked at the information board. "I don't think we should postpone the inevitable. Therefore I want the parents of those who were cremated informed today. It's not like the others where, hopefully, we can give those parents a body to bury. We can also use our time today, which I expressed yesterday, to inform the parents of the missing girls who remain on our list that we have caught the serial killer, and would someone clear those reporters and cameramen from the front of the station. How you do it, I don't care. Use any by-law, but get them moved."

"What about Felicity Roach, sir? She disappeared in 1933 but it was her work mates that reported her missing, not any of her family."

"A good point, Constable Bradley. It's unlikely that any of the women who worked in he shoe shop in Ware will still be there, after all it's fourteen years since she disappeared, and we know she was put in the incinerator. So I think we should leave the local police to trace Felicity's relations, if she had any." He looked around the room. "Any other business?" He paused. "Okay, the sooner we tidy up that part of the investigation, the happier I'll be."

After the briefing he made his way over to Parson's Wood. The security tape had come adrift from the trees, and fluttered in the wind. He tilted his hat in respect, then walked through the undergrowth and up onto the open heath land. He gazed across the wide expanse of grass land that seemed to stretch forever. There was a rough farm tractor track that someone could possibly drive a van along with care. He took a note of it before turning and heading back to the car, just as the dark clouds gathered and it started to rain. He sat thinking for a moment before returning to the police station.

Entering the incident room, he ordered that a police van should attempt the rough track up on Hatfield Heath. "I want to know where it starts and where it joins the B-listed road that runs parallel, approximately a mile away, and whoever is driving, take a colleague with them to keep a sharp lookout for disturbed ground." He rubbed his chin. "Perhaps they should take a detector unit with them. I know it's a long shot but you never know." He paused. "When you reach the other end of the track then turn around and retrace your journey, and continue with that until the light fades."

The two officers returned with nothing to show for their endeavours. "Okay, Constables, the same again tomorrow, only this time one will walk in front of the van, and you can swap when you reach the B road and track junction, then carry out that search until the light fades, and, incidentally, I don't have to remind you to take a flask and sandwiches. Also, dress for the occasion." Inspector Rupert gave a wry smile, that was soon to be wiped off his face.

The duty sergeant approached. "Sorry to disturb you, sir, but there is a Mrs. Peabody wishes to speak with you." The Sergeant saw the displeasure in Inspector Rupert's face. "She would not take no for an answer, sir, and insisted that she wait in your office, and that is where I put her, sir."

"Very well, Sergeant, forewarned is forearmed. I'll be through in a moment." He was in no hurry to speak to the barrister from London, especially when he knew what her visit was about. So he continued to give the following day's instructions of duties before venturing towards his office.

"Mrs. Peabody, sorry for the delay, it's due to the work load we have inherited." He sat down facing her. "Tell me, why the sudden visit?"

"Don't try to pull that one with me, Rupert. I'm here to inform you that we mean to press forward the case for wrongful arrest, and, on a brighter note, Peabody and Peabody intend to open up an office in Welwyn Garden City, where Desmond Simkin will be our branch manager. We still have to appoint a manager for our estate agent's office, but you will be seeing a lot more of me in the future."

Inspector Rupert stood up. "I would consider your intention to bring a charge of wrongful arrest, Peabody, because your son-in-law is not clear of us bringing a charge of wasting police time, and you as a barrister know the penalty a court imposes on those that do it. In regards to your new venture here in Hertfordshire, I'm sure it will benefit the local community with your expertise, so all I can say on that subject is good luck." Mrs. Peabody was about to speak, when Inspector Rupert held out his hand in a friendly gesture. "I'm sorry, Peabody, time is money. I'm sure you understand, and I am extremely busy at the moment, so I await your decision on the wrongful arrest charge." He watched the barrister fume, and knew he went one up when she refused his handshake then stormed out of his office.

The night flew in, so after dinner he decided on an early night, to be fresh for the coming interview with Eric Davidson and his solicitor. That came soon enough, as the morning broke and Inspector Rupert prepared for the interview, taking the written account from the safe he made his way to the interview room, where everybody was in attendance.

"Thank you for being on time, Mr. Butterworth, before we begin recording the formal charges, I would like to inform you of what was said on Tuesday, if you would like to read the account, that clearly states that your client Eric Davidson, made a confession of his own free will and was under no obligation to continue. Now we can press on with the formal charges or I can go to the canteen while you read the confession of Mr. Davidson."

He watched the solicitor flinch. "Entrapment, Inspector, nothing more and nothing less. A worthless lie." Eric Davidson nodded to his solicitor, who spoke calmly. "Very well, Rupert, let's get on with it."

Inspector Rupert was glad they agreed to press on. "Eric Davidson, you have been arrested on suspicion of murder, your victims will be mentioned step by step in this interview. However, for the record, I need your name, address, age and your place of employment, and where you were arrested."

Eric Davidson answered clearly and precisely to the relevant questions.

"Thank you, Mr. Davidson, now let's begin with your victims that you put in the Hatfield Refuse Dump incinerator, and let me remind you of your confession on Tuesday."

"Entrapment," the solicitor said loudly.

Inspector Rupert carried on, not wanting to give Davidson a chance to recover his thoughts. "Felicity Roach was her name, so, for the record, did you murder her, then dispose of her body by cremating her?"

"Yes," Davidson said in a whisper.

"Louder please, Mr. Davidson. So we can hear you, if you please."

The serial killer nodded, smiled and said "yes" in a loud tone. "Fucking slut deserved to die. Every one of them were sluts that god told me to wipe from the face of this planet."

"Thank you, Mr. Davidson, but please no more adages, for now, and, as I said we will go through this step by step, victim by victim. So now we approach the year 1938, we have Sophie Black, from Bishop Stortford, and Elizabeth Fry from Luton, do you admit to murdering them, and how did you dispose of their bodies?"

"I incinerated Fry, quite apt considering the name, and buried the slut Black in a field outside town."

"Thank you, Mr. Davidson, you are doing well. Now we move to 1940, and this appeared to be a quiet period for you. However, there was a girl called Polly Aniston, from Harlow. Do you admit to murdering her, and how did you dispose of her body?"

Eric Davidson held his finger to his lip and sat thinking. "I can't recall what I did with her, but I did kill the little slut. I probably buried her in some field close to her home."

Inspector Rupert nodded. "We'll come back to Polly later, but now we move to 1942. Nicole Fenwick from Stevenage, and Jane Riley from Letchworth Garden City." Inspector Rupert didn't get a chance to continue.

"I remember those two sluts quite clearly. I heard Riley Scream when I incinerated her, not what I needed, just in case there was a council worker close by. However, I never made the same mistake with Fenwick, or any of the others for that matter."

Inspector Rupert paused to take stock of what had happened. "So Jane Riley was alive when you switched on the incinerator?" He had to take a drink of water. "Okay, Mr. Davidson, let's move quickly to 1943. We have Maria Reynolds from Buntingford Village. Did you murder her and how did you dispose of her body?"

"Again, Inspector, I'm not sure where I buried her, but if it was a village then yes, I killed her, and would probably have buried her in a field close to the village."

"Let's stay with 1943 for a moment, we have already discovered the grave of John Wood. However, for the record, did you murder him with a cricket bat, and suffocation? A yes or no will suffice."

"Yes."

"Thank you for your honesty, Mr. Davidson. Now let's talk about 1944; this seems to have been a busy year for you, let me remind you of the names." He paused. "Lesley Hood from Hoddesdon, Emma Miller from Leighton Buzzard and Zoe Brooke from Hatfield. Do you admit to murdering those three girls, and how did you dispose of their bodies?"

"Zoe Brooke I remember, her being from Hatfield. It was easy. I killed her and put her in the incinerator. As for the other two, yes, I killed the little sluts, but what I did with them is anyone's guess. I probably buried them."

"Before we take a break, we will finish the morning interview with Sandra Phillips from St. Albans, who disappeared on the 8th of October 1945, another busy year for you, Mr. Davidson. However, I have to ask, did you kill Sandra Phillips, and how did you dispose of her body?"

"Yes I did kill the little slut and cremated her."

Inspector Rupert had noticed the glazed eyes of the serial killer, who occasionally wiped the saliva from his mouth after licking his lips.

"Interview will reconvene at 14.00 this afternoon, interview terminated at 13.00."

Inspector Rupert had to get out of the interview room. He stood up quickly and left Sergeant Buckingham to tidy up and do what was necessary. He went to the canteen for lunch, while trying to remain calm and wipe the morning interview from his mind.

The afternoon interview commenced on time.

"Right, interview commences at 14.04, and I must remind the prisoner of his rights, and that he is still under caution." He turned to face the serial killer. "Thank you for your frankness, Mr. Davidson, If I can just remind you of the last name mentioned before we broke for lunch, that name was Sandra Phillips from St. Albans, who you admitted to killing in 1945, and disposing of her body by cremating her. Let us continue with that year, which according to your own admission was a frenzied year of attacks on young girls. However, before we go through the names, perhaps you would like to tell us why from the early forties your frenzied attacks became more frequent, with occasional gaps, until you resumed your craving and continued to carried out the other murders? "

"Simple, Inspector, two reasons: one was that people had been bombed and furniture destroyed, therefore the orders got better as the war progressed, and two…" He smiled with glazed eyes. "The blackout and petrol rationing was in force which made it ideal for me to answer god's call and get rid of those sluts."

"I have to ask this in the presence of your solicitor: are there any other buried bodies that we don't know about?" The Inspector leaned back in his chair watching Davidson who looked at his lawyer for advice.

"I'll answer that for my client, Inspector. No, there are no other bodies buried that my client is aware of, so if we can continue and move on." The solicitor folded his arms.

"Certainly, Mr. Butterworth, that was my intention." He turned to face the serial killer. "Okay, Mr. Davidson, still in the year 1945, the war coming to an end, you stepped up your frenzied attacks, because the blackout would be withdrawn and that could blow your cover. You have already admitted that, so we now have seven girls that have been put in the incinerator. Are there any more you disposed of in this way?"

"No," came the curt reply.

It was obvious his lawyer had instructed him to be as brief as possible when answering the accusations. "Oh really, Inspector, my client has told you that there are no more bodies. I must protest at this line of questioning."

Inspector Rupert ignored the solicitor and continued, "Linda Symonds from Stapleford Village, Janet Findlay from Hemel Hempstead, Beverley Strang from Hertford, those were young teenage girls that went missing early in 1945. Did you kill them, and bury their bodies in some quiet location?"

"Yes."

Inspector Rupert nodded. "What about Alison Brent from Stevenage? We already have Cynthia Woods' body and grave but, for the record, did you kill those other two girls?"

"Yes."

He looked at the lawyer who was sitting stoney faced.

"As iterated to Mr. Davidson in his first confession, it would be helpful if he could remember the sites where those girls were buried. However, it is up to the home secretary and the Crown Prosecution Service to decide if Mr. Davidson can be released from prison, under guard, to assist us to locate his victims. I cannot promise anything due to the severity of these crimes, but it could make a difference in whether he gets solitary confinement or not. We all know how severe those prisons can be, especially to paedophiles and child murderers."

The Inspector took a deep breath before speaking loudly. "Eric Davidson, you are formally charged with the murder of John Wood. You are also charged with the murders of four older women, namely Felicity Roach, Sophie Black, Elizabeth Fry and Jane Riley. You are also charged with the murders of twelve young girls, the majority of which were teenagers, seven of them you cremated. A list of all of their names has been lodged with your solicitor, a copy has also been sent to the Crown Prosecution Service who will inform you, and your solicitor, of your court hearing date. You will be taken from here to a secure prison where you will be held until your trial date." He looked for a response from the serial killer and his solicitor. Getting none he said quietly, "Interview terminated at 16. 09." He sat back and stretched as Eric Davidson was led out to the prison transport. "Phew. I'm glad that's over, Sergeant. Now to keep the 'high heid yins' informed, then they can arrange a press conference for tomorrow. But tonight I'm going to have a few sherbets, and if any of the team wish to join me in the Fountain lounge bar, the drinks will be on the house." He gave a smile, left the interview room, then ascended to the fifth floor.

The investigation team trickled one by one into the lounge bar, and were handed their drinks order by Dot and John. The Williamsons were included in the free bar, with a buffet laid on for those that had not eaten.

Amadeus explained that this was not a celebration as such, but a way of releasing the pressure of the last few frustrating months.

Before he departed for home at a reasonable time, he advised the team to remember that a lot of disturbing work had still to be done tomorrow and over the days, weeks and months to come.

Next morning he was in the station early, the press briefing was arranged for 10.00 A.M., but he wanted to tidy up his in tray before the day got underway.

Sergeant Buckingham tapped the door and entered. "I've given instructions to the team sir, so they have been allocated their addresses to visit."

The Inspector looked at his watch. "My word, Buckingham, you are on the ball this morning, any absenteeism?"

"No, sir, all present and correct. However, I have to admit that I gave them a severe warning after you left the lounge, and it seems to have worked."

Inspector Rupert gave a wry smile. "I have this bloody press conference in the boardroom, a proper pain in the arse, all those from the upper floors, sitting smiling like Cheshire cats, licking up the cream, I ask you." He paused. "I know it is a bit soon. However, I might drive into London later today, then visit Eric Davidson in prison. I plan to strike while the iron is hot, and he is still basking in his newfound celebrity status. He just might help us find some of the missing girls." He waved a notepad in front of him. "I'll take this after I have listed the towns and villages on each page, then ask him to draw a reference map, with the names of any country lanes, which reminds me, any luck with the Hatfield Heath search? I am positive he disposed of some, if not all, the bodies up there, simply because of the quiet locality, and plenty of heath land."

"You have to bear in mind, sir, that some of those cases were so long ago, and he might have difficulty remembering, just like Davidson stated yesterday."

"Don't worry, Buckingham. I'm not going to beat the truth out of him, and I promise to have a prison warden present at all times." He walked to the wall safe. "This is two search warrants, Sergeant. I want Eric Davidson's house taken apart brick by brick if necessary. I also want the Crown Agency storage warehouse searched while I'm in London. I'll expect a report on my desk when I get back."

The morning, as always, crept by quickly as he made his way to the press conference in the boardroom that was already jam packed to the rafters with reporters, cameramen and women. Perched high in their towers were the television and Pathé news cameras that would be shown in picture houses across the British isles.

Inspector Rupert sat with his arms folded, like an obedient school boy, letting the Assistant Chief Constable waffle on about how it had taken a long time to find the serial killer, but with tenacity his team of officers had won through.

There were questions fired and answered. "Is it true, Inspector, that some fatal errors were made in the search for this serial killer, and if so would you consider resigning and taking up some other menial task?"

Inspector Rupert unfolded his arms. "If you crowd would care to look at when I took up the investigation after returning from the war, you will find that from 1939 to late in 1946, operations were scaled down for obvious reasons." He paused. "Yes, in my time, mistakes were made. However, sometimes clues will lead you down that particular path. As for resignation, that is out of the question since we still have a lot of work to do in finding those missing persons, which my team is working on at the moment." He paused. "As for another menial task, well I could hardly apply for M.I.5. or M.I.6. because you lot have my name and photograph on every front page. However, I might apply for the diplomatic service if push comes to shove."

There was a loud echo of laughter at his answer.

"Very funny, Inspector," the adamant reporter shouted. "So while your team are out doing the hard work, what will you be doing today?"

"I intend to drive to London as soon as this briefing is over with the intention of visiting Eric Davidson in prison. Perhaps he might now be keen to help, since he will have had a taste of prison life," Inspector Rupert said coldly. The drive to London was tedious, although he was glad to get out of the briefing, which had become a free for all with accusations directed at the "high heid yins".

He was shown directly into the governor's office where all was explained.

The governor pressed a button on his desk. A broad tall prison warder appeared. "Show the Inspector to the meeting room in prison block C, Anders. One hour maximum, Inspector," the governor said with authority." He took the paper warrant and gave it to the warden.

Inspector Rupert was stunned by the reception he received, after all they were on the same side, or were they? he asked himself as he was shown to the meeting room. "Thank you, Anders, if you could stay, this should not take too long."

The prisoner was brought in dressed in his prison bib and brace overalls. He casually sat down. "Well, Inspector, I thought you had finished with me."

"Not quite, Eric, we still have the question mark over the missing girls." He threw a bar of chocolate over, which Davidson eagerly snatched and put in his breast pocket.

Inspector Rupert sat opposite him and placed three packets of cigarette tobacco, along with cigarette papers and a box of matches on the table. Eric Davidson made an attempt to grab them.

"Uh Uh, Eric, that's for later, if I'm satisfied with what you tell me." He pulled the items back, then took a large brown envelope from his coat pocket, then removed his hat and coat.

"This is an A4 notepad, Eric." He opened it at the first page and showed the prisoner the sketches he had done. "This is the location of John and Cynthia Wood's grave at Parson's Wood, note the woodland drawing. It also has the date you murdered them. However." He flicked over a page. "Here on each of those pages we have the names and the dates those other girls were reported missing. I want you to concentrate and give me the locations where you buried those girls. Lanes, fields, anywhere that we can begin a search, and bring those dead girls home." He paused. "Remember what I told you. If you assist the police, I can try to make life easier for you on the inside when you are finally sentenced by the court." He paused and smiled. "Also, the snout and cigarette papers will be given to you when I am satisfied you have helped in locating the dead girls."

"What good will they do, Rupert? They're going to string me up anyway," Davidson said in a soft voice.

"Not necessarily, Eric. Personally, I think you'll be locked away in a mental institution, but that's not for me to decide. However, I can say that you will become a household name. *Eric Davidson, serial killer helps police to locate his victims' bodies*, you will have a bigger profile than Jack the Ripper."

"Do you think so, Inspector?" The serial killer was like a fish on the hook, and reeled in.

"I do, Eric, but that really depends on our meeting today."

The prisoner looked through the pages. "I will begin with the sluts. Alison Brent, from the Stevenage Orphanage, is buried along with Beverley Strand from Hertford and Janet Findlay from Hemel Hempstead." He paused. "Yes, they're buried in a field in Primrose Lane close to a hedgerow, a nice quiet spot, where I prepared each grave. Oh, there was a farm gate as I recall."

"Just write down the names and give a rough sketch of the location." Inspector Rupert watched him flick over the pages and sketch a detail of where the girls were buried. "Excellent, Eric you're doing well." Inspector Rupert was using all his cunning experience to coax the killer to reveal his secrets.

"Linda Symonds, now there was a sweet little raspberry, just ripe for the plucking. She was from the village of Stapleton, and I buried her close to a stream, outside her village." He made a sketch of the location. "Emma Miller, Polly Aniston and Maria Reynolds, are a blank, Inspector, as is Sophie Black, who I strangled in 1938. How am I supposed to remember as far back as that?" He thought for a moment. "There was a sweet little virgin called Lesley Hood, now I took real pleasure breaking her in. Yes, I remember the little vixen. She put up a real struggle, but I soon overcame her and strangled the little bitch. I buried her in the old disused barn where she succumbed to my advances, just outside the village of Hoddesdon. Her mother was just as sweet, that's why it sticks out in my memory."

Inspector Rupert knew he was lying about one of his earliest victims. "Let's talk some more about Sophie Black. You can remember strangling her in that year, but cannot remember where you buried her? Come on, Eric, try a little harder."

The prisoner leaned back in his chair with a smirk. "Sorry, Inspector, I have nothing more to add, I have given you what I can remember."

Inspector Rupert nodded, considering the vital information that had been given to him. But he still wondered how this serial killer could remember what he done with Elizabeth Fry's body, when he incinerated her in 1938, but had no recollection of what he had done with Sophie Black who he strangled the very same year. He sat for a moment. Were those three victims special to him? Did he want to take those three victims' grave locations to his own grave?

He stood up and pushed the bribery items to the prisoner.

"If you remember anything more, Mr. Davidson you will let me know?" He left the prisoner to his fate, and left the prison with a slight feeling of optimism.

It was an arduous drive back to Welwyn Garden City. There was a traffic accident on the London circular, and the traffic ground to a halt. It was late in the evening when he finally pulled into the police parking compound. He made his way home on foot, pulling his collar together, and battled against the wind and rain. He was glad that a hot meal was waiting for him, and after a long hot soak, he made his way down to the kitchen where Mrs. McGinty was standing ready to serve his soup.

"These irregular eating hours will be the death of you, Mr. Rupert," she said in a scolding fashion, trying not to be too hard on her tired-looking boss. "I'll be in my room should you need me," she said leaving him to tuck in.

Amadeus was glad of the peace and quiet as he finished his dinner, then poured a large brandy and soda. He then retired to the lounge with the evening paper.

Next morning he slept a little longer, much to the appraisal of his housekeeper.

He entered the office in a relaxed mood, looking for the search report. There was no sign of anyone in the incident room. "Where is everybody, Sergeant?" he asked the duty officer.

"Some are at Eric Davidson's bungalow, some are at the storage warehouse and some are out on the beat, sir. Oh, and one more thing, the Assistant Chief Constable wants to see you, sir." The Sergeant continued with his work.

Inspector Rupert thanked him for the advice, then turned and walked out of the station to proceed over to Hatfield and Eric Davidson's bungalow. The team were busy ripping up floorboards and prodding cavity walls.

"Where are Mrs. Davidson and her children?" he asked a constable who was signing people in and out of the bungalow.

"Gone to her mother's, sir; she took a train to Sheffield yesterday morning."

He nodded and walked into the bungalow. "Find anything of interest, Sergeant?" he asked, covering his mouth from the dust.

"Nothing, sir, and we are almost finished, just the kitchen floor to lift and that's it."

Inspector Rupert nodded. "What about the attic, has it been searched yet?"

"With a fine-tooth comb, sir, we started at the top then worked our way down."

"Okay we can move some of the team over to the warehouse. I just wonder if Eric Davidson kept a record of his victims. If not he certainly has a good memory, so check the book case and magazine stand."

"I hardly think he's going to leave incriminating evidence in a book stand or magazine rack, sir." Sergeant Buckingham said irritated. "I take it you have had a good night's sleep, sir, while some of us have been up all night."

"Just do it, Sergeant. I'll be over at the storage warehouse should you need me." He turned and walked out of the dust-filled room to the waiting police car.

There would be time enough in the day to organise a works detail to start digging where Eric Davidson had sketched. He thought that Primrose Lane in Stevenage sounded like the ideal spot to start, but first things first, the storage yard and warehouse of the Crown Agency. He pulled the car into the yard and got out quickly. Works vehicles were still operating, coming and leaving the yard. He ran to the security barrier. "No more vehicles or persons in or out until you clear it with me. Understood?" he spoke harshly, knowing that this should have been done immediately.

The security guard nodded as he lifted the telephone. Inspector Rupert listened to the conversation which had become one way. The security guard came out of the office. "My chairman is on his way, Inspector."

"Good, just make sure he does not enter this crime scene or I'll lock the two of you up, so help me." He ventured into the warehouse. "Who's in charge here?" he asked abruptly.

"I am, who are you?" a woman said in the same tone.

"Why are vehicles allowed to come and go from these premises?"

"We run a business from here. What's your excuse?"

Inspector Rupert shook his head. "Sorry, I'm talking to the wrong person. However, if you are in charge, you won't be getting any vehicles returning or leaving today, so you can shut down your operations. Then, after the staff have been interviewed and have given a statement, they can go home."

"And just who the hell might you be to start dishing out orders?" the woman said in anger.

"Detective Inspector Rupert of Hertfordshire Constabulary, now can you point me in the direction of a police officer?"

She gave a laugh. "Sitting in the canteen having a cuppa. Follow me, Inspector."

He stood at the door of the small canteen. "Right, you lot, out and line up outside the warehouse office."

It was a sergeant who moved first, then barked out an order. "You heard the Inspector. On your feet, all of you." There was a flurry of movement as they obeyed the sergeant's order. "Sorry, sir, you caught us on our tea break."

"Why was this yard and warehouse not sealed off, Sergeant? It is classed as a crime scene." He paused and addressed the line of officers. "Some of you, I take it, are from other stations and don't know me, so let me introduce myself." He walked up and down the line. "I am Inspector Rupert from Welwyn Garden City, who is heading this investigation. There will be no more tea breaks until this warehouse has been thoroughly checked. I also want an officer placed at the security barrier. No one leaves or enters without my express order." He stopped walking. "Okay, Sergeant, you can now explain how far forward you and the team are in the search."

"We have most of it done, sir. Some of us have been here since coming on duty at 06.00, sir, and we never got any instruction to shut down the Crown Agency warehouse, sir.""

"Then you should have used your initiative, Sergeant. However, I haven't got time to waste, so let's go and find that fat controller of operations, after you select a few officers to take statements from the work force. Ask about Davidson's visits to the warehouse, how often, that kind of thing."

"Right, you, you, and you, start taking statements. Constable Leech on the security gate, the rest fall out and continue with the search." She turned to the Inspector. "Follow me, sir. I know where the warehouse foreman is."

They walked in and out of passages until they heard voices. "That's her voice, sir. I'd recognise it anywhere despite the echo."

"Bugger off, Inspector. I have my instructions to keep the orders flowing," she said bluntly.

"Handcuff her, Sergeant. We can ask the questions at the police station." He saw the disturbed look on the controller's face.

"I need this job, Inspector, and my boss has given me strict instructions to keep this warehouse working."

"Cuff her, Sergeant. I don't have time for all this flummery."

"Okay, okay, you win. What is it you want?"

Inspector Rupert smiled. "Well we can start with your name and address, but I want to be specific, don't waste my time or you'll be in serious trouble." He paused. "Tell me, Rita, did your boss Eric Davidson visit the warehouse often, more often than need be?"

"Of course he did, he owns the bloody place, Inspector. Common sense should tell you."

"So he visited the warehouse on a regular basis?"

The controller stayed silent for a moment. "There were times he would stay after all of us went home, insisting he would lock up, after the orders for the next day's deliveries were checked. Why I don't know. The furniture packs are all sealed when Wood Press Mills make the delivery, so it's just a matter of loading them from one van to the other, and our own storage and delivery is an easy transaction."

"So he comes to the warehouse, just before it closes to lock up." Inspector Rupert raised his arms. "All this space, you couldn't hide a body though. It's far too open, and boxes and crates would be moved daily, so I think we might be wasting our time here now that I've seen the place."

The controller looked at the Sergeant. "You haven't been to the bomb shelter in the basement, have you?" she said, eager to please.

"Not yet, we still haven't finished in the warehouse," the Sergeant said in defence.

"Basement, bomb shelter," the Inspector said sharply. "Show me, Rita, you might just have earned a reprieve." They followed the controller to a door that led down to the basement floor level.

"This is where we sheltered during bombing raids, Inspector."

He looked around the empty, dimly lit floor space. "Nothing much down here." He shone his torch back and forth along the dirty whitewashed walls. "What are those tall cabinets for, Rita?"

"Oh, they're used for storing tape and string, some old records about who owns what, which date back to when Eric's father ran the company, but we hardly come down here, except in an emergency, if we run out of tape or string upstairs. This place gives me the creeps; you can hear the rats scurrying about."

Inspector Rupert walked over to the large cabinet door, and opened it slowly. The door creaked with the lack of oil on the hinges. He nearly pulled the whole tall cabinet over on himself. "Bugger," he said loudly, trying to hold the large tall cupboard upright. "Give me a hand, Sergeant," he said, annoyed with himself for getting in such a pickle. They steadied the cabinet until it became stable. "Get a couple of your burly constables down here. We might as well see what's behind it. Any ideas, Rita?"

The controller just shook her head. "Can I go back upstairs, Inspector? I think I heard a rat run for cover." The woman was obviously spooked.

"Yes, off you go, Rita. I'll be up in a minute." He gave a wry smile as he watched her move quickly up the wooden stair.

He shone his torch at the floor where the cabinet was standing and noticed that the dust had formed a ridge along with some scratch marks, indicating that this cabinet had been moved at some time or another. He took the decision to move it, and, with all his strength, eased the cabinet away from the wall. He shone his torch into the shadow and immediately spotted the door. He waited until the Sergeant appeared with two constables. "Right, lads, do your utmost and move the cabinet so we can open the door."

After it was moved, Inspector Rupert tried to open the hidden door. He noted that there were oil stains on the floor where the hinges had been oiled. "Ask the controller if she has a key for this door, if not get a wrecking bar, or a battering ram in order that we can see what is on the other side." He stood impatiently waiting for the door to be unlocked. "Okay, Constable, move this cupboard back a bit so we can get a shoulder against the door. It might just give." He moved to help them move the cabinet. "Let the bloody thing go, lads. There's nothing of value." They obeyed him and the cabinet crashed to the floor.

A constable spotted a key that flew across the floor from inside the cupboard. "Try this, sir. It might be the key we need." He handed it to the Inspector as the Sergeant arrived empty handed.

"Sorry sir I'll—" She stopped speaking as the Inspector unlocked the door.

He pushed it open and shone his torch into the dark void until he found the light switch. A dim bulb lit up what appeared to be an L-shaped room. He moved slowly towards the corner then gasped. He pushed the Sergeant back trying to protect her from the depravity that he had encountered. "Get onto Sergeant Buckingham who is, at present, searching the Davidson bungalow. Instruct her to get Constable Weatherspoon over here with our forensic team. He'll know who to bring with him."

"What is it, sir? You've turned as white as those surrounding walls."

"Something very nasty, Constable, have a look if you dare."

"Thank you, sir but I'll take your word for what you have found, and just stand guard until the forensic mob get here."

"Very wise, Constable, besides we don't want your size-twelve boots destroying the crime scene." He closed the door and sat waiting on the pathologist and the forensic team to arrive. He sat considering Eric Davidson, who had lied to him. There was no point in continuing his visits to the prison; he could not suffer the indignity of sitting beside the perverted monster, and would be liable to clobber him, after what he had just discovered in the hidden room.

Sergeant Buckingham arrived with other forensic officers. "I've contacted P.C. Weatherspoon who in turn has informed the pathologist, and, due to the urgency, gone to collect him at the golf club."

"I don't believe him, Buckingham, with everything that is happening around him, yet he finds the time to play golf."

"Unwinding, sir, so he shouldn't be too long. Meanwhile I'll take a look at what you've discovered."

"No, Buckingham, I wouldn't advise it." Inspector Rupert stood up and paced the open space of the basement. "Where do you think this basement is placed regarding the area above it? I'm trying to determine how nobody heard those women's screams."

Sergeant Buckingham looked upwards to the concrete ceiling. "I estimate that it's below the grass outside the gable end of the warehouse."

"That's why nobody heard the screams, and I would imagine that the concrete would be pretty thick. That would withstand a bomb blast, and with the door concealed nobody would ever think of moving the large cabinet where the key was concealed."

Sergeant Buckingham had never seen Inspector Rupert so distraught. "Why don't you take yourself up for a cup of tea, sir? I'll make sure nobody enters until Wilfred Ponsonby arrives." She took his arm and led him to the wooden stairway. "I'll send someone to fetch you, sir," she said softly.

It was an hour later when the pathologist arrived. "What's so important that this couldn't wait, Rupert?"

"Enjoy your game, Ponsonby? Forget what I just said, because a very serious crime has been committed that will even make you tremble."

They walked through the door, into the dimness of the L-shaped room.

The pathologist turned around quickly, trying to mask his disgust. "This is absolutely terrible, Rupert, committed by a complete psychopath, who would have killed, and gone on killing until you caught him. However, that's for the psychiatrists to determine, but I think you have to be congratulated and deserve a medal."

"Cut out the platitudes, Ponsonby and get on to do what you do best." Inspector Rupert stepped back into the shadow.

The pathologist pulled on his forensic mask. "The first thing we need to do, Rupert, is get a decent light bulb put in place so that it cuts out the shadows."

Inspector Rupert walked away, leaving the pathologist to study the three skeletons.

He returned a short time later and replaced the dim light.

"That's better, Rupert, now we have a clear picture of what has happened here." He kneeled down again. "This woman has been here for some time; I think between eight and twelve years. The foetus was born while she was still tied to the bed. However, the story does not end there, Rupert. The serial killer must have taken pleasure in trying to deliver the baby himself, but I'll know more when I get her on the slab back at the mortuary. This psychopath attempted to strangle her, probably after the baby was born, but failed, because she did not die of asphyxiation. She and the newborn baby died of oxygen starvation. Please note that these are assumptions only. I have to do a scientific study, to put in my report. However, the skeleton on the bed could have bled to death. As for the umbilical chord, well the rats and mice would have had a banquet at that particular time."

"The skeleton on the bed has a name, Ponsonby. She was called Sophie Black, from Bishop Stortford who disappeared in 1938. The skeleton on the chair can be one of two girls, judging by the state of the skeleton. It could be Polly Aniston, from Harlow who disappeared in 1940, or Maria Reynolds from Buntingford, who went missing in 1943. However, looking at the tattered dress I would say it's Polly Aniston from Harlow, but I'm keeping an open mind, simply because Eric Davidson has lied to me. Therefore I await your expert report." He stepped towards the bed. "So this woman gave birth here in the basement." He screwed up his face in disgust.

"There is another part to this tragedy, Rupert. Come closer and look through the inspection glass." He handed the Inspector the scientific glass. "There you can see the old semen samples that are faded. That dim yellow stain is when your killer had sex with the older skeleton before she gave birth. Now look at the semen stains on the other side of the bed; they show up as dark blue. Therefore, we can assume that your serial killer had sex with the girl you say went missing in 1943, while the skeleton of the victim tied to the bed was lying beside them with the small skeleton between her legs. You can confirm that by looking at the skeleton tied to the chair." He waggled his finger to bring the Inspector over towards him. "Look how terrified she must have been."

"I'll just take your word for it, Wilfred. So he forced the girl to have sex next to these two skeletons?"

"You're not usually so slow on the uptake, Rupert. However, there is little more we can do down here, so with your permission…" Wilfred Ponsonby moved the item that hung on the skeletal wrist. "Take a look at this bracelet, Inspector. There's a number on it."

"Leave that to the lab boys, Ponsonby. Now we need the police coffins to remove the skeletons to the waiting pathology department of transport. One more thing, if you please, would you cover each of them with a sheet of some description? We don't want the young officers to witness this carnage."

"Did I hear right, Rupert? My word, you are mellowing with age." The pathologist grunted, closed his bag and said loudly. "You still have work chits to sign, Rupert. So I refuse to do any work on those skeletons until you bother yourself with that." He walked out of the L-shaped room hitting his head on the light holder.

Inspector Rupert stifled a laugh and gave the order for the skeletons to be draped in a shroud before being removed.

When the police coffins were taken away, he ordered the forensic team in with the fingerprint department and a photographer.

"Okay, Weatherspoon, you know the drill: no reporters allowed into the warehouse until we're completely satisfied that no other bodies are buried here." He paused. "Right, Sergeant, I think we can bring in the landscape firm and begin down at Stevenage in Primrose Lane. You have the sketches so we'll start there."

After all the workforce had been interviewed and statements taken, an eerie silence descended over the area. Now was the time when the work would begin. That would keep him and Ponsonby busy. Inspector Rupert gave a wry smile as he drove out of the warehouse yard and back to Welwyn Garden Police Station.

Everything was now in place for the search in Primrose Lane, outside Stevenage. "Here, sir," the cry went up as the first corpse was discovered. The daylight was beginning to fade so arc lights with a generator were quickly installed, which allowed the labourers to continue with the search until another two young remains were brought to the surface.

Inspector Rupert turned to Sergeant Buckingham. "So Eric Davidson was telling the truth about this burial location. Get a road closure order in place, and seal off this location. Bring P.C. Weatherspoon over with the forensics team only if they have completed their work at the warehouse, then tomorrow we will move our search up to Stapleford Village. Davidson said he was unsure where he had buried Linda Symonds, but there can't be too many locations he could have buried her in, so that's our task for tomorrow with the detector machines." He paused. "Let's call it a day, Sergeant, but before we go, put a twenty-four hour watch on this burial site."

The next day began with a promising note. The sketch that Davidson provided revealed the corpse of Linda Symonds, buried on the banks of the stream, near Stapleford Village.

"If it continues like this, sir, poor old Ponsonby is going to be up to his neck in corpses." She apologised. "Sorry sir, just something to say."

Inspector Rupert smiled. "I just hope the bugger's not out playing golf this morning. That's all I have to say on the subject."

"No, sir, I checked the burial site at Primrose Lane, and he's busy now that the girls' bodies have all been brought out of the ground."

"Keep him mobile, Sergeant. When he's finished with them, just remind him that his presence is required here while we continue the search for Lesley and Emma Miller. I think we should concentrate on Lesley Hood next; Davidson was very explicit and precise about what he had done to her and where he buried her. So when the lads have finished here, move the equipment over to Hoddesdon. I'll go on ahead to find where the old barn is located. It shouldn't be too difficult to find."

The search for the missing girls had been a complete success except for one girl; Emma Miller from Leighton Buzzard could not be found, despite the search around the woodland and fields. A phone call was made to Eric Davidson in prison, hoping that he might disclose where he had placed Emma Miller in her grave, but it was a futile attempt as Inspector Rupert heard the serial killer laugh. "You'll never find her, Rupert." The eerie laughter echoed along the corridor of the prison and died away.

He replaced the receiver quietly, knowing that Eric Davidson was right to say that her young body would never be found. "Never say never, Davidson, you fucking perverted bastard." He found himself talking to the telephone on his office desk. However, it was now up to Wilfred Ponsonby the pathologist, the Crown Prosecution Service and the courts to carry out, what he, Inspector Rupert, had solved.

It was the weekend. Watford were at home in a league game, so he decided to travel there by the supporters' bus. However, that plan for his Saturday was blown out of the water.

Mrs. McGinty answered the soft knock on the door. "Come in, Mrs. Rupert. Mr. Rupert is upstairs shaving. Would you like a cup of tea, dear?"

"No thanks, Elsie. I'm catching the mid-day train to London with my dad and step-mum. I'll meet them at the station later. However, I need to talk to Amadeus urgently."

"Hang on, dear. I'll go upstairs and inform him you're here. Take a seat in the lounge; you know where it is."

Deborah walked into the lounge with bated breath, the lounge where things had started to fall apart in their marriage.

Amadeus appeared and kissed her lightly on the cheek. "Deborah, this is a surprise, how have you been?"

"I've been living up at Oakland Terrace, not far from here, just up and round the corner that joins with Oakland Drive and the avenue, but you were far too busy with your work, to notice and must be congratulated in bringing a serial killer to justice. You've become a household name all over England." She paused as she removed an envelope from her handbag. "I have come to inform you that I've accepted an offer from an aircraft engineer, who owns the villa I have been renting since we parted. I intend to go to the United States with him as his secretary, although he has hinted at marriage, but I'll consider that when the time comes." She handed him the envelope.

"These are divorce papers I have had my lawyer draw up, Amadeus. You can go over the content with your solicitor, and let me know if there is anything you disagree with. I'm sure we can come to an amicable agreement, and I want to state quite categorically that I do not want any of your fortune, which I am aware of," she spoke quickly. "I have met with the children and explained to them that I have no future here in England, and we have been separated for over a year now. I was going to post this through the normal channels, but you deserve better than that. It took me some time to pluck up the courage to come here. However, soonest said, soonest mended." She continued to stand. "You and the children will be made most welcome in my new house in the U.S. But right now I have to rush, since I catch the mid-day train to London."

"When do you fly out, Deborah?" he asked in a soft hoarse voice.

"09.50 tomorrow from Heathrow, flight Tango, Bravo, Zebra, 9544, with B.O.A.C. Everything paid for by Boeing, who Sydney works for: my travelling expenses, my hotel accommodation, even a hospitality suite at the airport. I don't want to say any more in case I start blubbering, so look after yourself, and keep in touch with the children." She turned and walked quickly out of the villa to a waiting taxi.

Amadeus stood for a while after the taxi had gone. He knew what he had to do, so he cancelled all plans for the football, and took a later train into London, to stay overnight.

Next morning he left early for the airport, by taxi, just in case the traffic was heavy, and he missed her flight. He found the Boeing hospitality suite. Walking in, he spotted Deborah talking to her dad. When she saw him, she ran and threw her arms around his neck. "I was hoping you would come, Amadeus. Oh, how I wished you would come."

Her dad gave him a frosty look, but her step-mum was polite. "Come, darling, we'll go down to the observation lounge and say our goodbyes from there, but now we should give Amadeus and Deborah a chance to talk." They both hugged Deborah before making a hasty departure, not bothering to look at Amadeus.

Amadeus refused the champagne on offer. "I'll just have a coffee thanks," he said to the black waiter. Who was neatly dressed in tails and a bow-tie.

"I'll have a top-up, Steven," Deborah said, handing the waiter the champagne flute. Small talk passed between the sad pair, and Amadeus hardly heard one word.

He sat considering how they could have ever reached this situation. He finished his coffee, just before Deborah's flight was called, and a Boeing representative appeared to lead her downstairs to the buggy transporter. Amadeus stood for a moment before embracing her tightly.

"If you ever need anything, you know where I am," he softly whispered in her ear.

Deborah could not answer him as the tears poured down her cheeks. She withdrew from his embrace, trying to hide the fact that her heart was breaking. She walked towards the representative without looking back.

Amadeus heard her sobs as she made her way downstairs, and something tugged at his heart strings.

He raced down to the observation lounge and looked for Samantha, her step-mother and her dad, but there was no sign of them, so he waited until the British Overseas Airways Corporation Boeing 707 aircraft was shunted out of its parking bay, then disconnected from the tractor. It made its way slowly up to the main runway for take-off. Something Amadeus had done so often in the war years. He watched the aircraft pick up speed, then lift up into the blue sky. He sighed as he watched the aircraft disappear beyond the horizon, leaving behind a very sad and disconsolate man, with only a love to remember.

THE END

Milton Keynes UK
Ingram Content Group UK Ltd.
UKHW010832190424
441445UK00004B/142